BLACKBIRD DAYS

HARPER & ROW, PUBLISHERS, New York
Cambridge, Hagerstown, Philadelphia, San Francisco
London, Mexico City, São Paulo, Sydney

1817

BLACK-BIRD DAYS

A NOVEL BY
KEN CHOWDER

Grateful acknowledgment is made for permission to reprint: Lines from "Thirteen Ways of Looking at a Blackbird," from *The Collected Poems of Wallace Stevens* by Wallace Stevens. Copyright 1923 and renewed 1951 by Wallace Stevens. Reprinted by permission of Alfred A. Knopf, Inc.

Designer: Ruth Markiewicz

Library of Congress Cataloging in Publication Data

Blackbird days.
I. Title.
PZ4.G545B   [PS3557.L3]   813'.54   79-1704
ISBN 0-06-011496-7

80 81 82 83 10 9 8 7 6 5 4 3 2

For Leonard and Phyllis

I know noble accents
And lucid, inescapable rhythms;
But I know, too,
That the blackbird is involved
In what I know.

—Wallace Stevens

It was the night, by my lights, that my brother Will went wrong—the night he went crazy, and stayed and stayed in his bath.

Since it was the longest day of the year, I imagine it was still light when Neal drove into Will's driveway. I can see him, forgetting that the springs of his car door no longer function, and giving the door a weak shove—not enough. This never irritates him (or else he'd remember?), but it always sticks in Will's craw; perhaps because of its inevitability. . . .

Remembering, Neal clicked the door shut. Without rancor, and without visible interest, he gazed down the crescent street, down the curving alley of maples, then up at the panel of sky glowing between two rows of swaying leaves. Lightning fluttered quietly in the distance; heat lightning, without thunder.

As I imagine it, Will sat sideways in the tub, patiently

1

watching the irregular corrugation of his skin, bony back propped up and long legs jutting over the side. Water dripped from his feet onto the tiles, making them glisten; what water remained in the tub leapt from side to side in solipsistic agitation. The water was blue-green, due to an indeterminate amount of jelly-like turquoise shampoo dissolved in its depths; Will himself was pink, and wore several fringes of suds—a vertical stripe on his chest, a small square epaulette on a shoulder, half a soapy goatee sputtering with air.

Will plunged a hand into the water like a violent child; then scooped up bathwater and listlessly let it trickle out between his fingers, in what I can only guess was a charade of loss.

His expression showed chagrin—and perhaps he envisioned, there in the bath, the monstrous difficulty he always had in tying his shoes.

Our father, Homer, was not without his bombastic side; and as he tightened his bow-tie knot (tugging with thumbs and forefingers, a small perfect movement exactly repeated each morning as he sat down to breakfast), he peacefully orated to himself:

"Morning at the Bard homestead: Howard rubs his eyes, but never wakes up; Neal sits shivering on the heating duct, but never warms up; Will tries to tie his shoes, but never succeeds. And Mrs. Bard is never for a second bothered that from her womb have stumbled would-be humans crippled by sleep, by cold, by sheer ineffectuality. Eh, dear?"

He patted his plaid bow tie with his pudgy fingers, and sniffed. Neal bit into his toast, and sat chewing atop the heating duct, while his free hand massaged a crew of small, white, lifeless toes; crumbs tumbled down through the grid, toward the furnace. Being the oldest, Howard asked what "ineffectuality" meant; Will looked up from the labyrinthine tangle of his laces, glaring furiously, and saw his moonfaced father calmly tapping the side of a soft-boiled egg with a knife—for our father had his boiled egg every morning, even on the day he left for good. Perhaps this image, this broken egg, was in Will's mind as he sat making the bathwater leap from side to side, on the day his own wife left, some twenty-six years later. Or perhaps not.

A mosquito, whining, landed on Neal's cheek. He slapped, got it; it lay in a little circle of blood in his palm. Neal inspected the insect's apparatus, turning the tiny hypodermic with his blundering index finger: Wonderful little machine, he thought. Very clever. But not worth the trouble. He flicked it off his palm into the long, sparse grass.

The front door was open, just as Lucy had left it. "Will?" Neal shouted, pushing the screen door open and letting it bang behind him.

"Tub."

"Back in the tub? What in hell?"

Two turns later he was staring at a slightly wrinkled, slightly red version of our brother Will—who didn't meet his stare, but went on peering instead at the water, through strands of black hair drooping down on either side of his nose.

Neal, who was always leaning if he couldn't be lying down, leaned against the sink. "You'll pucker to death, champion. A truly horrible death."

When Will looked up from the bathwater he saw a small, slight, fair man with an amused look on his sharp-featured face; the man slouched against the sink, looking much at home. He probably wore some of his gray suit, probably not all; Neal shed articles of clothing slowly but inexorably between office and bed, beginning with his tie. By this time he must have rid himself of his vest, and possibly his jacket, but in all likelihood there yet remained the light gray trousers of his eternal summer suit.

"Hot in here. Want me to hand you a towel? Middle shelf in the closet?"

3

"Neal," Will said gravely, irritated, "there's no need to try to rescue me. I'm *okay*. I'm fine. I like it here."

"That's fine," Neal said. "But if there's a flood you'll be the first to go"—although the fact is that it was the high side of Crescent Street, up the hill in Northampton, Massachusetts, and Will wouldn't have been anything like the first one to go. In any event, it wasn't even raining; the lightning, a long way away, was just heat lightning.

"No kidding," Will said through the veil of matted hair, "can you really become dehydrated from being in water too long?"

"Sure. Unless you drink some of it." Neal glanced at the blue bathwater. "Which I wouldn't recommend, champ. Want a glass of water?"

"There's beer in the fridge. Will you join me?"

"I don't think there's enough room in the tub." He coughed laughter. "No, sure I'll have a beer. Tell me," Neal said, his voice trailing back in from the hall, "how long you been in there?" Neal reappeared with two squat bottles in his hands. "You always get this kind?" Neal asked.

"Lucy bought it," Will said morosely.

"Marriage is hell," Neal proclaimed, but added: "It's all the same piss." He tilted and swallowed, made a face. "You could be a whole lot worse off, champ. She might come back."

"Unh-unh," Will said. "That's it."

Neal shifted uncomfortably; leaned, with the other arm, against the doorframe. "So how long you been in the tub?"

"I was here when she told me. I guess she figured I couldn't run after her."

"Smart."

"Sneaky. But not smart. I wouldn't have."

Neal looked away, studied a patch of space; then he clapped his hands together. "Well, you're *clean* now, at least. Want to come to the Flo for hot cakes and hash browns?"

"I'm not getting out just yet."

4

"What are you waiting for?"

"Not waiting. Time has stopped. I'm watching it not go."

One corner of Neal's mouth went into a smile. "How's that again? I don't know what it was, but it was quick."

"If you'd just suspend your humor for a second, I'll tell you," Will said. Neal nodded, but didn't retract his grin; and his gaze went from Will's eyes (which, gleaming like half-burnished copper, inspected his murky water) to the jagged cracks in the white paint on the wall, to the windows. Dusk was spinning threads of pink into the deepening blue; and on the inside a beige spider, presumably oblivious to the acuteness of its timing, had already begun to mark Lucy's absence with strands strung across a corner. It crept in circles, its scuttling steps chronicled by the traces of its trap.

Will seemed to enjoy talking to himself in Neal's presence. "I have this idea, this image: I've been murdered in my bath, caught in the net I made, gone down. What can be dredged up from the bottom? Everything, that's all. In my tub I can see clearly. Look: you and Howard and I, in our crewcuts and T-shirts and shorts, are walking along a path in the Maine woods; a porcupine waddles out on the thin branch of a bush, nibbling—the bark, I think. Lucy's just put down a dime at the fireman's carnival, the numbers on the wheel are rolling slowly down to twenty-three; I see she's going to win, turn to look at her face, to see her see, and her mouth has just opened in a perfect O—the same mouth I'm kissing in the graduate school library, among the *Congressional Record*s, while the Pakistani man who is writing about Senator Taft stares, as he always stares. And at the same time an osprey dives, and soars away mouthing a flashing silver fish."

Neal looked down from the spider to Will. "Champion," he said slowly, "what are you talking about?"

Will laughed self-consciously. "I'm just not leaving my tub yet, that's all."

"You know what Big Howie would say," Neal observed.

5

"Howard always says everyone is crazy."

"Well? He might be right."

"I think he is right," Will said, beginning to get excited again. "That's what I'm trying to say."

Neal looked doubtful. "I never heard you agree with Howard before," he said. "What's come over you? You want another beer? Hey, you haven't even touched the first one. The fans are in an *up*roar."

"You drink it," Will said. "No, let me have a sip first."

"Drink it all. It's good for you. I'll get another one." Neal steered himself expertly through the dark house. He'd never been afraid of the dark; he relished its teasing mystery in a familiar place—the refrigerator must be . . . just . . . here: ah. As a reward for himself he fingered, from the bright, shiny insides, a plump brown bottle. That despicable brand: Neal considered a quick trip to the package store. But Howard would never forgive him if he failed to get Will out of his bath —or so Neal might have been thinking.

"I've got it," Will announced. "You know how your whole life is supposed to pass before your eyes when you drown? Well, I'm drowning. Here comes the frost on the windows of the school bus. The locker doors are clanging shut. The yellow cake drowns at the bottom of the urinals. Billy Hubbard belches—"

"That's terrific, Will," Neal cut in. "Very good. You must be up to about age twelve now, right? Let me know when you get to—what was her name—the one with the big—"

"Jocelyn Stevens," Will remembered grimly.

"Yeah. She sure did."

I concur: Jocelyn Stevens certainly did. She was, it is to be suspected, a little retarded; or perhaps just easily led, an agreeable girl who hated to cause suffering, particularly in frisky boys with the sun in their loins on indolent summer afternoons down at Quimby's Hole. Jocelyn went swimming in her calico shirt; though she never let her head get wet for

6

fear of ruining her "do," the necessary, longed-for, blissful event was already accomplished. And Jocelyn rose from the river dripping jewels, her body haloed by sunlight; the awe with which she was regarded reached near-religious proportions, as did Jocelyn herself. No great wonder that, fashioned with such a lavish hand elsewhere, she should perhaps be less profusely endowed when it came time to construct the slow fastness of her mind.

"Jocelyn aside," Neal said, a bit harshly, "what good does it do to have your life pass before your eyes?"

Will cupped blue bathwater between his two hands, as if it were precious matter. "Memory is pleasure," he said; "even painful memory."

"What about boring memory?" Neal asked. He flipped a switch to watch his spider weave; but when the light came on, the spider froze. "Tell me," Neal said, "does it feel good to remember your entire inane existence?"

"It may not feel good, but it is good. It's going to help me change my life."

"Really? What will you do differently this time around?"

"I'm talking about the future, Neal."

"Right. The Red Sox next year. Their present difficulties disappear with the magical return of Ted Williams."

Will's apathy toward sports balanced Neal's ardor. He was talking about another future:

*"Neal. I'm leav*ing."

"Want me to get you a towel?"

"Not the tub. I'm leaving my job. And I'm leaving Northampton."

"How can you leave Northampton without getting out of the tub? I can just *see* the spectacle on Highway Ninety-one: a cheering crowd lined both sides of this interstate thoroughfare today as the intrepid Tubman continued to wend his splashy way southward—"

"Not likely you could be serious for once, is it?"

7

"No, not very likely."

"That's what I thought. Well, I am."

"Now that *is* likely."

"You don't even care to give me some brotherly advice, hunh?"

"Of course I do, champ—get out of the tub, dry off, come have hot cakes with me. Forget this nonsense."

"You sound like Howard again."

"Howard would never forgive me if I didn't."

"But what do *you* think?" Will always sounded passionately sure of himself, but often asked for other opinions. Neal, who tried for the most part to have no opinions, only doubts, found a tiny moth in circular pursuit of the light bulb, and abandoned his spider for it. But eventually he surrendered his ideas; he wasn't quick to tire of his joking, but he did tire, and put a stop to it himself.

"Well, you know if you leave UMass you're gonna have trouble finding another job."

"What if I said I didn't want to teach at all?"

"Why not? It's a pretty easy job for the money. The only one you're qualified for, not to mention the only one you have. You can't beat the vacations."

"I don't want it."

"What would you do instead, champ?"

Will almost said: Be an opera singer—a family joke that dated from a Sunday morning in the bath when Neal had unwittingly serenaded the entire family, gathered outside the bathroom door, and suffered their mocking applause on his lame completion of "O Tannenbaum." But it had taken Will too long to get his brother serious—the thought caught in his craw, that even on the day Lucy left it was tryingly difficult to get Neal to stop joking. Now that Neal had "simmered down," as our mother used to put it, it was best not to get him going again.

"I'm going to write about birds," Will said. "I think David

Fowler will pay me to do a column in his newspaper. Maybe I could collect the columns into a book."

Neal didn't say, A *bird-watching* column? which was the first thought that came into his head. He didn't ask how Will could keep up house payments by writing a weekly column for the Deerfield newspaper; didn't ask how much Will knew about birds, or cared about them. Instead he asked: "So why do you want to leave?"

Will looked intently at his brother. The shadow of Neal's head on the wall behind him looked like Australia. It was because his cowlick had sprung up again, Will thought; it always did in the evening. Will felt a rush of warmth for Neal; he wanted to explain himself, so Neal would nod in understanding; for there Neal was, slouching in the doorway, with the same boyish face, the same cowlick—the same boy, in fact, who had taught Will how to catch frogs. Will said: "I want to leave because the whole kit is ridiculous. Because I'm tired of my own pretension. Because there's something that makes me angry every single day.'

"What's that?"

"Yeah. That's what I want to find out."

"Writing about birds will help you find out?"

"It's not the writing about birds. That's just to make enough money to get by. It's the looking at them."

Neal shook his head. "For Chrissakes, champ. What would Howard say?"

"Howard would say, 'Tell me, Will, exactly what do you intend to do about the house? You do have financial commitments in this world.' "

"Okay, you got it. But what about that?"

"I'll sell it. Without Lucy's salary I couldn't meet the payments anyway."

"Unh-hunh," Neal said dully. "Suppose not."

His face looked pale, now, in the glaring artificial light; pale and not pleased.

"Does that annoy you, Neal?"

Neal roused himself. "Not at all. I'm just tired of standing around your bathroom watching you shrivel. You didn't happen to hear about the murder of the football player by the vegetable man in the North End bar?"

"You know I haven't."

"The vegetable man went to the john. When he came back, the football player had taken his seat. So the grocer shot him in the neck. Remarkable murder. A quarterback."

"What's so remarkable about it?"

"It was the only occupied stool in the whole bar." Neal laughed.

"Your murders always have punch lines. That one isn't true, is it?"

"Of course it's true," Neal said, sounding offended. It was true, though Neal had neglected to mention that the stool was the grocer's lucky one, that the Derby was about to come on the bar TV, and that the grocer had bet his life savings on the race. All in all it amounted to justifiable homicide, according to Neal. "So do I get a chair now, or do I pull out my pistol? Or do you jump out of there and come eat?"

"There are chairs in every room."

"But this one, where you entertain your guests," Neal commented. "Very handy." He went back to the kitchen; this time he turned on the light. Neal, unlike Will or Howard, rarely allowed images of the past to penetrate his present; or else he would surely have been entertained by the bittersweet apparition of the Sunday midmorning, two years before, when Howard brought chilled champagne to the brunch, and there in the sunlit niche of the kitchen the four of them (nearly five; Lucy was seven months pregnant) stood in a circle around the round table, toasting Will and Lucy's new house, Will and Lucy's new baby, Will and Lucy. Lucy brought out a bright red tablecloth, swirled it in the sun like a matador's cape; and everyone admired the way the silver-

10

ware shone against it; and they devoured all the smoked salmon; and Neal told a murder; and Howard noticed that the kitchen wanted painting. It still wanted painting. But Neal never noticed, and he didn't notice now; just as he somehow failed to see the happy group as they had been arrayed there, laughing again and again, their champagne sparkling in the sun. He found a chair, hooked it with his arm, and lugged it into the bathroom. It banged once or twice against the walls of the narrow corridor.

He sat in the chair backwards, his arms folded, and started in again. "What's so great about birds, anyway? Planes go a lot faster. Why don't you be up-to-date and write a plane-watching column? A rare Russian MIG, presumed to be a stray visitor from its normal Siberian nesting grounds, flashed its bright scarlet plumage in migraine flight in this area last week, members of the Aerobond Society reported. . . ."

Will was nettled. "I don't think I could explain to you about birds, Neal."

"Why not?"

"I just don't think you'd understand."

"Sure I would. I like birds."

Will wasn't about to be mollified. "No, I don't think so."

"Sure I would. What's the big mystery?"

Will wasn't sure what the mystery was. When he looked into it he could make out the black and white face of a kestrel, black tears painted under staring eyes, like a harlequin in a fury; the kestrel spread his slate blue wings and soared against the sun, his tail glowing a rich red-brown. Was this the mystery? Will thought about bringing in Icarus and Daedalus; but that speech would be more to Howard's liking. The kestrel hovered, fanning his tail and beating the air with the tips of his wings, searching for prey.

"I just like birds," Will said, and shrugged.

"So do I. Is that enough?"

"It's an old wish, to be able to fly."

11

"We can *do* it now, champion," Neal said softly. "Remember Kitty Hawk?"

"That's not the kind of hawk I'm interested in."

"Can't say that I blame you. It's a two-bit town. Lots of used cars."

Will said something to provoke Neal. "The way I feel about birds is—well, it's almost religious. You wouldn't understand."

"No, I sure wouldn't," Neal smiled—not provoked, and not believing Will at all.

They sat in silence. Neal, looking in vain for the moth, watched his spider complete preparations on its loose, asymmetrical web; Will dipped his wrinkled fingers into the bathwater, testing, it seemed, the heat, as if his submerged legs were no longer capable of providing an accurate indication. In the meantime a pockmarked, humpbacked moon rose into the sky on the other side of the house, its reflected light made imperceptible by the brighter ones of the streetlights —yellow-green interlocking circles, marching up the curving street.

Will refused a final invitation to dinner. Neal rose to go. "Don't bother to see me to the door," he said, smiling again.

"Thanks for coming," Will said forlornly, suddenly depressed. It seemed to him that his ideas, even perhaps his emotions, never stood a chance against Neal's wisecracks and omnipresent good humor. He felt somehow deflated; as if even his misery had been shown to be just a way of puffing himself up, a pretension. But that wasn't the case; he was honestly miserable, wasn't he? What an absurd position to be in: honest misery! Damn it, why did he need justification to feel the way he did?

Neal went out. A second later he was back. "She took Sarah with her, didn't she?"

"Yup," Will replied gloomily.

"That's too bad."

12

"Yup."

"Is Lucy staying on at UMass?"

"She didn't say. I didn't ask."

"Did she say where she was going?"

"Where else?" Will made a face. "To mother."

"That's funny," Neal said. "She doesn't even *like* her mother."

In the yard Neal stood listening outside the bathroom window, hoping to hear the stuttering snore of water swirling down drain. He stood a long time, his patience fortified, perhaps, by the fragrance of the rhododendrons flanking him. Fireflies hovered in tremendous number, blatantly attempting to expose the lurking intruder with their pinprick luminations. It had grown dark, despite their efforts. Finally he heard the vulgar noise of water and air in competition for a small space—snorting, Neal thought, like two professional wrestlers: the outcome already assured, but the maximum fuss to be raised in accomplishing it. Neal barely had time to be pleased before a new sound was heard: the din of water again thundering from the tap.

I give up, Neal said to himself; what was it our father used to say to Will? "Do what you want. You will anyway." But Neal had to admire Will: no matter how ridiculous the things he did, that was really what he wanted to do. Who else could say that? Neal considered his own office desk, its rows of pencils, its stack of yellow pads, its tiresome, blurring documents, wills, divorces, and taxes, waiting for him; I hope no one ever asks me why I'm a lawyer, he thought. But maybe that was the point of being a lawyer: nobody would. Except Will.

Adele Sleeper at twenty-eight hated to think of herself as a professional waitress, though she'd never had another kind of job. All you had to be was sweet and good-looking and the tips would roll in, Delsey sometimes said, and though she didn't believe it herself for one second (you had to be a goddamn *dip*lomat sometimes, and a slave), it made her mad that people would nod when she said that; well, shit, she couldn't do *that* all her life, if that's what people thought it was. Delsey was a waitress because she liked working nights, and because she liked people, and because she liked to flirt a little bit. When people asked her what she did, she always said she was a floozie—which in a way was a lie, because she got pissed off when the customers came on strong, but in a way was true, because she asked for it. She had to admit that she asked for it. She liked men, and she didn't; some of them, He-Man men, made her want to vomit—and then they would turn this way or that, or laugh, and she'd have to admit that they were kind of cute. But you never knew how men would act. You really never knew. This one here, for example, who came in sometimes and sat by himself: she liked him, he was sort of funny in a stupid way, not too tough-guy; she didn't mind him looking at her, she knew she was pretty cute, she hoped to God they'd look; but then you never knew, like she said, the ones in business suits were the worst, he was in his late thirties maybe—the ones who came in and sat by themselves, they *were* the worst. Any second he might be all over her. The idea made her queasy; when she poked the menu at him all her lights were out.

He waved the menu away. "We want something really good to eat tonight," he said. He motioned to the empty booth. "I'm treating," he added.

"Oh, really?" she said, not interested.

"Yeah, it's a special occasion; it's a Happy Not-Anniversary dinner. Tonight we haven't been married for exactly two hundred and seven years."

"Your birthday or something?"

"No, I'm a Libra. What's yours, Delsey?"

"Quarius. Hey, how'd you get my name?"

14

"I just guessed. You look like a Delsey."

"A likely story," Delsey said. "Who might you be?"

"Aimee Semple McPherson," he said. "At your service. And this is my charming wife, Minnie."

"How do you do?" Delsey said sarcastically.

"Very well, thank you. Well, what's good to eat tonight?"

Delsey pointed with her little finger to the scrap of paper clipped to the menu. "The chicken à la king is on special," she said. "It's real good," she added.

He shook his head vigorously. "Unh-unh," Neal said. "No birds."

Will stayed in his bath. I wonder what it was that finally got him out. Dripping, he rose, wrinkled and rosy, and teetered out to the hall toward a towel. He didn't feel very well; he was dizzy, a wobbly sailor still on sea legs. He wrapped his towel around his slender middle and lurched into the living room, where his cigarettes, perhaps the direct catalyst of his landward evolution, lay on the coffee table. He landed beside them, dropping with a crash into a tired armchair. A book on the chair's arm slipped off, and slapped the wooden floor; a glass on the other arm, half-filled with flat beer, rocked perilously back and forth for an unlikely amount of time, and then rather arbitrarily fell. The glass bounced, intact, but emptied its contents—for an instant the beer made a hillock on the floor, then sank into a flat circle, sending a tongue sliding out of one side to lap at Will's foot like an affectionate old dog. Will paid no attention. He pulled a cord dangling below a lampshade, blinked, and dialed hunching over the telephone—in much the same way that he used to hunch over his soup, making our father fulminate from the head of the table.

Someone answered.

"Hello, Mrs. Burnham? I hope I didn't wake you. Is Lucy there, please?

"Yes, it's Will.

"Well, why don't you *ask* her if she wants to?

"Could you just go check?—if she is awake I'd very much like to talk to her.

"Listen, Mrs. Burnham. Mrs. Burnham. I'm not *going* to make a scene, Mrs. Burnham. I just want some information.

"No, I don't think you know it. I'd like to talk to Lucy. Could you ask her, please, if she'll talk to me?

"Look, I know, uh, I know you're in a delicate situation. We're all in a delicate situation. But I'm really not trying to cause any trouble, Mrs. Burnham—Mrs. Burnham? Hello? Aah, shit."

He replaced the receiver as calmly as he could. Will was not above violence to objects—in fact he enjoyed it, espoused it, felt it served a practical purpose—but he chose his objects carefully; so the destruction of the object wouldn't add to his unhappiness, or his violence wouldn't have any effect on the object. In this latter case it was Will himself who suffered damage; blessed damage, for it took his mind off his anger.

He was tired of punching the closet door, an exercise his knuckles disapproved of ever more strenuously with each repetition. Instead he ended up quietly crumbling cigarettes into an ashtray. He found it somehow satisfying to reduce a thing to its inarguable components, its atoms; besides, it smelled bad, and he liked his rage to produce manifestations for his senses, to impose on the macrocosm something . . . distasteful. Waste itself was distasteful; and he had very deliberately crumbled a half-dozen cigarettes, for his murderous intent extended to the whole pack (he would quit smoking), when the phone rang, startling him and rousing him from his sulk.

Lucy was curt, angry: "It's me. What do you want?"

"I just wanted to talk a little bit."

She was immediately exasperated. "Go to sleep, Will."

16

"I can't. I've gotta ask you couple questions."

"What questions?"

Will tried to think. "Are you staying on at UMass?"

"You can't sleep because you had to ask me that? Yes, I'm staying on. I'll see you in the fall."

"N-no—" Will started, tremulously, and stopped short.

Lucy hesitated. "Will," she began, but she too had trouble continuing. Finally, though, she was able to; Lucy was an able person. "This conversation. There isn't any—Will, there isn't any—"

"You're right," Will said, beginning to snicker, an embarrassed reaction to his own tears.

"Can't you stop laughing?" Lucy said, as if his laughter had been going on for a long time, and exhausted her.

"Okay," Will said. "Okay. Listen, I love you, hunh?"

Lucy sighed. "Unh-hunh. Okay, good-bye."

Will didn't reply; he listened for the click of disconnection, holding the phone away from his ear, imagining that the sound would be so loud as to be uncomfortable. Instead he heard Lucy's voice again. "I love you too, Will. Don't call again."

He put the phone down sharply. "I won't," he said aloud. He picked up a cigarette. "Right," he said crisply. "Enough is enough. That's that." He gestured with his cigarette and practiced again on the empty room: "That's that." He listened for a second, seemingly pleased that there was no reply, no dispute. Then loudly: "That's that." The grandfather clock ticked on a bit more slowly; the refrigerator ceased its hum; but otherwise no response. "That *is* that," Will said, and smiled, surprised. He closed his eyes and let his head loll back on his shoulders for a second. Before his echo had cleared out of the damp summer air of the empty house, he had shouted: that that was that; and for a minute he went on shouting: that was that, that was that.

17

Then, looking around him, he felt startled and satisfied, as if he had waked at last from a long dream complete with blissful resolution. He noticed without annoyance the sticky dampness of his bare foot; and in a state of exhilaration, almost, he trotted off to the refrigerator for a beer.

2

Bright black crows called warning to each other when Neal turned onto the dirt road; still cawing insolently, they glided alongside the road with languid beats of their ragged wings and swooped into the evergreens by the farmhouse. Glossy black eyes glittered in among the matte green of the pine needles. Curious, brazen, the crows watched Neal watch them; and were still watching him when he turned away and walked up to the vast old white clapboard house.

Neal wasn't an unhappy man, I always thought; he had a general affection for what he considered a world without redeeming value. Although not on record as ever having expressed respect for any person or thing, he had suffered, as he put it, from a number of strong attachments and inclinations. His rabid support for the baseball Red Sox has already been noted—a state of affairs to which Neal himself attributed his overriding pessimism. He liked small children (though not babies), biographies, airplanes, old movies, new

19

movies, virtually any alcohol, humorous crime, and machines of clever construction or astounding function. He had few convictions, and among these was the conviction never to act on any of his convictions.

Neal's habits ran a certain peculiar gamut. Neal was a churchgoer, like Howard. A poor singer to say the least, he went to church just to be able to sing in public, in company, and not suffer the awful embarrassment of being heard. Even so, he claimed the distinction of being one of the few in Northampton to have been shushed while dutifully (if unmelodically) singing a hymn. From time to time he changed his house of worship in order to remain to a degree anonymous.

Neal, an unmarried man, was proficient at amusing himself. This was not difficult, for he was easily amused. When asked to state his religion on forms, he filled in Vivisectionist; under Race, he put Daytona 500; for Occupation, Deity. He spent long hours writing short, useless letters to magazines and newspapers. For example:

Dear *Sports Illustrated,*

I find myself unable to keep up with you these days. Who the devil *is* this Benjamin Disraeli character, and why is he always asking for more money? Doesn't he know that it isn't the ballplayers that the public pays to see, but the ballgame?

> Yours truly,
> Mary, Queen of Scots
> Pittsburgh, Pa.

Or:

To *The Reader's Digest:*

Your stand on taxidermy (re Vol LVIN, No. 7) is really absolutely repellent. That you seem to have no respect for moral decency is one thing, but your use of taxpayers' hard-earned money to increase your ill-gotten gains is quite another! Is there any chance of you going out with me this weekend, hunh? If not, please cancel my subscription posthaste.

Regretfully yours,
The Dalai Lama
Fort Worth

I warned Neal that his antics would lead to trouble. He replied that it would serve him right, and was therefore unlikely. In the long run his unconcern was shown to be well-founded, for he never heard a peep out of the law about this epistolary vice. On the other hand, he never succeeded in getting a letter into print. The futility of such an enterprise would have discouraged some, but as Neal put it, he believed in futility as an end, not a means.

His pessimism often stood him in good stead. He predicted the most dire happenings, but neither hysterically nor gloomily; he was cheerful in foreseeing a given apocalypse, and much amused when it came about. In part he could be pleased by his own prescience. We hurried for the train, desperately late, Neal claiming that we would miss it, and we did miss it; as we watched the train recede in the distance, emitting a dawdling puff of smoke, Neal pulled his handkerchief from his pocket and sat, heavily mopping his brow. "I feel much better," he said.

Neal, not good with time, missed a number of trains. "You're late," Will said on the front porch, smiling and extending his hand.

"No I'm not," Neal said, puzzled, shaking it. "I said midmorning, no?"

"You said *Saturday* midmorning."

Neal was sure he had said Sunday. After a second he replied, "Pretty stupid of me, hunh?"

"Forget it," Will said, still smiling. He watched Neal stare curiously at the house. It was as if Neal were there to inspect,

21

to judge: Neal would go back to Howard, discourse on what Will was doing with his life, and Howard would nod, puff a pipe. Knowing Neal, what he had to say wouldn't be vindictive. Nor would it be positive.

"Pretty place," Neal said.

"It's a nice enough old house. A little creaky, a little lopsided, but it works. People can live in it."

"Looks comfy."

"It's that, anyway. But mostly it's a tremendous relief to live in a house where you don't have to meet the payments."

"I'll bet."

Neal wasn't buying it, Will thought. But what did that matter, who was Will trying to please? Will felt the familiar first tickling: slight pressure in his temples, trickle of saliva into the back of his jaws, distant thunder in his ears. A small shudder went through him. Something had caught in Will's craw.

"Would you like to meet the Petersens?" he asked.

"They around?"

"Surely," Will replied.

Surely? Neal wondered.

The Petersens were both small, weather-beaten, and in the kitchen. They looked to Neal as if they had been clipped from a Frank Capra movie, examples of the Good Life on the Farm: they were short, square, getting on in years, but could still be called handsome—Mr. Petersen with his huge, crew-cut head, massive craggy face with gray eyes and white brows; Mrs. Petersen with her sharp chin, button nose, and tight gray bun. His overalls and straw John Deere hat were inevitable, Neal thought, even if her khaki trousers and paratrooper boots were not. She was watering plants, and he sat at the table with coffee mug in hand and the morning paper sprawled in front of him; flies buzzed about everywhere, but congregated in the greatest numbers along the sunlit window squares and around the acrid Mr. Petersen.

Will made graceful introductions. He put his arm around Edna's shoulders, and she laughed uncomfortably. Pete shook Neal's hand firmly, and told him that his brother was the best laborer they'd ever had: though skinny, Will was, Pete claimed, real strong—strong as an ox, by Christ.

That was hogwash, Will said; Pete was just trying to build him up so Will would haul bales by himself. Pete admitted as much—winking elaborately at Neal. "Maybe your brother can give you a hand," he said. "He looks kinda powerful himself."

"Never touch the stuff," Neal said. "Anyway, Will was telling me something about bass in your pond."

"There's three or four left in there, all right," Pete said, trying to nod and slurp coffee at the same time. "But you best just content yourself with bluegills. Those bass that's in there is the smart ones. They loop your line around the locust tree that's laying under the water there in that corner of the pond, and away they go. They didn't live to be that size for nothing, I tell you. I must of hooked each one of them, personal, half a dozen times. They figure I'm about the stupidest fella ever lived."

"They're big, hunh?" Neal was becoming excited. "You sure you don't mind us going after em?"

"Why I surely do not, no. You go right ahead. Have a good ole time being made a fool of."

"Course the rowboat's no good anymore," Edna put in quietly. "Want some coffee? Pete never does get around to fixing things."

"I'll get around to it, I'll get around to it," Pete claimed, waving his rather short arms.

"The rowboat's no good?" Neal asked. "How do you fish?"

"Well, I haven't for a couple-three years," Pete confessed. "I been pretty busy, what with trying to keep up the farm and all."

"I guess," Edna said sharply. That was the end of her sen-

23

tence; apparently it conveyed criticism, disbelief. "Nobody seems to be able to figure out how you go about keeping it up, Pete Petersen; some people surely got the idea it means cribbage playing and beer drinking on Ralphie Warner's porch. Sanka okay for ya, Neal?"

Neal winced. "Sure," he said.

So there was to be no fishing that morning, a late July morning when it would have been just perfect, Neal sighed, to be sitting in a rowboat rocking with the breeze, the water rippling and the beer cold. He allowed his daydreams to stretch out and include the sun on his bare back, the gently idling motion of the sparkling water, a lake of time; and then his idle thoughts were carried on by their own momentum, and he saw himself sitting on his bed painfully dabbing cream onto his throbbing scarlet shoulders. His daydreams didn't go so far as to include fish. Neal fished every year, and he never caught a thing; not since he brought home the three gray, rank suckers from the polluted pond behind Calhoun's, and Homer made Howard sneak them way out in the woods, for the raccoons. But as I remember it, even the raccoons weren't much attracted, and the forest stank for days, Howard thought; perhaps even weeks; it was difficult to tell if you were smelling them or just thought you were. Since then Neal hadn't caught one thing, and in fact he had had very few bites. That was one of the reasons why he liked to fish.

Will had a few things to show Neal, he said. They could come back and have coffee later. Neal agreed cheerfully, and went trotting off in Will's wake. It always irked him that his younger brother was so much taller, and had been so at an indecently early age: before Neal had time to extract a just quantum of fraternal awe (as partial compensation for that vast amount extorted by the towering, muscular, athletic, intelligent Howard).

"We have new piglets just today," Will said over his shoulder. They passed a sty; three pigs lay on their sides in a

24

morass of mud and potato peelings. "Trying to keep cool," Will said appreciatively. The pigs seemed to have been drawn by a caricaturist: tiny legs and corkscrew tail sallied forth from a windless sail of body (sheer belly), small dim eyes squinted above huge white snout. A pig disinterestedly pointed the flattened, hairless end of its snout at Neal as he passed; then lay back, exhausted.

Will opened the barn door. A wall of stifling heat met them. "Pigs don't pay," Will announced. "The Petersens just keep a few because they like them."

"Sounds like criminal law," Neal said. "You don't make a dime in criminal. I'd advise them to try torts."

"Pigs are really kind of wonderful. They're very smart."

Before them, in a stall strewn with hay, lay the sow and her piglets. The piglets scrambled for teats; sucked frantically, squeaking in high piercing yips. The sow grunted and closed her eyes. Remains of the placenta filled a corner of the stall, a dark, mucous pool in a nest of hay; two black and white cats watched the goings-on calmly from another corner. Neal was inclined to believe that these porcine proceedings had a distinctly satirical, mock-Christian aspect; while for Will its religiosity was no farce. "Just today," he repeated, marveling.

What was that there, dangling in Will's hand, a gray tool like pruning shears? His long arm reached out and snatched a pink piglet, which howled in terror; the cats looked up blankly; the supine sow didn't stir. Will pried apart the piglet's jaws, revealing several sharp little teeth. "They have them from the time they're born," he said. He inserted his tool and maneuvered it around one of four long fangs. Will squeezed, and with a crunching snap the tooth flew into the air; it landed in the other corner of the stall, at the foot of a cat. The piglet shrieked; the cat batted at the tooth with its paw. "You have to do them in the first three days after they're born, or it gets complicated," Will said. "They can really take a chunk out of the sow if you wait too long." He snapped off another tooth, twisting his wrist. This time blood spurted from the mouth of the screaming piglet. "A little too close to the gums," Will commented, shaking blood from his fingers. "I'm just learning," he added, and a third tooth flew out of the piglet's mouth. "I still haven't been able to do their balls yet. Pete loves to do that part, though. I don't know why, but he does." The pig almost squirmed out of Will's hands. He caught it on one knee and held it against his chest. "Just one more, pal," he said to the pig.

"Does it hurt?" Neal asked. "Maybe they're so young they don't feel it."

"Oh, it hurts, all right. It surely does. They're never too young to feel pain." He yanked at the last fang; it broke with a loud crack, and sailed across the room, much to the fascination of the cats, one of whom almost sprang up—but thought better of it, and assiduously licked its paws instead.

Will took a red felt-tip pen from his pocket and pulled the top off with his teeth; he scribbled a W on the side of the piglet, and put it back against its mother's side. The piglet grabbed a teat with its mouth and went unconcernedly back to its business.

Neal asked, "What's the W for?"

"Well, there are quite a few of them here. Almost a dozen. We mark them so that we can tell which ones have been done."

"Why with a W?"

Will smiled sheepishly. "It stands for Will."

Neal didn't mention, and perhaps he didn't think of, and there is even the possibility that he didn't remember: how Will, to our mother's weepy distress, had carved his name into the back of an eighteenth-century rocking chair—perhaps in a kind of triumph, and perhaps a kind of rage (it was the week our father left).

All Neal said was, "Why should it stand for Will?"

26

"So Pete will know it hasn't had its balls cut off yet," Will said flatly, and reached for another piglet.

Will had something else he wanted to show Neal. He led his brother back to the house, up the back staircase to his rooms. There was a tacky kitchenette, a square, empty study, bathroom, and closet toilet; and then the white, spacious bedroom. In one corner a large cage stood on the table; a drab hawk stared sullenly from inside it. "His name's Harwood. He's an immature Broad-winged," Will said in a pleased voice, as if showing Neal a marvelous toy. They approached the hawk, who moved only his head. "Better not get too close," Will whispered excitedly. "Don't look right at him." The bird was a dull dark brown above, on his wings and back, and pale beige, streaked and spotted with brown, below; not much to look at, thought Neal. Before the bird's opaque stare Neal felt curiously helpless. It was a sensation he had had once before—when he watched Sonny Liston, the heavyweight fighter, come up the aisle in Lewiston: the monolithic body was shrouded in a white silk robe, but as Sonny stalked past on his way to the ring, Neal had been caught for an instant by his expressionless face, by his hard brown eyes glaring from behind a wooden mask. In that second Neal felt overmatched by the mere presence of a stronger being, and he shrank in his seat. To his surprise, Clay easily knocked Liston out; but Neal had already lost his bout.

This small, distant creature had that same power: Neal was transfixed. As if pulled by the hawk's eye, he stepped toward the cage. The bird sprang nervously away, crashed against the back of the cage, and fell in a heap of feathers. Harwood picked himself up holding one wing out away from his body; and now Neal could see a thin sling supporting the wing, and gouts of fresh blood popped through old scabs at the wing's base. The hawk tried to shake free, but succeeded only in spraying blood all over his cage and around the room.

27

"I should have been more insistent," Will said grimly, his lips pursed. "He's still pretty shy." The hawk tried to flap his wings again. He was bleeding freely; dark, almost black blood. "A woman in Colrain read my column about hawk-watching," Will explained. "Did you read that one? 'Raptor Rapture'?"

"Unh-hunh," Neal lied.

"She called me up. Harwood had smashed her kitchen window. She was afraid to pick him up, but she sat beside him, while he lay bleeding on her front porch."

"Surprised he's still alive," Neal said.

"Unh-hunh. It's not legal to keep him. But I'm not trying to domesticate him, just cure him. The local vet fitted him with the sling, but now he's shaken half out of it. I'm a bit pessimistic, to tell you the truth."

Will was more than a bit pessimistic—he was broken-hearted. But he didn't guess Neal could understand or be interested in that. He searched his brother's calm face; it would be futile to apply for kindness, for sympathy, there. Neal was cold, that's what he was; when you peeled away all the layers of jokes, there was—nothing. Nobody. All he had were defenses and more defenses—Will was becoming angry now—and that's why Neal had never married, had never even been serious about a woman; nor for that matter about anything. Will told himself that he loved Neal; but his brother too caught in his craw.

And now Neal was sitting at the tiny formica table in Will's kitchenette, playing with the sugar cubes and his coffee; Neal dipped one with his fingers, watched it suck up the liquid, and soften; past his shoulder Will could see the hillside, dotted with Holsteins, black and white against the green green grass, and farther down, the pond sparkling among the pale, swaying cattails. Dark, puffy clouds gathered in the distance, moving slowly closer; later it would rain, rain hard; there would be lightning. Will stole a glance, as if he were stealing away: as if the sight of the bright warm world could ease him, could uncoil the tight muscle of his heart, could dissolve his dis-ease like . . . hot coffee and sugar cubes. "So it wouldn't be so final," Neal was saying, looking into his coffee cup and away from Will.

"The payments would be met," Neal went on; "and you don't, I assume, require a substantial influx of money at present, do you?"

"You sound like Howard," Will said, though not sure what Neal had said.

Neal chuckled. "Pretty damn good, champ. Howard's idea, I admit. But maybe he's right—just this one time?"

"What did he do, ask you to come up here?"

"That's exactly right. You go on to the next round."

Now Will was more interested. "How did he put it?"

"Oh, he blustered a bit. He put on his walrus suit. He did a little soft-shoe, you know. There was faint applause. He wasn't unkind about it."

"Come on. What did he say?"

"Well, he said the usual thing. About burning dams behind you. He said not to rule out any possibilities."

"Just like that? No Howardly invective?"

"Nope. Just like that." Neal cleared his throat. He recalled Howard's booming voice: "Next week Will will want to be a university man again," Howard had said. "He'll give up this back-to-nature nonsense and remember that he has a mind. Will is destined to be a peasant for just so long."

"And so?" Will said to Neal.

"And so, like I say, he said that I should try to get you to consider renting the house, and trying to get a leave of absence from UMass."

"All right. I hereby consider it."

"No, hunh?" Neal hadn't expected him to listen.

"Try to impress upon Howard, would you, that it's just that possibility that would be dangerous."

29

"Why? Because it's tempting?" Neal asked, temptingly. Neal believed in temptation, or so he said; he made it standard practice to give in.

"Yeah, because it's tempting," Will said, "because it's the easiest thing to do. But not the best."

"Oh well," Neal said cheerfully. He could see that Will was in an argumentative mood. "Everyone to his own lousy baloney, hunh?"

"Besides," Will said—chewing the inside of his cheek, intent (I believe) on convincing himself—"I've already written my letter of resignation to UMass."

"Did you send it?"

"Not yet," Will said. "I, um, don't have any stamps."

Howard was right, Neal said to himself. Will was destined to be a farm laborer for only so long.

"Don't send it, Will. The fans will love you for it."

"I hate sports fans."

"They'll love you, champ."

Neal was dangling another sugar cube above his cup. How many was he going to put in there? By the time he got around to drinking it, the coffee would be cold. What was Neal thinking about?

"Hey Neal?"

"Hey what?"

"Do you know what I dream about?"

"Of course I know what you dream about, you nasty bastard."

"No, you know what it is? I dream about the way Lucy used to lock the door on her way out. She always used to fumble with her keys. I've dreamed that about five times. And whenever she opens her mouth she seems to say, 'I read something in the newspaper today.' Really ridiculous stuff. Do you ever dream about stuff like that?"

"No, I can't say as I do." Neal rarely remembered dreams; he believed that he rarely had them.

"It's as if someone is shining a light into the secluded corners of my past. If I dream about stuff like that, think about how the important things must be churning around in my subconscious. Can you imagine what I must be repressing?"

"Probably nothing at all. You're not too good at repressing."

"I wish that were true," Will said soberly. Neal was finally drinking his coffee, if only to hide behind the mug. "I don't want to dream about Lucy and the keys anymore," Will said. "I'm so damn tired of her fumbling for her keys."

Neal put down his coffee. The cup rattled against silence. Sunlight cut through the kitchen, and fell on the hawk in his cage. Harwood blinked.

"I guess maybe you should sell the house," Neal told Will. Will almost started. "You could buy a season ticket for the Red Sox," Neal added quickly. "Next year."

Will was pleased: "So you think next year is the year, hunh?" he said sympathetically.

"Yeah," Neal said. "No," he added.

He reflected. "In theory," Neal said at last, "I believe anything's impossible. In practice, I'm not so sure."

After lunch they talked for a while, probably about Howard; then Will took Neal downstairs to say good-bye to the Petersens. They found Pete stretched out on the living-room sofa, his stockinged feet propped up with pillows. The television set glowed; a man's voice whispered something about a break to the right, there was a silence, and then a smattering of applause. "Watson is twelve under," Pete said by way of greeting. "But he won't win. Nicklaus is only two shots back, and he's comin after him."

Will, embarrassed, didn't reply; what did Pete care about golf, for God's sake?

"Watson might win," Neal said. "He's a good one. Nice irons."

"He surely does, though, don't he? Straighter'n I seen since Hogan. Nice boy, too."

"Even nicer than Hogan?" Neal said; Pete laughed; Will gathered with some small displeasure that this had been a joke.

"Want a frosty?" Pete inquired.

"Surely," said Neal.

"Make yourself to home," Pete said, motioning to a yellow armchair, where Neal sat down.

"I thought you were about to leave," Will said.

"This is the Open," Neal explained. "I forgot all about it."

Will didn't bother to ask what the Open was; he rarely asked a question when he wasn't interested in the answer. Neal and Will had been children together, and there had been many opportunities for these various questions to be asked; but Neal's propensity was invariably matched by Will's indifference, and vice versa. In my opinion this was due more to their different natures than a desire to antagonize. As boys they shared an interest, however peculiarly manifested, in the opposite sex, in frogs and crayfish; but apart from that they had nothing in common. Except their brother, Howard.

Under bygone normal circumstances Will would have retired to his room, to read, or to the woods, to explore. Here he might have shared a portion of the silence with the brooding Harwood, or donned sweatclothes for a jog; or perhaps hauled Pete's bales in the hayloft, where the sunlit air was so thick with dust and chaff that it glowed, golden. Will liked his solitude; he usually filled it with energetic enterprise, remembered later in warm, romantic hues—golden glows. He labored at a desk, a pen still capped in his restless fingers; his blank page gave him an opaque stare; on the windowsill an ocher vase sprouted dry flowers; the sunlight poured into the windows, and came out, transfigured on the opposite wall, as a bright rectangle; the wicker fruit basket on the table, containing two jaded cherries, bathed in yellow light.

32

Nothing passed; nothing changed; except that Will took in more and more of his surroundings, bit by shining bit, until he must surely burst: there was more of it than him. But he didn't burst, he didn't move, he didn't unscrew the cap of his pen; he just went on collecting the beautiful, the perfect, the luxuriant world. There was no stopping him; and perhaps, he thought, he could get it all. Perhaps he could stop time— could stop time by remembering everything perfectly, by keeping the image of the past presently before him—nothing would pass—nothing would change: he unscrewed the cap excitedly; it was gone.

Will decided to watch golf with Neal. Will wasn't often polite, but he often tried to be. He got too worked up, too angry, to keep track of the niceties. At times he could be as polite and charming as Howard; he wasn't always wrapped up in his own world, despite what Lucy said—he could be painfully aware of others. At this moment it wasn't painful: Will saw the familiar glaze settle over his brother's features: in the presence of the television set Neal was no longer present. He was instantly submerged. Reactions reached Neal's features as if coming from a great depth; as if he had been emptied of all but a small part of his intelligence, and in his dotage could only smile vaguely, wrinkle one eyebrow, and blink weakly. Will pulled up a wicker chair, laughing a little; because he was amused by the picture of Neal in doddering senility, and because he had for a second the glittering impression that he was the only person left alive in the room— and he laughed softly, exultant.

"He's gonna bogey this one too," Neal murmured unhappily. "That damn Nicklaus'll win. He wins everything."

Will in the early evening found himself subject to a flood of remembrance. His memories went almost as far back as he did, sometimes further than he thought they could go (diaper rash—Howard holds up the can of talcum powder for his mother and peers curiously at Will's reddened parts); but for the most part they focused on his life with his wife. Obscure, trivial moments came before him with a shocking clarity; they possessed a more vital, irresistible reality the second time around. Here too, limpid as day, were their arguments. Will, jealous of the department head (Archer, whose buck teeth made him look like the village idiot), dragged Lucy out of the cocktail party by her elbow; Lucy, late one late fall evening, pulled on her coat and stalked out of the house in her bare feet; they sat over herbal tea and told each other they were full of crap. Not one of the arguments was anything but absurd, absurd and ridiculous; what had they been arguing about? Will gave Harwood a strip of raw meat; he held it in his needlelike talons, and didn't move. Perhaps Will would read for a while; he could try that Pynchon novel again. Perfect thing to get your mind off—

And then it seemed transparently obvious to Will that just a little twist would be necessary. They were not so different, Lucy and he; surely not irreconcilable. There was no need for such drastic measures. Lucy was being too dramatic; things could always change for the better. Always things could change for the better.

Possibly literary criticism: more soporific. Where did that Frye go? He found a fat paperback and switched on his dim lamp.

Lucy had read something in the newspaper today: a small article, hundreds of people were dead. She was disgusted: the President's small daughter fell down, and her Band-aid was on the front page; and here hundreds of people were dead in South America. She had already fed Sarah and done a wash. Now she had to put her to bed, first mentioning the existence of the toilet, which Sarah did not need, because she had already deposited her material in a handier receptacle. Lucy sighed. The phone rang.

Soon she asked Will why he had called.

"I've just seen blue lightning," he said. "And now it's raining cats and dogs."

"I thought you're not supposed to use the telephone during electrical storms."

"Oh, well, the lightning's over now."

"I can still hear thunder."

"Yeah. Well, just for a minute, hunh?"

"I have to put Sarah to bed soon."

"Give her my love, okay? Lots of love."

"She says your name a lot," Lucy admitted.

"Oh yeah? I say her name too. I say it a lot. To tell you the truth, I'm pretty lonely." For a second Will waited. "Otherwise I'm doing pretty well," he volunteered.

"That's good."

"What about you?"

"Fine. I really have to go, Will. I don't much feel like talking. I'm not feeling too well just now."

"No? What's wrong?"

Lucy shook her head at the telephone. "No, actually, I'm fine. I just have to go."

Will started to ramble. He told Lucy about Neal's visit; then hurried on to the hawk and the piglets. "I watched the sow give birth," he told her. "There were eleven piglets. Must have been excruciating for her, hunh? I thought about you a lot while I watched it."

"Lovely compliment."

"No, she was beautiful. She was extraordinarily beautiful." He stopped, remembering. "For a pig," he added.

"It's Sarah's bedtime."

Will hurried on, moved by a sudden surge of desperation. "It's the same process," he said. "It's always the same—the same miracle. But the difference is that humans love. That was what kept occurring to me: I love my wife." Just at that moment Will felt an unaccountable twinge of doubt: did he love his wife?

Lucy spoke slowly. "I think I want a divorce," she said.

35

3

Howard was the crossword-puzzle editor for a New York
newspaper; when ambitious he contributed an occasional
book review. This occasion seemed to require greater effort
these years; there was more to say, really too much to say,
and yet for all his strength of intention his umbrous prose
seemed to lose all direction; and then there were fewer and
fewer books worth troubling over. He occupied a small cubicle off an enormous room where a thousand typewriters chattered; and in the ceaseless roar Howard was alternately
amused and disturbed by certain small repetitions. It seemed
that every day he found himself crossing out the clue "Summer drink" and replacing it with "Humorist George." Sometimes, more rarely, he drew a line with his fountain pen
through "Humorist George" and whimsically wrote (the
typewriters clacked out a thousand words at once) "Summer
drink." It was true Howard was tired of some words, small
convenient words that constantly buttressed his puzzles; the

tiresome erne, the omnipresent nene, the infamous esne. But it had to be, that was the nature of words, there was no jai _____ without its alai, and it would be impossible to perpetrate outrageous puns, or weave subtle tapestries of half-meaning, without occasionally calling Humorist George to the rescue in some tight (if banal) spot. Howard was tired, but not tired out; not finished, not yet.

The realist could add that he appreciated his salary, used it, and needed it. We don't need to go into numbers, certainly, but those numbers made him comfortable and gave him a kind of satisfaction. Howard dressed well, it was I think generally conceded, although he showed an unusual weakness for bright buttons on his close-fitting dark suits. He did not shrink at the sight of a famous label, nor at its imposing price tag. In his brownstone, too, he had exercised his formidable taste; and though the plans were verified and executed by a distinguished decorator, and the results were maintained by a housekeeper, they were his plans and his results. Most of the rooms were dominated by wooden furniture (Shaker, or nearly), Persian-style rugs, and seventeenth-century Dutch art (photographic reproductions of the Leiden *fijnschilders,* Fabritius, and de Hoogh—but one fine, genuine Seghers etching). Howard's studio was an exception: in the large white room he scattered modern furniture, also white; left the floor bare but for palmy potted plants, and adorned the wall with two large examples of minimal art. Howard was proud of his house; but I'll stop talking about my house.

About Howard himself it can certainly be said that he hated children, liked church, and had been an oarsman. At forty he was no longer as fit as he had been as bowman for Harvard. But the stomach's not too bad yet, Howard thought, slapping it; he could still run a brisk mile if he had to. Fortunately he didn't have to.

Why did Howard attend church, since he didn't figure to

be joined there by God? If God wasn't in attendance, something else was; something as elusive, and nearly as imposing. In the trappings of ritual Howard found the richness, the substance and quality of life as it had long been lived; in an empty century the old rites had a stately pathos, a touching decorum. A good Catholic service, complete with ponderous Latin and thunderous organ, reminded him pleasantly of the Queen of England: cannons boomed, and onto the balcony stepped a middle-aged lady wearing an odd hat, waving a stiff arm; Howard waved back, inspired and saddened. We have accomplished, lately, the fall of man, and this lady still waves, Howard thought; only later adding the adverb *gallantly*.

This sentimental man's office door opened one summer morning and into his cubicle regally, gallantly stepped our mother. Always tall and thin, in her sixties she pulled her straight gray hair back from her forehead, her skin drew in around her sharp bones, and, looking at her, it seemed possible to deduce her skeleton.

Howard held her chair, and she sat gracefully, dabbing her forehead.

"I wouldn't bother you in your office, as you know, Howard, but I have a message I didn't want to give you over the telephone."

"What message might that be?" Howard asked placidly.

"You remember your father, don't you?" our mother asked in her social voice. Certainly Howard remembered his father; he had been fourteen when his father left. Gravely Howard nodded.

"Your uncle said your father would like to see you. All the boys."

The last time Howard saw him, Homer was carrying suitcases out to the taxi. He didn't wave; Howard let the draperies fall back over the window.

Howard was forty years old. He thought about this for a while. "Which uncle?" he said at last.

"Your Uncle Elliot."

"Elliot." That was the one who had sent the birthday cards, the money. "Did he say why?"

"No, dear." She adjusted a glove on her knee.

"Where is Homer?" Howard asked, using the first name, as we all sometimes did, deliberately.

"Flower Fifth Avenue."

Flower Fifth Avenue? he repeated to himself. The name was familiar—

"Flower Fifth Avenue *Hospital?*"

"That's right, dear," she said, and expelled her fluttering cough.

There was no point in reprimanding his mother. "Well, what's wrong with him?" Howard said as calmly as he could.

"I don't know. Elliot wanted to tell me, but I asked him not to. Elliot was always blunt."

"Must be serious, don't you think?"

Our mother began to twist the handle of her purse. "Well, I suppose so," she said reluctantly. Her eyes searched Howard's desk. "But it would be just like Elliot to make a great hue and cry over a kidney stone. Elliot's extremely excitable; you might never know."

Howard smiled. "You don't want us to go, do you?" he teased, rubbing the tips of his fingers together.

But Howard was never very good at teasing; or perhaps too good. His mother's upper lip quivered; she replied, "No, I *don't,*" coughed delicately, and burst into tears.

Howard was appalled, appalled; he jumped up and bent over her as if he had spilled something on her dress. She spilled a few drops, and sniffled. "I've never had the strength for boys," she said, wiping her eyes with her handkerchief. "Howard, I do wish you'd been girls."

"You were stronger than Homer, Mother."

"Homer," she said, and shook her head. She dabbed twice more and turned to Howard, composed. "I have recollected

39

myself," she said. "Now please tell me whether you intend
to visit your father."

Howard judged her recovery. She appeared calm and settled; for all his manners, Howard didn't see why he shouldn't
tell her the truth: "Yes. Yes, of course I do."

"But why?" she cried. "All he did for you was send—"

"It wouldn't be right not to." An urge came to Howard to
put up his hand, bottle up the argument he felt coming. But
from his mother, whose tears were drying on her bones,
there came only a dry look. No imploring would be done.

"I won't belabor the point, Howard," Mrs. Bard said, allow-
ing herself a last sniffle. "I will merely promise that these past
few moments have contained my final tears for that man:
whether he dies, or no."

"Perhaps that's fair," Howard judged.

She didn't usually work lunch. Neal had never seen her in
daylight.

"So who are you today?" she asked.

Neal stood up. "Allow me to introduce myself. Dwight D.
Eisenhower." Same stupid joke, he thought.

"How do you do?" Delsey said, ceremonious. "Have you
chosen yet, President Eisenhower?"

"The usual."

"What's that, Nixon again?"

"Pretty funny," he admitted. "What else can you do?"

"A roast beef platter. You get mashed potatoes and peas."
She poised pencil against pad.

"Okay," Neal said, without enthusiasm. "And a salad."

"Toss salad," she said, scribbling. "To drink?"

Neal smiled as if she'd made another joke. "Do you fraternize?" he asked.

She smiled back easily. "No," she said.

"Heineken's."

"Russian, French, or Italian on your salad?"

"I'm a romantic, Delsey. I only come here to see you. Italian."

"Ask me again sometime," she said, taking his menu.

A minute later she brought the beer. "Well, do you fraternize now?" he asked.

Delsey laughed a little. "No," she said.

"I'll ask you again sometime."

In the afternoon Howard called. He said, "Shouldn't we all go see the old man together?" and Neal thought, He's afraid to go by himself.

"I'm not going," Neal replied.

Howard sounded shocked. "For heaven's sake why not?"

"You know I hate New York. The Yankees, remember?"

"Neal. This doesn't have anything to do with baseball."

"No. And I don't have anything to do with the 'old man,' as you call him."

"Don't you think you should?"

"Listen, Big Howie, I don't think I should do *any*thing I don't want to do. That's one of the primaries, remember?"

"You're talking like a child, Neal. At some point you'll have to grow up."

"Why? Homer didn't."

Howard paused. "I'm very sorry you feel that way."

"I'm sorry too," Neal said cheerfully. "Just not very sorry."

"Not sorry enough, that's certain," Howard growled.

Neal apologized quickly, and changed the subject: "So when are you going to come up here, Big Howie?"

"Christmas," Howard said mechanically. "With Mother, for the service."

"You're going to miss Will's piglets."

"I'm not worried. He'll always have piglets of one sort or another. Sarah, for example."

"He doesn't have Sarah now, remember?"

41

"He will again. We'll see how long this business lasts."

Neal whistled. "I'm proud of you, Big Howie. You've become something of a cynic in your later years."

"Just an even forty," Howard sniffed. "My prime."

Pete Petersen answered Neal's ring. Will was out doing the afternoon milking, would call back later. By the way, Pete, how's your game? This meant golf, and Pete gave a detailed, too detailed, reply.... Neal put the phone down, his feet up, and gave himself to a reverie: he saw Will yanking rhythmically on some unconcerned cow's mammae, the resultant stream's tinny noise in the inevitable bucket, the short three-legged stool and Will's absurdly long, sprawled legs. The cow, in Neal's vision, chewed the cud; Will, tobacco. Neal knew about the existence of milking machines, but he didn't allow them entry into his image, which pleased him just as it was. A moment later he went on to insist that Will clean out the slops: so here came Will with a square shovel, pushing manure down the receding length of an endless cement trough, past the latter portions of an infinitude of cows. Neal remembered the case of a man accused of stealing cow manure in Vermont, only a few years ago; of course (it was too bad) the judge threw it out of court—presumably in fear of Exhibit A. What was it we used to call cowpies? Meadow muffins.

Will said, "It's good to hear your voice." Neal cleared his throat, told Will about our father. Will listened silently; the request caught quickly in his craw.

"The bastard leaves us without a word when we don't know up from down, then expects us to run and hold his hand."

"Nobody said he *expects* us to come."

"He does, though. You know he does. He always *expects.*"

To his own irritation Neal found himself being conciliatory. "I don't think it's too surprising. Most people would want the same thing."

42

"But for what? Some foolish kind of forgiveness? Last rites?"

"Maybe. Look, I don't know, champ. I'm just relaying the message."

Will went on more calmly, his anger dissolved in curiosity. "Maybe he just wants to look at his descendants. So he can watch time pass backwards."

"Unh-hunh. Right. And maybe he wants to give us each a piece of chocolate," Neal put in. "But it's up to you, anyway. I wash my hands of the whole deal."

"Are you going?"

"Nope. You?"

"Homer can shove it up his absentee ass."

Neal chuckled. "That's the way I thought you'd look at it. Anyway, how's it going?"

To Will it must have seemed that everything was coming apart at once; as if the little demon who was master of his anger were playing a game, betting for mastery of more. Will's rage, usually a dove that glided straight to a spot and nestled there, seemed to want to fly off in every direction. Harwood was bleeding freely now, each day growing more lethargic and inert; Lucy seemed about to slip away from Will forever, just when he needed her back; lately, Will admitted, he wasn't sure what he was doing, he found it impossible to write, he wasn't sure he shouldn't just go back to UMass in the fall. But he had already sent in his letter of resignation. He felt as if he had resigned from more than that. Aches, pains, came to his body more freely than ever before—he digested nothing without internal struggle. He watched with fear as the weight in the bags beneath his eyes inexorably increased. When he looked in the mirror, all he saw was mortality.

Now our foolish father was gathering his happy band of offspring around him in his time of need. Nothing in the

43

apartment left for Will to kick. All the destruction that could be borne had been accomplished already.

"It's going okay," he told Neal. "But I have one problem. I need a lawyer."

"Is it first-degree?"

Will ignored him. "Do you do divorces?"

Neal chose not to heed the implication. "I do a little of everything: some tax law, a few torts, a bit of probate, a divorce here and there; everything this side of criminal. What can I do for you?"

Will said, "Lucy wants a divorce. What do you think of my chances?"

"Chances of what? Contesting the divorce?"

"No. Sarah."

"Bad. It's No Fault, right? Or is it Cruel and Abusive?"

"Don't know."

"Should be able to beat alimony, but you'll have to fork out child support. Just a few bucks, though, since she's working and you're not—"

"The hell I'm not. Pretty hard, too."

"Okay, okay. I just meant she has a higher salary."

Will let it pass at that. "What I want to know, Neal, is what about custody?"

"Custody?" Neal snorted. "Not a chance in the whole wide world, champ."

"How come?"

"Lucy is the *mother*, Will. *Mo*-ther. You know what that means?—just everything, is all. The only other criterion is income, and she's got you there, too. Forget custody. They'll give you visiting rights. Try to talk Lucy into giving you Sarah on the weekends or something."

"That's not exactly what I had in mind."

"It's a tough break, kid," Neal said. "But that's the story from here, sports fans."

44

"Damn blind law," Will growled. He added a lame, "Thanks for the help."

"Don't thank me," Neal said. "Send me a check."

Will finally decided he wasn't even angry. Of course there was a more intimate connection between mother and child, an emotional umbilical. Income with a capital I, that legal criterion was to be expected too; law was based on money, Will recited, holding the binoculars up to his eyes. Money was the means people used to relate publicly to each other; and law was the set of rules for those relations. The sentence came to him as if he were still teaching; it had no meaning, he judged, or if it had meaning it had no use. He scanned the cliff: no use. Crows, about eight crows. A flock of swallows darting over the field. Will turned back into the woods.

He left the path and wandered along a stone wall; a bluejay noticed and protested. Will climbed the brow of a hill, heading for a dense dark cluster of evergreens. He had a longing to see something rare, to be shown a sign of the marvelous. At the foot of a Douglas fir he sat down. He tried to be quiet, let it come. He needed, he thought, a little plain-and-fancy rejuvenation. The shadows of the forest grew with the early evening; songbirds quieted; crickets began to repeat their single shrill note. A downy woodpecker sailed through the dappled light and landed on the gnarled branch of a dead apple tree; rapped at the branch three times and swooped off. A nuthatch appeared with a fluttering noise and attacked the same branch; crept slowly down its crooked length, occasionally prying the shaggy bark with its awl-like bill. The nuthatch turned and slowly retraced its patient steps; Will, less patient, had already looked away by the time the bird reached the beginning and flew off. Was this all? Will wondered; where would his column come from? Was it to be two chickadees and three pages about the universe? Chickadees hopped from branch to branch, peering at him, twittering.

Well, the universe didn't have much to say for itself. What would the Greeks, who read portents from the doings of birds, have said about two chickadees?—about an absence of omens, a future that gave no signs, no hint even to the wise? One of the chickadees said its name. Disgusted, Will stalked back through the underbrush toward the cliff, hoping for a hawk.

Crows jabbered harshly from atop the cliff. The sky was blank, blue. A few wisps of cloud clustered around the sun, just at the horizon, but there were no hawks. An empty day, now nearly gone; and on Will's notepad, beside "8 crows, swalls, chick, nuth., downy," he wrote "Lucy," as if he were carving it on the dead apple tree.

From the midst of a shimmer of flying drops the old man came out of the sea. At first Will thought he was our father; but as he came closer, Will saw the long red face, skin dotted by bursts of livid color, and the great eyes like saucers, and he knew it was Mr. Burnham. "Time for Middaysies," Mr. Burnham trumpeted happily. Will turned; his eyes left Mr. Burnham's baggy, unfashionable bathing suit, and for a moment he saw only sand and the line of surf, and then, as if carried on a carousel, he was given a glimpse of the dunes and long, waving grass. At the end of the arc he found Lucy and Mrs. Burnham sitting on a beach blanket; Mrs. Burnham was holding out a martini for her husband; Lucy patted the blanket beside her; Will sat. Will had noticed the peculiarly jovial style of the Burnhams that morning: Mr. Burnham had called him "pal" twice, and Mrs. Burnham had tittered when she dropped the salad. It was really very curious. Then he found Mr. Burnham eyeing him; Will examined the egg sandwich in his hand for solutions. Mrs. Burnham had chopped off the crusts, and suddenly Will understood that Lucy's parents knew he'd been sleeping with their daughter.

But the afternoon was long, the picnickers drank a Thermos of martinis, and Will wasn't careful: he lay his head to

46

rest (it swam in a sea of its own) in Lucy's lap. Above him he found two distinct layers of clouds, passing in opposite directions; then, through his closed eyelids, he still saw the ball of sun, this time igniting an orange sky. Perhaps he drifted in sleep, or merely drifted, and above his head the jocular façade had slipped, and perhaps there were hurried whispers of anger or hurt: Will woke to changed faces. Propping himself up with a hand on Lucy's knee, he found Mrs. Burnham's sharp face tightened around the lower-case *o* of her mouth, and Mr. Burnham's apopletic face sputtering angrily. "You— you teen-age gigolo!" Mr. Burnham sputtered.

With both hands Mr. Burnham gripped the soft brown carcass of a roast chicken; trembling, he lifted it over his head and heaved it at Will's bare chest. The chicken displayed a surprising amount of bounce. From Will's chest it bounded nimbly onto Mr. Burnham's inner tube, rebounded onto the sand, and rolled halfheartedly over on its side.

Will laughed, which he was not meant to do. That was another mistake; mistakes like these dominated his relationship with the Burnhams. Until of course Mr. Burnham became ill.

In the hospital bed Will saw his own father instead. White-coated doctor; angelic nurse; hopeful, serious smiles on the faces of the visitors. The nurses and visitors moved aside to give him room, him, the bereaved. Will bent over the bed. Homer lay there perfectly still, with his chalky moon face and his tweed jacket and bow-tie the perfect image of the man who broke his boiled egg with a knife the day he left. Except that his eyes were closed. Will understood, gazing up at the blank face of the cliff, now entirely in shadow, that these eyes were not to be opened—either by Homer, or anyone else. It was forbidden to pry them open and watch the blank eyeballs. Not even a little peek? Will said to himself, trying to be amused. But it was not amusing; no good to try to be like Neal. Will lingered at the little scene of an imagined bedside, and try as he might to make jokes, he still gazed at this moon-faced corpse with a mixture of ruthlessness and pity. Small unfunny details cropped up, like the curve of the rims of Homer's ears, or the deep shadowing above the eyes. It was no use, Will thought at last, trudging back toward the farmhouse; no use to disavow the connection, disown the man.

A yellow nimbus circled the porch lights as he approached: white moths, gypsy moths, flew in and out. Will had heard that moths were attracted by night lights because they used the moon as a guide, and artificial lights ruined their sense of direction; they went haywire, made circles around their false moon. Where had he heard that? It didn't seem likely. How did moths fly when there was a new moon, for example. But it was a nice idea: flying by false moons. He opened the screen door and turned off the light, wondering where the gypsy moths would go, now that he had switched off their moon.

Harwood blinked sleepily, ruffled. He doesn't look so bad; he's eaten most of his food. A few red remnants lay scattered about on the newspaper; Harwood shook his meat before he ate it, like a puppy with a slipper. Sad to see a bird of prey look "cute."

Will called Neal back. Will was going to see their father. Cheerfully Neal said, "You don't want to do that: it won't feel good."

"Feeling good isn't the point," Will said.

"Tell you what. If you feel like taking a trip, we'll go see the Sox on Sunday. I'll pick you up and we'll drive down to Fenway. It's a doubleheader. The Orioles."

"That doesn't sound bad, Neal," said Will (he was thinking of bright songbird emerging from woven nest), "but I've already made up my mind. You know what *that* means." He waited for Neal's laughter. Neal didn't laugh. "I won't go with Howard, though. I want to see him by myself."

48

"Why see him at all, champ?"

Will had his answer ready. "I want to ask him why he left."

Neal grunted. "He probably went to the Red Sox double-header."

"Probably. But I want to ask him anyway."

"Okay, buddy. Do what you want; you will anyway. Maybe Homer will give you that piece of chocolate."

He had already given Will some; but Howard had taken it. Outside Charley Miller's store nine-year-old Howard gently lifted a long, slender Hershey Bar from four-year-old Will's back pocket. Just back from the war, our father chatted, puff-chested, with Charley within. Will demanded his candy bar back in his biggest voice; but when this demand was met by silence, Will merely turned away. . . .

Two hours later Will turned away from the phone, resisting it. The telephone itself was the problem: if he didn't have an extension right there in his apartment, he might be content. He wouldn't keep harping on the past. It was connection that plagued him—all he had to do was twist his finger a few times in the obliging disk and be connected to Lucy, to Howard, to Mother, to everyone that he no longer wanted in his life. There was just one place in the world now; it was hell.

According to Will he slept soundly; and he was only awakened by a faint but persistent ringing. He discovered himself squatting beside his bed. Something was draped over his shoulder; with one hand he clutched something to his stomach; between two fingers of the other hand he held something hard. He inspected the hard something dangling between his fingers: telephone receiver. He looked down and uncurled the fingers holding something to his stomach: alarm clock. The final something was a sleeve of his long johns, dangling unreasonably over his shoulder.

Lucy answered the telephone. "Hello?"

Will heard a voice. "Hello?" he said into the receiver.

49

"Will?"

"Unh-hunh. Is that you, Lucy?"

"Are you all right? Where are you?"

"I'm fine. How are you, Lucy?"

"Do you realize what time it is, Will? Is this some kind of joke?"

"No, it really isn't. I—"

"You had me scared half to death. Do you know what time it is?"

"No, I don't. As a matter of fact, I was just asleep."

"So was I. So are most people at quarter after four in the —no, Mom, it's okay. It's for me. Go back to bed, okay? I'm sorry. Yes, it is. He's not. It's all right." Lucy put the phone down. When she picked it up again she said, "You know, you can't do this kind of thing, Will. Not even to me."

"I was just trying to tell you—Lucy—"

"Crazy isn't funny anymore, Will."

"No, I was just trying to say—"

"It's not fair, you've got to stop this kind of—"

"Lucy, let me say something."

"You've got to stop *pes*tering me, Will."

"Will you listen for a second? Christ, you don't even listen for a *sec*ond."

"At four o'clock in the morning? You're damn right I don't."

"Okay, okay, I'm sorry. Just listen. I'm trying to tell you something. It's all right."

"It's *not* all right. You go on as if I haven't said anything. But I don't want you to call, Will. I don't want to talk to you. Can you get that through your—"

"For Chrissakes, Lucy!"

"—head? You've got your problems, I've got my problems, everybody's got their problems." She stopped.

"That's very true," Will said quietly.

"Well? Are you gonna stop calling me now?"

"It was an *ac*cident, Lucy. I called you in my sleep. When I woke up I was holding on to the phone and talking to you. Honest to God, I didn't *mean* to call. It sounds ridiculous, but it's true."

"Oh, for Christ's sake."

"Listen, it's true. I'm sorry I called—it was an accident, but I'm sorry, okay? I apologize, okay? But it's true."

"I know, I know, nothing is ever your fault. You're never wrong. Always innocent."

"Well, you're always fumbling with your goddamn keys, Lucy," Will spat back, hanging up.

Will slept well the rest of the night. No Lucy, no keys; he saw a row of rounded hills covered thickly by short grass. Small wildflowers, buttercups and violets and edelweiss, sparkled everywhere under a white sun. In the dream he thought: So this is the moon. Good.

Howard's sleep was more difficult to attain. Lying in his bed, Howard was plagued by Homer in his; Howard's only distraction came from the occasional sounds of a sadly quiet corner of the city. Cats had already been in and out of heat; apparently no fires were to be had; even the police seemed to be taking the night off. No garbageman would bang for hours. So Howard tossed and turned in his hard bed, and thought—perhaps in a somewhat mannered, pedantic fashion—about death.

4

Seemed like lunchtime. Neal stuffed his papers into the crowded top drawer of his desk and was out the door, whistling the theme from *Star Wars*. The law, on this breezy, bright Thursday midmorning, was an imposition; Neal, despite the prescience of a handsome fee, was not interested in helping his quick-fingered dentist construct a tax shelter out of a multitude of fast-depreciating buildings. When prying into clients, the dentist wore enormous spectacles, onto which he attached another pair, these square. Neal opened. Dr. Stark held out a tiny mirror, and Neal saw, reflected in its concave curve, the distorted image of squat Dr. Stark—in his bespectacled spectacles a complicated nightmare insect, plumbing the murky depths of Neal's large mouth. Reading Dr. Stark's informal, illegible notes (jotted onto the back of appointment reminders with a splashing fountain pen), Neal shuddered with the recollection of that tiny portion of picture: the distorted dentist, a multilensed mantis. Neal appreciated the principle of accelerated depreciation of property; but he would rather, he thought, have lunch. He would always rather have lunch. It was eleven o'clock.

He was walking slowly down the hill from Smith when he was passed by Lucy walking quickly. When she turned to face him she had already brought out her narrow, but charming, smile. Neal wondered if she could have failed to recognize him; but that was Lucy, she had her mind in a number of places, none of which was necessarily where she was. And there she was, smiling, wearing a blue leotard and a wide-belted blue skirt, her summer freckles out: Neal was ready to forgive Lucy far more grievous offenses than she was ready to commit.

"Hiya," she said.

"Howdy, ma'am," he replied, and doffed the hat he didn't have on. "Going my way?"

"Always am, mister."

"Long time no seek, hunh?"

She dropped the game, if not the smile. "I wasn't sure we were still friends. I hadn't heard."

Neal wasn't quite ready to do the same. "Oh, I don't guess little marital squabbles could have much effect on more important relationships, do you?"

"You're not even a little angry, hunh?"

"Angry? Hell no. I'm after you now, Lucy. You're fair game."

They were both smiling. Neal checked Lucy's multitudinous freckles: cute. She was attractive in a skin-and-bones way; small, but energetic, perhaps. For the first time Neal looked her over as sexual prospect; he tried to do so as coldly as possible. Tits, ass, legs, lips, what would she be like in bed. It didn't quite work. Lucy retained her forbidden aspect—when Neal put her to bed, she wore flannel nightclothes and slept soundly.

Lucy seemed to know what was going on. "Fair game, maybe," she said, "but easy game, no."

"No problem," Neal boasted. " 'When the going gets ridiculous, the ridiculous get going.' My high-school football coach told me that. Send me in there, coach."

"You didn't have a high-school football coach, Neal. You went to prep school and you were assistant manager of the soccer team. In the winter you were assistant manager of the basketball team, and in the spring you played golf or something."

"Tennis," Neal corrected. "JV tennis."

"That's right, I remember the story of your doubles partner breaking his racket over your head."

"That was a lie," Neal said. "But since we're discussing disgusting old times, shouldn't we have some greasy lunch together? Got a half-hour?"

"I'm not hungry, but I'll watch you eat. We can go to the Soup Kitchen." Lucy had gone to Brandeis with the owner of the Soup Kitchen, Potch Baker. Potch was a short, curly-haired avuncular man who looked like a pudgy Bob Dylan. He was always gregarious and tired. His wife Tikki made terrific blintzes.

They sat at a small table toward the rear of the long room. Caribbean rock was thumping over the speakers; Neal tapped his foot hesitantly, not quite in time. Potch came over to wet Lucy's cheek with a warm kiss; Neal felt a twinge of jealousy, which he immediately disowned.

Potch turned to Neal. "I think I know you," he said. "I don't remember what context it was in, but I know you."

"It probably wasn't me," Neal said, not quite looking at Potch. "I don't frequent contexts very much."

Potch scratched his shoulder through his T-shirt. "It's Neal, right?"

"That's right. Patricia."

"Neal Patricia," Potch cackled. "As I live and breathe. You

54

were great, you really were. You won an Oscar, didn't you?"

"Yup. For *Duh.* My greatest role."

Potch pointed at Neal, saying to Lucy, "You've got a walk-ing *Mad* magazine here." He added to Neal, "I'm not being critical. I'm the kind of guy that still likes *Mad* magazine. You can ask my wife."

Someone called him from the kitchen; he shouted back, "All right already," and got out his pad. "What do you guys want? I don't recommend the gazpacho. We just made a new batch, and it hasn't had time to get good yet."

"Coffee and cheesecake for me," Lucy said. "Real sin."

"Sin's good for you," Neal said.

"Hey, I like this guy Neal," Potch said to Lucy. "He's not Jewish, is he?"

"I'm afraid not," Lucy said. "He's a lawyer."

"That's close enough. What do you want to eat, Neal?"

"Chili and Greek salad. And cheese blintzes."

"Ethnic, very ethnic," Potch commented, walking away. "We need more lawyers like you."

"How well did you know this guy at Brandeis?" Neal com-plained.

"Pretty well. Not well enough to want to sleep with him. Why? You like him?"

"Sure, sure I like him. I just can't figure out what he does for a living."

"You're jealous, because he makes jokes too. I hear nobody is allowed to make jokes in the same room as you."

"Did Will tell you that? He's hardly ever tried. But listen, Lucy, how well do you have to know someone before you sleep with him? I'm all excited now."

Lucy grimaced. "I don't want you all excited. And I think I'll never know you well enough. Sorry I mentioned it."

"Why? What does Norman Mailer have that I don't?"

"Nothing, of course."

"Are you trying to tell me that you love me?"

Lucy was suddenly serious. "Yes, in a way. And your brother."

Neal stopped too. "You want me to tell him you said that?"

"Don't bother. He already knows."

Neal picked up a cut-glass ashtray from the table and turned it around between his hands; he ran his fingers along the edge; he held it up to a sunbeam, where it sparkled. "Seems that the lady in question is trying to tell me something," he said, not looking up from his ashtray. "Would the lady in question like to talk about her lovelife?"

Curious thing about Neal, Lucy decided: As soon as he has to stop joking he gets worried. Never serious without being embarrassed. Lucy liked shy people; the early quiet suited her. It was always quite a while before she had much to say to a person.

Will had been painfully shy when they first met. Pleasantly but not dreamily she remembered his dark, angular face, his beautiful brown eyes shining beneath close-cropped black hair. In class Will seemed to burn with the desire to speak, and never said anything. He squirmed uncomfortably in his chair; occasionally sputtered out low, wet, nonverbal noises; when called upon, he curtly shook his head. Lucy went to Anglo-Saxon 461 just to watch him fidget and say nothing.

"The lady in question is no lady," she said to Neal. "And she doesn't want to bore her friend."

Neal looked up from his ashtray, whose facets threw a shower of pinpoint glimmers around the room. "I think I wouldn't mind talking about life with my brother. If it doesn't bother you, that is."

"How could it bother me? After all, Will's been the main topic of conversation for a dozen years. What Will thought; what Will wanted; how Will felt today. He's a guessing game, you can never tell whether he'll be in ecstasy or a sulk. He used to pull me up and down with him, like a Raggedy Ann doll with strings attached. To me the hard part was that there

56

didn't seem to be a *reason* for him to feel one way or another. I looked for a long time, too. It disturbed me to think that Will's games might not have rules; I was brought up on causality, and here I was, married to a series of spontaneous circumstances."

"Well, it's a spontaneous generation," Neal claimed, grinning. "But I don't agree. I think Will's games do have rules. It's just that he doesn't know what they are." Potch brought Neal a bowl of salad; a black olive eyeballed him from a drift of feta cheese. "As a matter of fact, I don't think they are games. Or if they are, Will isn't playing; he's the ball."

Lucy shook her head. "I felt like the ball most of the time. It hurts to get kicked back and forth like that."

Neal poured oil and vinegar on his salad; he started off with too much oil, so he added, reasonably enough, too much vinegar. "Can I make a sexist comment?" he asked.

"You always do."

"Thanks. Here it is. It takes a woman to look at a game and take the ball's point of view."

"Now just why do you think that is?" Lucy asked.

"Because they're full of hot air?" Neal tried. He slid some cheese onto the back of his fork and stabbed a bit of lettuce. When he put it into his mouth, the back of his jaws ached. I wasn't ready, he thought; I forgot to salivate.

"I think Will *is* the one playing the game," Lucy said, absently watching Neal chew his food. "To get back to Will," she added, and laughed. "We didn't mention him for nearly a whole half-minute. We have to watch that, he'll die of inattention. Anyway, it may be true that he doesn't know what he's doing, but he doesn't try to stop either. He's a child: me-me-me. And he's still going through stages. He's a bird watcher; a farmer; a poet. It's sort of a mundane dreamworld. There's nothing permanent, and nothing real either."

"I'm not so sure about that," Neal said. "He seems to carry his dreams pretty far into the real world. I went up to his farm and watched him snap off a few piglet teeth, for example."

"A few what?"

"The teeth of some piglets. They have to break them off so they won't bite into the mother. Which reminds me, how is Sarah? I miss that girl, you know."

"Come see her in Springfield any time you want, if you can stand my mother with her. You remember my mother? She's the kind of person who calls herself Mommy when she's talking to her dog—you know, 'Mommy is going to give you your little supper. Don't you want Mommy to give you your supper? Yes, you do.' You can imagine how she treats Sarah."

"Has she got her today?"

"No, she's at the day-care center. Sarah, that is."

"How's the growing-up business?"

"Oh, not too bad, I guess. I've given up trying to toilet-train her for the time being."

"No luck, hunh? Lois Culbertson made Randy walk around without any clothes. He was toilet-trained in about two weeks."

Lucy wrinkled her nose. "Too brutal for me. Besides my mother still has her one day a week. Do you think she could deal with a horrific circumstance like that? She'd practically spill her drink. I'd have to call off class to attend to the atrocity."

"What are you teaching your collegiate pinheads this summer?"

"A rehash of freshman composition for backward scientists, and a course called 'Women in Sex.' That one 'traces the graphic portrayal of sex in both pornographic and straight literature': sado-masochism, rape, lesbianism, the whole shmeer. It's very well-attended."

"Heard any good rapes lately?" Neal asked through the last bite of salad. "I got one for you. Did you hear the one about the rapist in England a few years ago, the Cambridge one who did university women?"

58

"This is a joke?"

"No, it's a crime. A series of rapes."

"You always say these things are true, Neal. Would you tell me if you were making it up?"

"I wouldn't, but I'm not. There's no need to invent crimes; every day fantastic ones are being committed all over the world. The only difficult part is finding out about them."

"Like in Chile."

"Yes, like in Chile. Or like in Denton, Texas, where last month a masked bandit held up a delivery truck at gunpoint and made off with a hundred and eighty frozen anchovy pizzas. Speaking of chilis, here comes mine." Neal held a spoon expectantly in his fist. "Thanks very much." He nudged some onto the spoon and placed it cautiously on his tongue. "Hot," he said. "Good. Mmm, let me tell you about my rapist, Lucy. Wonderful *modus operandi*. He wore a satin-lapelled jacket, complete with spats and top hat; when a victim answered his knock he tipped his hat and bowed. There was a hood underneath, with two words sewn on top, in silk letters: 'The Rapist.' When he bowed, his victims saw 'The Rapist' staring them in the face."

"They must have been totally terrified."

"Not terrified enough, apparently. Sometimes they invited him in. By the way, in your seminar do you take up the question of whether there's such a thing as rape?"

"Unh-hunh. Also whether sex is ever anything but."

Neal, chewing, chuckled. "Might not be a bad defense for a rapist," he commented. He thought for a second, and then dismissed the thought. "No, there's no question, this man did unusual harm. He got more violent as he went along. He never actually killed anyone, but he hurt them. He used objects." Lucy shivered; then she frowned. She was used to grisly details, she told herself: to the bland, grisly details. "Curiously," Neal went on, "this rapist kept getting away, despite the fact that he worked in a limited area, and a crowded one at that. The police had what they thought was an accurate physical description of him; a woman put up a struggle, grabbed his black hair, and it came off. He was blond underneath the wig. They still couldn't catch up with him, even after students began volunteer patrols up and down all the narrow back streets."

"What happened to the woman who put up the struggle?"

"He hurt her."

"How?"

"This is really good chili, by the way. With a blunt object, I think. I'm not sure. I wasn't really interested in that part."

"Unh-hunh," Lucy said, pointedly.

"Finally they caught him. One victim screamed, and they managed to cordon off the area. They didn't let even one person out without questioning. This little old lady on a bicycle tried to run the police barricade. In her saddlebag they found top hat and tails, hood and wigs. I can tell you're not in the mood to appreciate it, but I enjoyed the fact that our rapist had gray hair, after all. He always wore at least two wigs."

"You've got yourself an unusual rapist, all right. Now tell me something, Neal: was he convicted?"

"Unh-hunh, don't worry. He confessed. In fact, he had already confessed a hundred times. He was a middle-aged clerk, happily married, who lived in a tiny village outside Cambridge. He used to get drunk at his local pub every night, and in his cups he claimed to be the notorious rapist. Of course no one believed him."

"That part I believe," Lucy said. She winked; but as she watched Neal slopping up chili sauce with bread, she couldn't help but feel: he told that story to put me at a disadvantage. And he's accomplished that, old Lucy's at a loss again. She knew about all the weapons available to a woman, but there was always the one: the most basic, yes, the best. It didn't even matter that a man might never use it; the knowledge of its existence was self-serving, terrible. Lucy closed her eyes. For God's sake, she told herself, I'm thirty-six. When am I going to get rid of my virginal vulnerability?

Neal wiped his chin, chuckling. Lucy said to him, "Exactly what is it about that story you find funny?"

Neal looked up and down her thin face, smiling, trying to coax a smile in return. "It's not the rapes, if that's what you're implying. I like the sign on his forehead, the wigs, the lady on the bicycle, the little man sitting boasting in his pub with no one believing him. The rapes are the only part I don't like."

"Are you sure?"

"No, of course I'm not *sure*. That's just what I think. But I'm not much interested in my subconscious, in what I *really* think way down underneath. I don't know if anyone can ever tell what they *really* think."

Lucy's lip trembled, as it did when she had something critical to say. "I'm not talking about your secrets. It's not that you're hiding anything; just that you're ignoring something, maybe. You say, on the one hand, that it's a true story; and then you go ahead and pretend that it's an amusement, a fairy tale. What you don't seem to care about is that there's a powerfully real side to it, and that part isn't funny at all. A man came into these women's lives, out of the blue, and raped them; they answered the door, just as you would answer the door any day, and a berserk person came in and *hurt* them. That's in your story, but you don't seem to notice; that's the central reality in your story, but you claim to be more interested in the paraphernalia." She stopped, started again softly: "I hate to tell you this, Neal, but suffering is real."

Potch came and took Neal's chili bowl and silverware away. "You want blintzes now, right?"

"Yes please. With coffee."

"That's how they all do it around here," Potch said, shaking his head. "Like it's dessert. My grandmother used to give us blintzes for breakfast."

"Wonderful to have a grandmother like that," Lucy said.

"Wonderful? Unh-unh. My grandmother was cranky as hell. The only reason she gave us our blintzes was so she could stand over us and bitch while we ate. We were too busy eating to answer her. But it was a lousy atmosphere to eat in, you know?" He moved on to the next table, where two Smithies had sat down. "Well, what do you want?" he said. "I don't recommend the gazpacho."

Neal yawned. "I could use the coffee," he said, and smiled again. "I think what you said about paraphernalia is absolutely right, pal. I'm a paraphanatic. But if I were any other way I'd be terrified to read the newspapers. Those rapes involved suffering, sure, but what crime doesn't? Or war, or repressive government, or plain old poverty and disease? There's a whole lot of suffering going on out there." He smiled again, lamely this time.

"I guess I take it too seriously," Lucy said.

"Oh no, that's your trick, Lucy. If you took it any less seriously Will and I might beat Howard and you at badminton. What would Howard say to that?"

"I'm not worried about Howard, but Will would be a problem. He'd be impossible to live with for a week."

"I thought he was always impossible."

"Close to it. But he had his compensations."

Neal leaned forward in his chair. "Tell me about his compensations."

"You probably know them already. I'm more interested in my cheesecake. When do you think Potch will get around to lugging it over here?"

"No, come on," Neal insisted. "I want to hear what's good about my brother."

The cheesecake wasn't immediately forthcoming. Lucy gazed down the length of the room (it was filling up), past the leafy plants, outside. Through the glass storefront she could see heads bobbing along above the counter; when they went by the open door, heads sprouted whole bodies beneath; then heads and bodies were gone.

"I think I liked Will for his body," Lucy said. "He's good in bed. He has a really nice little ass, and long, gorgeous legs. His only bad point is his chest."

Neal politely smirked for a second. But he was disappointed, you could see that. "Those are his only virtues, hunh?"

Let's see. In April 1953 our Granpacky Singer took all three of us (Howard, Neal, Will) to Washington, D.C. He mumbled something in his quavering voice about cherry blossoms (none remained to be seen), about our great government (it took the shape of pale, splendid, unapproachable monoliths, buildings to feel lost in), about taking the train down just as he had done as a boy, sixty years before. We were fourteen, eleven, and nine; on the train Neal sat with Granpacky, while Will was assigned to Howard's safekeeping. Will was in an extraordinary state of excitement: he chattered gaily on about the toothpicks that held the sandwiches together, avidly watched the banalities of New Jersey roll evenly by, cheerfully made up stories about each person in the car, relaying them to Howard in a conspiratorial whisper. Two in front of us is the President, traveling with his nephew, a small fella who likes dogs; to the side that's a gypsy fortune-teller, and when she goes to the toilet at the end of the car she inserts a golden ring in her nose and admires herself in the mirror; her companion is shot out of cannons, he always lands on his feet; between them there's a kidnapped eight-year-old, heir to millions (diamonds, railways, rodeos), who is going to jump to his feet and cry for help, we have to be ready. . . .

Howard listened, trying to be older and wiser—he succeeded at the first, failed at the second. By Baltimore he realized that the glowing-eyed boy next to him was capable of something that he, Howard, was not. At the time he wasn't sure what it was; he merely multiplied his pretended boredom, and arrived in Washington in low spirits.

But now Howard knows the origin of his envy; he's put it in a form, if he hasn't exactly put it to rest. Will was capable of extracting mystery from his (normal) life. It might be a fiction, but Will's life seemed richer, more vibrant, than Howard's own. Howard felt that Will was good at feeling. I do try. But even now it seems that what I am doing could be better done by Will—if you were just able to do it. . . .

Lucy did not list this among the virtues she enumerated for Neal. She spoke of Will's ardor. She went on to note that he was willing to share the household duties, and did his best, though of course neatness didn't come naturally to him: on occasion, however, he outdid himself. Yes, sometimes he did. Potch brought blintzes, cheesecake, and coffee; Lucy recalled a dinner Will prepared for the department head, Archer, and his wife. Without prompting, Will taught himself to bone a duck so it could be stuffed and sewn back together; he made a truffle *farce,* a charlotte Malakoff, and served by candlelight. Lucy mentioned his pleasant grin, boyish and exuberant: pride is charming, she commented. At least Will wasn't boring; he was too difficult for that.

"Is he a good father, you think?" Neal asked, wondering why he was asking.

"Oh, he's very good," Lucy replied; then had the realization that her enthusiasm was at least partly due to the cheesecake her tongue was rolling around in her mouth. "At least, he's a lot better parent than I am. I hate having a kid, and it shows."

Neal stopped chewing in mid-blintz. "You kidding?"

Lucy smirked. "I see I've finally succeeded in shocking you. You didn't know that, hunh? Having a child was never my idea. It was an accident; I was between birth-control methods."

"But couldn't you have—if you really didn't want—"

"I guess I could have, yeah. But Will wanted it very badly, had always wanted it; and I *was* thirty-three, you know, and I figured—and besides, I didn't want another abortion. One of those is enough for a lifetime."

Neal stared into his coffee cup and didn't look up. Lucy watched. "You didn't know about that either, hunh? I guess Will is pretty secretive. I knew he wouldn't tell Howard; but I didn't think he kept secrets from you."

"Will believes in privacy," Neal mumbled, tipping his cup up so that he could watch the grounds slide along the bottom.

"*You* do, anyway," Lucy answered. "Hey, speaking of privacy, did you hear about the letter the Duchess sent me?"

"My sainted mither?" Neal asked, trying to recover his spirits.

"Just today," Lucy said, reaching into her bag. Neal thought: "Just today": like Will's piglets. Marriage is a serious connection, he went on to himself, amused at the grave tone he could adopt when speaking to himself.

Lucy pulled out a folded piece of pale blue stationery. Neal recognized our mother's handwriting immediately: looping consonants, full circles instead of dots over the *i*'s.

" 'Dear Lucy,' " she read aloud,

"I have heard, through Howard, of the recent events concerning Will and you. Naturally, I was very sorry to hear of it, sorry for everyone involved. However, my biggest concern is with the well-being of Sarah. Will and you are grown, and can fend for yourselves, after all, but the emotional difficulties Sarah will encounter may do more serious damage. In recognition of this, I have a proposal. At first you may consider this mother-in-law meddling. But if you consider my proposal carefully, on its merits, your conclusion may be more agreeable.

"I have noticed—could not help but notice—the irritation

65

you have always felt at being forced to care for the child. I do not blame you for it. For a bright young woman with a career a child can be a difficult and a tiresome cross to bear.

"I am not bright; I do not have a career. I do have a great deal of time and an ample portion of resources. I propose to you that you allow me to care for Sarah. I can do this in Manhattan, or if you wish, move back to Cummington, where opportunities for you to see Sarah would be more readily available. If at any time the arrangement might fail to suit you, you would be free to withdraw Sarah from my custody, after a short period of notice.

"I do hope that you will consider my idea carefully. If you do you will realize that I am actually trying to *liberate* you, Lucy! Though I understand your general lack of concern for such matters, I would like to add that materially Sarah would be very well off indeed.

"I have not spoken to Will about my offer. Would you please do me the kindness of replying directly to me? If you accept, I will, of course, inform my son of our arrangement.

"You may possibly be angered by my plan. If this is the case I ask you to remember that my interests are only the sum total of those of all parties involved, yours certainly not least of all.

"Yours truly,
Eunice Bard."

"Well, what do you think of that?" Lucy asked.

"Pretty funny," Neal said.

"You didn't laugh."

"I laughed inwardly. Way inwardly. What do I think? I think it's—what was the phrase?—mother-in-law meddling?"

"Wait a sec, Neal. I heard you made a profession out of seeing both sides."

"I do see both sides. I think that rude, meddling old woman might be right."

"So you advise me to accept her proposal?" Lucy asked, smiling delightedly (Why? thought Neal).

"No," he said. "I advise you to do what you want. How does Howard put it? 'Leave all doors ajar.' Do what you want, but try to do it in a way that doesn't rule out your doing what you want later too."

"Meaning what?"

"Try to give yourself the freedom to change your mind. Hell, I'm not making any sense. I guess I just think you shouldn't be nasty to the Duchess; she's not as unbreakable as she looks."

"If that's what you mean, that's fine. I agree. If you mean I should be careful so I can change my mind, I don't."

"How come?"

"I'm not *going* to change my mind; I *know* I'm not." Neal shrugged. She added, "I think that's just plain hypocrisy. You can't go around covering up what you feel, just in case."

"Actually, you can," Neal said. "You just have to have an iron bladder. I, for example, was three times voted Bladder of the Year by the Northampton Jaycees." Lucy didn't laugh. Not funny, Neal thought. "You're right," he said. "It is hypocritical. But take it easy on my sainted mither anyway. There's no reason not to."

"I will," Lucy said. She gave Neal a wink. "Don't let it get around," she stage-whispered, "but I'm not totally nasty. Way down deep I'm sort of nice, in fact."

At the moment Lucy looked sort of tired. Her collar-long umber hair, usually meticulously ordered, pointed in all directions; a few particularly rebellious strands had even crossed the plumb line of her part, fallen in a looping arc on the forbidden side. Her shoulders sagged, Neal thought, or perhaps imagined; shadows surrounded her fine blue eyes. He registered a ripple of pity, an emotion that often came to him in his dealings with people, though he didn't always register it, and almost never expressed it. Pity was the last thing Lucy wanted from Neal; so he put it as admiration.

"You're more than sort of nice," he said, glowing. "You're very nice. Terrific, in fact."

That word *nice* was almost painful; when Neal voiced sentiment, it choked him on its way out. The great emotions escaped very rarely, but once in a while he suffered smaller ones, like this, to lumber on their ponderous way—never without a twinge.

Very nice, he had said. Lucy was wondering what that meant (Was he joking again? Was he making some dim kind of pass?) when Neal asked her if she felt like going to the movies that night. "It's a great double feature, in South Hadley. The first one has Edward G. Robinson as a riveter, and in the second Gary Cooper is a scholarly professor."

He's after me, Lucy thought. "What are they called?" she asked.

"Two Seconds and *Ball of Fire.* With Barbara Stanwyck." Well, Lucy thought, what would it be like? She tried to imagine Neal as her lover, and had trouble. *"Ball of Fire* is a Howard Hawks film," Neal continued. "Gary Cooper and some other scholars, old men, are cloistered in a library, writing an encyclopedia. Barbara Stanwyck is the dance-hall girl who hides out there to escape the cops." Lucy tried again: pictured Neal's face coming close in dim light; perhaps candlelight, perhaps moonlight; she watched his mouth pucker. "She teaches the old men to mambo, I think. Or maybe boogie-woogie. It's a terrific flick." Neal saw that Lucy wasn't listening. "If you like that sort of thing," he ended lamely. "Well, do you want to go?"

"I like you, Neal," Lucy said.

"That means yes?"

"No, I think it means no," she said. "Don't ask me to explain, because I can't."

Neal let a short silence go by; then felt the urge to end it. "I understand," he said cheerfully.

"Do you?" Lucy asked, pleased and surprised.

"Of course not. Let's get the check, okay?"

Neal reached for his wallet; Lucy hauled her bag onto her lap. Neal felt it would not be worth the inevitable bother to offer to pay for her cake and coffee; she might agree, but she might want to put up a fight. Let her pay for her own damn coffee, Neal thought, with a certain unprovoked resentment.

"Heard from Will?" Lucy asked casually, as if she were talking about the check, and it occurred to Neal again that Howard might be right.

"I called him earlier in the week," he said. "Oh, I forgot to tell you something—something sort of grim. I guess I put it out of my mind, is all. Our long-lost father has cancer of the stomach. He's just about had it and wants to see us. I called Will, and I think he's going down to New York."

"My God, Neal. How long ago was it that you last saw him?"

"I went up just a couple of weekends ago. I told you about the piglets, remember?"

Lucy looked strangely at him. "Your *fa*ther, not Will."

"Oh. I was eleven when he left. I saw him just after breakfast. Then I went up to my room to read Superman."

"Not since?"

"Nope." Lucy listened for a note of self-pity in Neal's voice, and couldn't find one.

"When are you going down?"

"*I'm* not. Will is. Tomorrow, I think."

"Are you that bitter, Neal?"

Neal smiled. "What bitter?"

Lucy shook her head, shaking off his smile. "Bitter enough so you won't see a dying man?"

"I'm not bitter," Neal said patiently. "I've already had this discussion with Howard, okay? If you're not careful, you're going to wind up sounding like Big Howie, no matter what your politics are. If these guys are interested in corpse watching, that's their business; but I'm not, and that's mine."

69

"Okay," Lucy said. "But now *you* sound like Will."

"Maybe. But at least I'm not angry." They were talking about Will again, Neal noted passively.

"Oh, Will's anger is imaginary. It's just something he made up one day because it suited his image."

"You think so?" Neal asked, who didn't think so.

"Possibly. I know he thinks it's real. But then he thinks he loves me, too."

"You don't think so?" Neal asked, who thought so.

"He loves something, certainly. But he made that up, too. It's an imagined Lucy, not the real one. I'm trying to be a real one."

"Will the real Lucy Burnham stand up, please? I have to get out of here. Bert might even notice I'm gone."

Neal pulled into the huge parking lot. It was almost empty; weekday night, Neal reassured himself. He clambered out of his car, pushed his door, pushed it again; it shut. Gallows-shaped lights, immensely tall, spread yellow pools on the asphalt; walking through the interlocking circles Neal noted with pleasure a pair of shadows, one leading him on and one trailing him. The leader lengthened, growing dim, while the follower became shorter and darker, sharper. He passed directly under the gallows, there was a moment of confusion, and then the two shadows exchanged places: the small dark one took the front and the long dim one was relegated to the rear. Neal slowed his stride, turning his head quickly back and forth to see both sides at once. Finally he placed himself at the center of the ellipse of interaction, and stopped. There: his shadows were identical. A fine symmetry, Neal thought, and turned to admire his rear shadow, a spindly gray caricature; it's not everyone who is bracketed by mockeries. One more look. They're tall, at least, Neal conceded; but something's missing—a little life, maybe. Neal began to wave his arms, watching his grotesque, flickering companions dancing

70

like the shadows of flames on a wall. Neal heard a car rumble behind him; without turning he quickly lowered his arms and walked stiffy into the cinema.

He bought his ticket, glancing around the lounge. The Kane Cinema had two theaters, and in the first a new Bergman film was playing; some twenty young people formed a ragged line, waiting for someone to open up. Neal ambled past the refreshment stand, eyed the popcorn, and couldn't resist. Buttered, yes; he took the waxy cylinder and went to stand alone by a second set of black doors. The college kids straggled into the Bergman film. Neal waited a few minutes, with a faint feeling of nervousness, almost alone under the glaring lights of the lounge. Ruefully he watched the uniformed girl selling popcorn and candy; he had almost finished his already. He'd be damned if he was going to buy more popcorn. Where was his doorkeeper? Could this door really be meant for Neal alone? At last he realized that no one was coming; that very likely his films weren't playing; and in a tiny gesture of frustration he gave the door a tentative yank. It opened. The theater was lit with the familiar prefatory glow; out of the speakers in the corners came Fats Waller's chubby voice, the tinkle of his piano; three couples lounged in the last half-dozen rows, leaning on each other. Neal let out a chuckle of delight. He strode grinning down the long slope of aisle, and sat down in the fifth row, center. And he was still smiling broadly when the lights suddenly brightened, then died; the curtain shuddered, a humming motor shunted it aside; music blared briefly; when into a sparkling white square leapt a black and white shield, symbol —no, vanguard—of the movie to come.

5

Today the nene flies higher than the erne; disaster and her progeny wandered through Howard's office. Howard's Friday, it seemed, would never end.

The trouble was the puzzle. The Friday puzzle came out garlanded around with Saturday's clues. Useless clues, fruitless efforts for Howard's constituency. Catastrophe had never reached these dimensions in the crossword-puzzle department. Howard's previous worst had been the occasional deleted clue (serving to stimulate the expert, Howard reasoned), or a few misnumbered ones (no real problem for anyone). Those were mere sniffles, but this was the plague. Howard ignored his suddenly hyperactive telephone: in musing desperation he took to attempting alternate solutions for this ugly amalgamated duckling, pinning near-misses to their uncomfortable quarters and hoping for the— "Impossible, absolutely impossible," he muttered, letting his pen clatter on the desk, and splatter. There was no question about it,

"Mauna——" meant Kea or Loa, but here five places were allotted; then the "European capital" scheduled to be Sofia on Saturday had been offered no spaces at all; and here were other, eternally empty spaces, with no clues, where no answers would ever fill in their blanks—it was heartbreaking; it was sheer nonsense. Who was responsible for this?

"It's not my fault, Warren," Howard said into the telephone, which he had finally relieved of its urgent jangling. "No, I have yesterday's mock-up here, everything's in order." He didn't have the mock-up, it so happened, but he was reasonably sure of himself, reasonably sure; it must have been someone in paste-up—it simply would not be like Howard to make that awesome a mistake. "Of course it is," Howard was saying. "I *know* a lot of people do it, Warren. I always tell you it's my puzzles that sell your newspaper." The cacophony of typewriters was particularly horrific this morning. "I'll write an apology for tomorrow. The best I can do is apologize, correct?" Howard listened a moment, and twitched, a mix of boredom and irritation. He tapped his glossy desk top with the back end of his pen, staring fixedly off into the distance; but his gaze came to that obnoxious group of young Yalies (cub reporters, Howard comforted himself) herded around an open newspaper, laughing and pointing. Howard craned his neck to see if the page was . . . but abruptly changed his mind, looked away. Let them laugh and carry on. Howard would not give them the satisfaction of his merest interest. "If you absolutely have to ascertain blame," Howard said to the telephone, "you could always try the proofreading department. Well, no. As it happens I don't think they're responsible for actually *doing* the crossword. I suppose not, no."

What did it matter? Howard wanted to ask, not entirely characteristically. If his youngest brother were here, Will would certainly chime such sentiments, would want, as ever, to establish what *was* important to Howard; and Howard, no doubt, would counter that this was exactly his job—how he earned his living, what he *did*. It was of no importance whether it affected the world or not, nor how. One doesn't butter one's toast in the morning with regard to the universal consequences—Howard (who liked toast) was always answering Will with such sentences, their subject in the impersonal, to parade his objectivity.

Howard had no toast. He sat behind his office desk and tried to struggle away from the impression that he was taking his brother's side in an argument against himself. The point here, he argued, was that the puzzle was *out*. This morning already occupied the past tense; the difficulty was not likely to recur; what good to fix blame?

Howard was twelve. He perched next to his father on the chaise longue of the Cummington porch. Maple wings fluttered everywhere in the air. Will came in red-faced from long, strenuous pursuit of swirling seedpods; he clutched a handful. Will stared distrustfully at the object in his father's lap. This newspaper seemed to be of unusual interest to Howard; one part of it was not only the vertex of two attentions, but attracted a yellow no. 2 Faber pencil as well, whose chiseled point was poised barely above, hovering like a bird of prey. "What are you doing to that?" Will asked Howard.

"We're doing the crossword puzzle," Howard said proudly. "You get clues for words, and if you know you put it into the little spaces."

Will pondered this for a second. Then he asked, "What good is that?" He was only seven, and he was asking the good of things. Perhaps that was *why* he was asking; except that Will never stopped asking Howard that question.

Our father said that in a year or two he would show Will, too, how to do crossword puzzles, that one tiger was all he could handle at a time—giving Howard a paternal but comradely nudge, producing a prideful smile. Our father had a deep voice, great thick arms, broad shoulders, and a prac-

74

ticed bedside manner, and Howard was very comfortable on the chaise longue.

Will turned away, not interested. "Just a couple more years," Homer mused to Howard in a sonorous, pleased voice —as if he were watching those years pass even as Will closed the screen door and set his maple wings whirling in the wind, like helicopters.

"I'm out to lunch, Louise," Howard said into the telephone. "No more calls, please." He thought for a second. "In fact, I'm out to lunch until four o'clock, and then I've gone for the day. Thanks very much, Louise."

Will never became interested in crossword puzzles. It was curious, Howard thought, that someone who loved literature as much as Will never evinced an interest in words themselves. Will was too lost in feelings to remark form, Howard thought. But he admitted that just this moment his job too seemed like hell—oh, it was an inoffensive hell, and at least it was a private one (infinitely preferable to the thunderous anonymity of the next room); even, perhaps, a bearable little hell. Possibly that was the worst of it: it was bearable, eternally bearable, and Howard, having glided into it, might never wriggle out. And what good *was* that? When did the words lose meaning, shackled in their boxes by rows of intersecting letters? Probably just a bad day, Howard; the elevator opened, and Howard stepped toward the revolving door, the sharp click of his heels on the tile floor following just two steps behind him.

It would be interesting and symmetrical to be able to report that Will, who was sitting with knees propped up in an air-conditioned bus, was at the same moment deciding that it was curious—unfathomable, in fact—that someone who loved words as much as Howard never showed much interest in what they meant; more, in what they *intended,* how they were put together to form more than their mere selves. . . . But Will was trying to look up the short skirt of the chunky

75

teen-ager across from him. He wasn't trying to pick her up, he told himself; he was just trying to look up her skirt. It was a good, honest occupation. He wasn't sure why he was engaged in it—underwear didn't excite him, and he wasn't wild about teen-age thighs, nor glistening pubic hair. There was just something about a short skirt that called for looking up; or else something about Will, the cultural phenomenon, about reactions developed in the adult male (the media again, he claimed). Look, male sees skirt, male looks up; objectionable or not, those are the rules. Do attractive women really despise admiration?

But the girl in the bus seemed to mind. Will wouldn't have been so persistent if he'd been able to look outside without having to confront the dulling green haze of the window itself. He bent down to peer out through the small pellucid portion of his window. He rode through Connecticut in a glass coach; Connecticut was veiled in a low sky the blue-tinted white of skim milk. The sky, the mist, hardly moved, and to someone unacquainted with Highway 91 it might have been annoying; but for Will the mist was a blessing, lessening as it did the familiar seen in favor of the rare imagined, and softening as it did the sharp outlines of what remained to be seen.

The bus emitted Will, admitting him to the routine thunderous tumult of the Port Authority. It must be said that Will had never been comfortable in the big city. The goings-on excited him; but it was too much, too much sensation. You could say the city was the only vital place to live; but living here was like—well, it was death, he said "death" to himself, but was caught by the vision of a lecture hall and a throng of tittering faces. They always laughed when you said "death." So Will told himself that living in New York City involved a willingness to not mind, to turn away from an unesthetic outer world and construct an inner one, a reality of . . . Will yawned. UMass seemed a long way off.

He took subways cross- and uptown, affecting the rushed, brusque air of the city-dweller; no expert, he turned the wrong way as he left the uptown train. Of course no one paid the slightest attention; you could be a hippo and not get a second look. And if he was no expert, he was no hippo either. This thought made him giddy, gave him a curious gaiety. He was no hippo, Will repeated to himself; with high heart he went up the hospital steps. It wasn't until he passed through the front door of Flower Fifth Avenue Hospital that he had the sense of where he was and what he was doing. Then the antiseptic hospital smell, the glare of the long bright hall receding into the distance, and the quiet murmur of suppressed noises gave little shocks to his senses. With a jolt Will remembered his father. The woman at the front desk told him: "Three twenty-eight."

The elevator opened, and Will turned along the corridor, disregarding the numbers pointing this way and that; something disoriented him, and he stepped, for the minute, down the first corridor that came to him, walking in a bright haze of lights. The hollow noise of his bootheels on the tiles preceded him down the hall, two steps in front; he followed, curious to see where they would go.

A tiny, ancient woman was sitting at the end of the corridor, her chair turned to face down the length of it. She looked at the floor and continually nodded her head to an inaudible question. When Will approached she turned her eyes gratefully to him, still nodding. She was remarkably small, almost a dwarf. Her tiny legs were braced with a complicated steel apparatus, her feet encased in grotesquely large shoes. Having approached this far, Will reasoned, it would be impolite to turn away without saying something. But he didn't say anything; he just came closer, and put a tenuous smile on his face.

The woman nodded, and said, "I said, I can't hear very well."

77

Will nodded back. He stretched that smile.

"I said, I can't hear very well."

Will did more nodding. He came even closer to her, towering over her bobbing head, while he waited for something to occur to him that he could say. She raised the grizzled remains of her eyebrows expectantly; an extra set of folds furrowed her forehead, joining an extensive network, a wealth of wrinkles. Her head was about the size of Will's two fists. On top, in a sparse nest of dull gray hair, Will saw a purple ribbon, in a bow. The loose ends of the ribbon trailed against the back of her skull.

Will leaned down toward her ear. "I like your ribbon," he said loudly.

"Ah," she said, as if she finally understood.

Will had the thought that he might pat her head. His hand wavered over her; then he pulled it back. Instead he started back down the corridor. He turned, waved. The woman's gaze returned to the floor.

Will followed the pointing numbers to 328. A nurse stood at the doorway, as if she were expecting him. "He's asleep," she said. When Will didn't respond, she added, "He's under heavy sedation, of course."

"Is it permissible to have a look?"

"Of course, of course," the nurse answered, seemingly surprised by Will's question. "Go in and have a look, of course."

Will paused at the entrance. "How is he, by the way?"

Again the nurse seemed surprised. "Well, just at the moment he's under sedation. He's asleep."

Will waited for her to go on, but that was all, apparently. After a moment he said, "Of course," and went in.

An enormously fat man lay on his back in a bed near the window. The sheet covering him rose from his chin in a great billowing swell over his stomach, tapering down to the small bump of his feet. A yellow blanket was folded neatly at the foot of the bed.

The face was a puffy round thing, red with pinpoints of bristly white beard. The fat man was jowly; cheeks overlapped chins, and chins rippled into neck like a series of laden hammocks. There was a bushy, beetling brow; Will noticed that the patient no longer shaved the spot where his eyebrows knit together. He still had his full head of hair, streaming back from a low forehead. He'd always been proud of his leonine mane, and now that it was white it was even more impressive. Yes, in his sixties—1912, Will remembered —Homer was more impressive than ever. There was so much more of him, Will remarked, gazing at the vast expanse of sheet covering the hump. He was not so handsome as he had been, of course; he was no longer handsome at all, as a matter of fact; but now—now Homer was a phenomenon. Will guessed that the deep voice had dropped another octave; that it used the first-person plural; that the lengthy reflection that always marked his manner had stretched to full silence, the quiet of the dreaming man.

Of a summer afternoon this man, now grown so fat, used to drive slowly up the driveway, gravel popping under his pudgy tires. The car parked, then sat silently in an aura of heat. One had the impression that the driver was waiting so as to heighten the excitement of his arrival, or to reflect on what had just been done; but probably he was merely arranging papers in his briefcase. The door opened; a leg swung over; a second leg appeared, and the man pivoted in his seat; then he emerged, wearing a suit and dangling a briefcase beside him, smiling like a banker. He took a public breath of air; he shut the car door. This was all accomplished. He paraded down the lawn to the front steps. Homer was home.

This man, who now had hammocks for chins, used to sleep in the rope hammock between the apple and cherry trees, on weekend afternoons when the weather was fine. Occasionally one of his male children used to come along and swing him gently, scanning his face to see if he was really sleeping. He was always really sleeping; he was an able sleeper, an adept. He lay down with his hands folded in his lap; for a minute thumbs twiddled. Slowly the thumbs stopped badgering one another; Homer's mouth fell open; and from somewhere behind his nose came a low, whistling snore.

Lying, much larger, in the hospital bed, he still slept with open mouth. He wasn't snoring, but his breath was loud and rapid, as if he were constantly being surprised in his sleep. His breathing amplified the silence into which it fell—a powerful silence, clean as a white sheet.

Will looked away. He catalogued the bedside cart: gleaming white bedpan, pitcher of water, Dixie cup with straw, box of tissues, furry little cactus in white plastic pot, two unopened cards. Why does he need a straw? Will wondered. What can our father still do?

A fine thread of spittle dangling from Homer's upper gums swung back and forth in the wind of his respiration, and landed on the first chin. Will leaned over to wipe it off. His hand, clutching a tissue, poised over the shiny spot, but then dived back in his pocket, tissue and all; Will's hand went out, but couldn't quite touch.

Will walked over to the dim window. One could see Central Park from there: a few stray benches, a crow in a crippled apple tree, the asphalt paths glistening with rain, and the floral sundial, which on days like this one told no time at all.

A black umbrella moved toward a sodden bench. She sat under the open umbrella; water dripped from every spoke. She fed the squirrels, it looked like peanuts. Even in the rain squirrels came running; they never changed. Tremors ran through their tails; they held the nuts in their two hands; these things never changed, Will repeated.

He gazed at the sundial: he saw a shadow fall on the nine. But that could not be, it was still afternoon, it was raining and it was still afternoon. No sign of the sun in the dingy sky. Oh yes, there it was, a whiter patch of cloud.

He grew impatient. Homer wasn't going to wake up. But Will didn't want him to: it seemed right for it to be this way. Our father sleeping, Will staring out the window, fitful rain; just like old times. Will and his father never knew each other. The umbrella moved off, trailed by two squirrels; the fat man slept, huffing and puffing. Will didn't know why he was even there; attending his father's slow demise was much like watching golf on television.

He passed the same nurse in the corridor. She pushed her cheeks up toward her eyes; this must be her smile, Will guessed. "Hopefully he'll be better after tonight," she said. "At the moment he's under a good deal of sedation, of course."

"Of course," Will said, wondering what would happen tonight. But not about to ask.

Howard wondered what was keeping Will. He relaxed in his smallish living room, feet up, highball beside him, ice just cracking in the tall glass, soda still fizzing. I should have had a gin and tonic instead, Howard was thinking when the phone rang. "Hello?"

"Howard Bard?"

"Speaking."

"This is Will Weng, Mr. Bard."

Howard had a moment of shock: it was the former cross-word-puzzle editor of the *Times* calling to lampoon him for the mix-up. The shock was soon superseded by annoyance; Howard hadn't thought Weng capable of such a paltry prank. Coolly Howard replied: "Good afternoon, Mr. Weng."

"May I remind you that it is evening, early evening, but nonetheless evening, Mr. Bard?"

"Pardon me?"

"Evening, when the woodcock mates, or attempts to?"

81

At last Howard recognized the voice. "Don't you *ever* stop?" Howard asked, exasperated.

"Hey, Big Howie. You're slowing down in your later years."

"I wish you would restrain yourself now and then. Humor pales in direct proportion to its density."

"How are you, Howard?" Neal asked, unperturbed.

Long-suffering Howard sighed. "Not absolutely happy. Newspaper mishaps."

"Oh yeah? Like what? The Sunday magazine turn down another article?"

"Just a little mix-up with the puzzle."

"What, they drop a clue again?"

"It's a fairly technical problem, and this has been a long day. Let's not go into it, shall we?"

"Whatever you say, boss. Will there?"

"As yet there's been no word from him. Perhaps he's been led astray by an attractive wood pigeon."

"Been sharpening your tongue again, hunh? Great. You two'll go at it tooth and nail."

"Nonsense. What do Will and I have to argue about?"

"You'll argue about nothing, just like always."

"No, no. For my part, I'll be pleased to see that skinny miscreant." Howard paused. "I trust he'll be as amenable."

"He won't," Neal said cheerfully. "May the best man win. Watch out for his right cross."

"We're too old, and too civilized, for fisticuffs. I'm sure it'll be very pleasant." Howard waited for Neal's profession of disbelief, but it wasn't forthcoming. "Why did you call?" Howard asked.

"Just wanted to nurse the talking wounded," Neal said. "How long is Will staying, anyway?"

"So far as I know, a few days."

"Have him give me a call, hunh? And as for you, Big Howie, you turn over a new leaf. Don't you drop those clues, you hear?"

82

"Rest assured," Howard said stiffly.

"Bye Howard. Happy trails."

Good-bye, Neal. Sentimental Howard tried to remember the moment when Neal, his cowlicky deputy in all endeavors, first heard a different drummer. It was after they built the treehouse in the apple tree; Howard overruled Neal's architectural schemes, and the treehouse collapsed in a windy week. Shortly after that Neal patiently agreed with Howard about the bicycle to buy, then went off and got a different one. His bright red Schwinn. Tenderly Howard remembered the fluttering rainbow of plastic streamers flapping from the handlebars; the glittering orange reflectors plastered on every possible surface; the playing cards affixed to the frame, brushing against the spokes and making a staccato chatter, hopefully akin to a machine gun's. The vehicle did attack the senses, flashing and rattling, when Neal rode by (standing on his pedals, grinning seriously), went up the hill, and was quickly out of sight: Good-bye, Neal.

Hello, Will. Howard peeked into the fisheye peephole in answer to the bell. In it he found a distorted version of Will, gigantic face staring at Howard from atop the shrunken afterthought of body.

Will didn't look much like that. He was very long, long and bony. Parts of him flopped: his straight black hair, which tended to be greasy, flopped over his bright sienna eyes; his limbs, which were thin, flopped from their joints, as if not perfectly secured. All the same, Will was not denied a certain grace—lightness of step, ease of balance. In Howard's opinion it was an attribute they shared.

Unlike anyone of near relation, Will had sallow skin; at times it seemed golden, at others sickly and jaundiced. In part this depended on the expression of his face, a face that was sometimes dull, tired, and serious, and sometimes intense, excited, and serious, but rarely given to frivolity. Even his laugh had a peculiar gravity about it, as if he sat in judgment of a joke, and decided to find it funny. Will's deep-set eyes (circled by shadow), high forehead, fine nose, and thin lips gave a weight to his moods; suggested an earnestness that might equally have produced his mien, or been produced by it.

What I seem to have difficulty including in my description —possibly because it was a cause for envy—is the sensitive glance that came from Will's dark visage; a bright, alert regard giving the impression that Will saw, and understood. Much easier to mention are Will's blue and gray houndstooth jacket, clashing with red-and-green-plaid cotton flannel shirt, his brown corduroy trousers, his bulky hiking boots with crenellated soles. His bare head was damp. Will had just turned thirty-five.

The two brothers sat beside each other on the living-room sofa, talking quietly and familiarly. Howard offered Will a drink; Will refused; relented; Howard happily abandoned the last swallow of whisky and soda to join him in a gin and tonic. Peanuts appeared in a pewter bowl; while Will talked he jiggled some in his palm. He talked idly about the woman he had watched feeding squirrels in the rain.

"How was he?" Howard asked.

"Asleep," Will said. "And very fat."

Howard wondered aloud what would be a good time for them to see Homer. The plural was taken for granted.

"I want to see him by myself," Will put in quietly. He marshaled his arguments, and bit the inside of his cheek.

Howard bristled. Howard thoroughly calmed himself, and took out his pipe. Howard formed his reflections. There was no reason for acrimonious dispute; after the difficulties of the day, or (taking the long view) after the difficulties Will and he had always had. There had never been a reason for that. It was time the two of them got on. Howard proclaimed it to himself. Howard lit. Here they were, middle-aged (yes, Howard), still acting like unrepentant children, still sulking in their respective corners; Howard puffed.

"Oh well," Howard said. "That's your decision, of course. That's most certainly entirely up to you." He smiled briefly.

Will assumed that Howard abandoned his company only because it wasn't really wanted. He said something to the effect that he was glad Howard understood; he mumbled, and it was difficult to understand precisely what he said.

These peanuts were particularly salty. "Want another one?" Howard asked, waving his empty glass.

Will looked down to the glass in his lap. It was empty too. He held it out to Howard, who padded off noiselessly.

Nice pictures. Not a bad apartment. Little bit too . . . static; immobile. Like Howard.

Will could have been thinking almost anything while Howard was in the kitchen, whacking the bottom of the ice tray, screwing open another quart of tonic. I am the type of man, Howard said slowly to himself, who buys his gin by the half-gallon; but I do not buy my gin by the half-gallon.

He handed Will his glass. "I've forgotten the lemon," he said, but he didn't go back to get it. Instead he turned to Will, looked him squarely in the eye, and asked: *"Am* I the type of man who buys his gin by the half-gallon?"

Will considered Howard's question, and Howard, gravely. "I would say so," he replied.

Howard nodded. "What else am I the type of man that does? Excuse me. What else does my type of man do?"

Will was still looking carefully at Howard. "Is this the beginning of an argument?"

"No, not at all. Not at all. I am in a very happy frame of mind." Magnanimously he added, "I'm very glad to see you, you know." Will did not quite return the compliment, but he seemed on the verge of it, and he did smile. "No, not at all," Howard said again. "Just the opposite, in fact. I was hoping to have a frank and good-humored discussion. I would like to see," he said grandly, holding his glass up as if to propose a toast, "how the game is played Will-wise in the soul."

Will seemed a little startled. Howard proceeded unchecked. "I no longer know you well. Or perhaps I know you, but it is without—without your knowing it. Without your *permission,*" he added happily, lighting upon the right word.

"I'll go get the lemon," Will said. When he returned he noticed that there was very little drink left in Howard's glass. That there wasn't a lot in his own.

"Are we agreed, then?" Howard asked.

Will dropped a slice of lemon onto Howard's ice cubes. "Agreed to what?" he asked—not truculently, I hasten to mention, merely confused.

"Well, you might be somewhat curious yourself," Howard said, smiling at Will. "You might wonder at my thoughts, perhaps. Am I right? Or am I an open book? Is old Howard an open book?"

On this too Will felt he had to reflect. At length he said, "No, I suppose I wonder."

"Ah," said Howard—like the old woman with the ribbon. He glanced over. "I see you are in need of liquid refreshment," he said politely. Howard rose and carried his own glass off to the kitchen; he came back with a single drink, and sat down, cradling it. When he looked over, ready to resume conversation, he remarked Will's still-empty glass. "Sorry, sorry. Here, take mine," he said, hurriedly pushing his drink along the length of the coffee table. "Make yourself at home," he added vaguely.

"Well, Howard," Will said, "what would you like to know?"

Howard jumped up and returned to the kitchen. His voice came around the corner: "Oh hell. We're out of peanuts." Will heard the sound of the refrigerator door opening: then a tinny rattle; and then the door shut again. Howard pulled the lever on the ice tray, and there was a satisfying crunch. He tapped the bottom of the tray over the sink. The ice cubes fell out one by one and clattered against a cup and saucer.

Shortly he was back. "Oh hell," Howard said again.

"What's the matter?"

"I lost my lemon. How could I have lost my lemon twice?"

Will said he didn't know.

"Resign yourself," Howard said to the glass, "to a lemonless fate." He took a sip. "Good," he judged. "Hardly needs it." He crossed his legs. "I'm hungry," he added.

"Are you ready for my secrets now?" Will tempted.

"Aren't you hungry? It's eight."

"I thought you wanted to talk," Will complained, surprised at his own disappointment.

"Oh yes, of course," Howard soothed. He sat up straight, leaning away from Will. "Well. What do you think of me, Will?"

Will laughed. Howard tried again. "Who do you think I am? Seriously."

Will reached for his glass. Finding it, he wrapped his hand carefully around and lifted it off the table. "Howard," he said, shaking his head for emphasis, "I think you're the Received Opinion."

Howard seemed to consider this carefully. "That's very good, Will," he said. "But what do you mean?" He took a long swallow.

"I suppose what I mean is—you know how in sort of sciency writing they always say 'we'? Like 'We don't yet know the basic building block of atomic structure'? Well, Howard, I always think the other person they're referring to is you."

"Do you?" Howard asked, sounding both flattered and puzzled.

Will swished his drink in circles, though it no longer needed mixing. "I hope you don't mind, Howard, but when I see History with a capital H, I translate it as 'what Howard thinks.' "

"That's very kind of you," Howard observed tentatively. "I

do believe, I believe, that everything has an historical perspective. Perhaps that's why you think that."

"Neal says that everything has a tax angle."

"Oh, we're both right," Howard said. He stretched. "What secrets of mine do you want to hear? It's your turn." He got up and went to the toilet. When he came back he took both of their glasses to the kitchen.

"That's enough booze for me," Will said immediately, realizing that he hadn't spoken loudly enough for Howard to hear. Instead of repeating himself, he too tottered to the bathroom.

Will was still buttoning his fly when he asked, "What do you think about what I'm doing?" He imagined Neal's response: Button your fly all night if you want; just don't ask me to get involved. Will laughed—though he probably wouldn't if Neal said it.

Howard was seated on the sofa beside a bag of Fritos. "They're stale," he said. "But help yourself."

"I don't much like them. They taste like styrofoam."

"Peanuts are better," Howard agreed. "But these are better than none." On a faint impulse Will reached into the bag. He popped Fritos into his mouth one by one; chewing gingerly, he felt the same awkward unfamiliarity one does when making a trial promenade in a new pair of shoes.

"So what do you think of what I've been doing? Working at the Petersens' and all," Will prompted.

Howard sat wiggling the corners of his mouth, as if a struggle between opposing views were going on underneath, and he was being careful as to which side to let out first. Finally he said, "I think you're a very fine fellow, Will." This was enough to have said for a moment; his mouth gave some more small jerks. "I'm very fond of you. I want to tell you what I think, but first I want you to know that I'm your staunchest advocate."

Will nodded impatiently. Howard nodded back, his eyebrows wrinkling in sincerity, and said, "Your objections to the mundane duties of your life are still valid, if somewhat stock. One would have thought we'd left behind the temptation of uncivilized existence in the nineteen sixties." Will started to object, but Howard plodded on. "Listen, Will. Listen, my friend. You're an intelligent and a thoughtful man. But you're bent on transforming your life into the most adolescent of soap operas. Your search for *mean*ing is ridi—tell me, have you sat down and thought at all about what a cliché you've fallen for? About how you appear to the world?" Howard waved his arms one time more than he had to. Perhaps he forgot that he was no longer speaking.

Will waited until Howard had finished a swallow. Then he said, "From a given angle, anything can look ridiculous. My answers are hardly original, it's true. But originality is pretty hard stuff to come by. I was very tired of my particular mode of existence, and I didn't intend to sit around speaking of meaninglessness over tea until some esthetically apt solution took up the chair next to mine."

"But *your* solution is a rather obvious one, don't you think?" Howard said, face slightly red.

"Obvious is about the best I can do, Howard."

Howard now chuckled soothingly. "Very good, Will. So you prefer the active course, as usual. You stubbornly make your outcry. Fine, fine, I understand. What you are doing may be admirable. Admirable but perhaps dangerous; or unproductive, which is worse."

Will shrugged. "The choice is pretty straightforward. Kierkegaard said: 'There are two ways. One is to suffer; the other is to become a professor of the fact that another suffers.'"

"You would prefer, I suppose," Howard said, "that everyone suffer."

"I don't know about everyone. Just me. When I teach, all I do is deaden feelings—mine, my students', and those of the writers whose masterpieces I reduce to three forty-five-minute lectures. The same lectures, every year."

Howard held his drink up to the dim light, and filled his lungs with air. "You forget sometimes, I think, no doubt you forget, the nobility of teaching. The no*bil*ity. You are, after all, the bearer of light; you pass the torch. In an illiterate age, with atavism hard upon us, you quietly keep the faith. Call me History if you like, but it is *you* who transmit the lessons, the wealth, of history: you who keep alive the great tradition." With a flourish he swilled down his drink.

Will frowned. "Sounds good," he said. "But teaching is a job. What I do is tell a lot of kids who don't listen a lot of things I don't believe. And I correct spelling mistakes on their handwritten papers."

Howard appeared concerned. "Why, what don't you believe them that you tell? I mean, what do you tell them that you don't believe?"

Will wasn't sure why he was drunkenly chattering away about something in which he professed disinterest.

"I tell them it matters," he said. Howard said nothing.

"I don't believe the facts matter," Will added, half noting his half-pun.

Howard ate ice cubes when he felt no prohibition against it. "What *does* matter, then?" he mumbled, crunching, and probably, Will thought, not caring; it would be like Howard to crunch and not care.

"Moments matter. And kindnesses; intentions; feelings; extraordinary sights; memories," said Will, reciting his list.

"Those *are* the facts," Howard said, spitting a big piece of ice back in the glass.

Neither of them was quite sure what Howard meant; nor, in fact, what Will meant; and neither seemed to have anything to add. At last Howard asked, "Are those the things you want to write about?" Will answered, "Yes," and Howard said, "Good"; and they both felt a bit better.

But Howard still wasn't sure he understood why Will had stopped teaching, unless it was because he was tired of correcting spelling mistakes. How could Will turn his back on literature when he wanted to write? One becomes a great poet by reading, not by going out into the world intent on feeling—feeling something or other, God knows what. One could be sensitive from now till doomsday and one wouldn't write even one—

"You know, Howard, you should do more serious writing," Will said idly. "You love words. You'd be a great craftsman."

Howard's wave of criticism subsided. "Don't you believe my inspiration might be suspect? I'm not readily subject to revelation, you know."

Unfortunately, Will—tactless as ever, without a stitch of conscience—said, "Possibly. You may not be a great writer, Howard. But you should try."

"What should I try to be, adequate?"

Will drained his gin again. He would stop drinking now, certainly. But even that had been too much; his stomach was notoriously weak. There's always a point, he said to himself, when you know you should have already stopped.

It was the George Pratt system. George was the mechanic who worked on Will and Lucy's car; George had it down to a science. "There's a torque wrench for this, but you can just do it by feel," George explained. "How do you know how far to tighten it?" Will asked. George shrugged. "It's pretty easy, I guess." He fitted his wrench onto the bolt. "See, you just tighten her"—he turned his wrench— "tighten her just till—" With a loud crack the engine head split in the center. "Till she breaks. Tighten her till she breaks; then back off half a turn." It wasn't long before Will discovered the universal applications of the Pratt System: take it past the limit, and turn back.

"Well?" Howard asked. He sounded impatient.

"Well what?"

"Should I aim for adequacy?"

"Oh no," Will said. "Try to be a great writer. Then back off half a turn."

Yes, more coffee. Without politeness he added: Please.

The night before this rainy morning Will drank too much. Hazily he remembered the fog that accompanied him toward the stumbling end of the evening; he liked that fog, at the time. He liked the little space that cushioned him from his drunken body: found it pleasurable to knock knuckles against forehead and not feel a thing, not in forehead, not in knuckles. But now dues had to be paid. His local universe ran riot; with world-weary eye Will watched its persistent spinning. He woke early, exhausted, aching, dying for a drink of water. Will swore he would never touch the stuff again—an oath he often took under the pain of a hangover.

It all came back to him, and he pushed it away; puddles of city light that spread behind the rain, puddles in the street that spread light, raindrops that kicked up bubbles on shiny sidewalks; and among these the pressure of Howard's sonorous voice, like a cold hand on his collar, more constant than the rain. The restaurant was good, lamb was his favorite; but

Will elected not to think about that. His memory drifted back a bit further, and lighted like a persistent fly on his obese father, the mountain beneath a sheet. . . . Will waved his hand, trying to scatter the images. As if he could dispel them like dreams, just by coming to.

Will searched for a topic, a resting place for his restless thoughts: a source of sweet, simple delight. But this morning Will couldn't find a dream that wasn't already soured. For Will that was a terrible, a crippling deficiency—a dearth in dreams.

Maybe just a little toast.

Howard certainly was chipper this morning. What an incredibly ugly bathrobe he had there. Purple with silver trimming, for God's sake; and his hair was thin on top. Poor Howard: whistling, coffee pot in hand, balding, robed in purple, stupid slippers, his fussy apartment, a crossword-puzzle editor; he was getting old. Will pitied Howard very rarely; but it seemed he would have to shortly, and for a long time; for soon it would go by Howard, and Howard wouldn't even know it.

Will pitied everyone when he had a hangover, most of all himself.

"Are you going to see the old man this morning?" Howard asked, jocose, pouring himself more coffee.

"Will you stop calling him 'the old man'?"

"Why is that bothersome?"

"It makes me sick, that's all."

"Might you be mistaking the residue of last night's alcohol for moral stance?"

Will growled and buttered his toast.

He was only half through the slice of toast when he thought perhaps he'd lie down again. He staggered down the hall, flopped onto the bed, and propped his aching calves on a pillow. He drifted off quickly, without having chosen to sleep. Nor did he choose his dream. In the dream he saw Howard sitting in an old armchair in the apartment above the Petersens'; Howard sucked on a long, thin pipe like those in Dutch genre paintings. When Will came in Howard looked up and emitted a perfect smoke ring. The ring rose tremulously before him, and with a self-satisfied smile Howard nudged it with his pipe; it disintegrated; Howard said, "See?" As if in answer Will strode up to Harwood's cage and opened the door. *"He'll* get your smoke ring," Will said; but instead Harwood leapt from the cage with a scream and crashed through the window. Will ran to the windowsill: Harwood soared toward the horizon, blood dripping from his wing. Without getting up from his chair Howard said, "He'll make it. They always do." Will knew that they didn't, that Harwood wouldn't; and his eyes brimmed with bitter tears.

When he woke, he could only remember Howard smoking the long pipe and the perfect smoke ring rising; something else, vague and imperfect, troubled him.

Will raised himself up in bed and found himself face-to-face with a crow. The black bird perched on the windowsill and peered in; he gazed from corner to corner, examining the contents of the room, and his eyes met Will's. Here too the crow found matters of interest to him: vermiculated tracery of red running through the wet, milky white of Will's eyes; barely visible webbing of white that softened the brown of the irises; opaque, pulsating pupils, which at the very center of Will's eyes mirrored for the bird his own dark, glittering ones.

They're the brightest birds, crows. He probably won't move until I do; then he'll cry bloody murder. Will bent forward; the crow cocked his head, and stayed. Will waved his arms; the bird stayed. "What are you doing out there, you old crow?" Will asked; and the crow tapped three times on the windowpane with three sharp, assertive jerks of his head.

"Were you talking to me?" Howard asked, opening the door. The crow flew off noiselessly.

"I was talking to the birds," Will said.

94

"Were they talking back?" Howard asked.

Will searched Howard's gaze for some sign of complicity; but this, apparently, had been a joke, a little Howard sort of joke. "Not yet," Will replied. "Did you know that when Virginia Woolf had her spells, the birds sang to her in Greek? They must have been special birds. I think if New York birds could talk they'd say 'What da hell ya doing, joik?'" He grinned. "Wonder what Virginia would say to that?"

"It would probably be Greek to her," Howard said, pulling a pipe from his pocket, sucking on it.

It was late afternoon by the time Will made his way back to the hospital. The long rain was over; the clouds, lighter now, were rising in a well-rinsed sky, and below them a line of dazzling blue glittered promisingly along the horizon. The energetic sun seemed about to work its way free: the last row of clouds (a shining silver lining) was barely able to contain it, and shafts of bright and yellow light streamed out, gilding the afternoon. The wet city began to dry. Dark splotches on the blue and yellow awning of the Sabrett hot-dog cart shrank away from the umbrella peak; drops slithered down from the back of a park bench onto the seat, reflecting a curving, elongated willow tree dripping and drooping over a pond. Will looked around for a rainbow; this was weather for it. But in New York, Will summed up, there was never a rainbow.

The nurse was surprised to see him. It seemed the nurse would be surprised by everything he did.

"You needn't have come, of course," she said. "You could have just telephoned."

"How is he?"

"Oh, he's conscious. The pain operation was a success. They're very good with that one."

"Can I see him?"

95

"If you want, I suppose so. I suppose I don't see any reason why not." Her cheeks went up toward her ears.

"That's very kind of you," Will said uncomfortably. She seemed to agree with him. Will wanted to ask, "How kind?" but stopped himself.

Our father was flat out. A plastic tube ran from a hanging bottle into his nose; the tube was full of yellow fluid. Our father's eyes were half-open. The eyelids looked to be holding up a constant weight; from time to time they sagged shut, and it was only with a visible fluttering of the lashes that they managed to half open again.

Homer's face seemed distorted, as if under great atmospheric stress. At first Will thought of astronauts; then compared Homer's weary expression to that on the face of a man whose brains, at the other side of the photograph, were on their way out of his skull.

Will stood there by the door. Homer's head turned slowly. There was no sign of recognition, Will thought. He took a few steps forward. Still the moon face gave no sign; but one arm, lying on top of the sheet, raised itself from the bed. Will watched it move; he noticed pinstriped pajama sleeves. After what felt like a long time he realized that the hand was motioning to him: it was beckoning.

Will walked unsteadily toward the bed to touch his father —he wasn't sure where. In the end he held out his hand for a shake. "Hi," he said brightly. "How are you?"

But he could hold the hand in the air for just so long; at last he put it into the one that lay on top of the sheet. He gave a squeeze, and let go.

"Come closer," Homer said, in a hoarse and gravelly voice.

"I'm here," Will claimed. His father's lips moved again, but this time nothing came out.

"Pretty nice place you got here," Will said, pretending to look around. Today the bedpan contained a small quantity of lustrous purple-black liquid, with bits of duller, green material. Will looked away, back at his father.

Homer's lips were still moving. Will put his ear close. All he heard was breathing: gentle sighs.

"I heard your operation was a success," Will said, perhaps a little loudly. His voice bounded off the walls and came back to him, mocking. Will wanted to say something hopeful to his father, or something affectionate; but then he'd have to listen to it as it came back off the walls.

He said, "Lot of rain the past couple of days." A pause. "Nice for the ducks." Pause. "Not as if I'm a duck."

Pause, pause, pause. What else was there for Will to say to the walls? He said he'd read Homer his mail—then he realized that the two cards were underneath the bedpan. Will couldn't help it, he made a face, grimaced as he gingerly lifted up one end of the pan, and sighed with relief when he managed to pull the envelopes out. His father wouldn't notice, though. Would he.

"This is one from Claire Mudgett. Was that Mrs. Mudgett's name, Claire? She didn't look like a Claire. Let's see. She writes: 'My poor dear Homer, it is so awful to hear about you. It makes me so very sad, very very—' " Will read the rest silently. "She doesn't have too much to say. She hopes you'll get better." Will added, "Soon.

"Let's see. The other one is from the Bakers; I don't know them, do I? I don't think so. They say that Ed's kidney is coming along fine now, and they thank you for that. They're finally moving back to the suburbs; the Island. Bethpage. Their new house has a swimming pool. They hope that someday you'll be able to come out and go for a duck. Eleanor is going out to the University of Oregon this fall. She wants to be pre-med. They hope you get better soon too. Lots of good wishes. Lousy handwriting."

Homer stirred. His hand left the sheet; again motioned Will closer. Will bent his head. The voice was stronger:

"Come back tomorrow," Homer said. Will nodded. "Maybe this"—Homer's hand drifted slowly in the air, and finally pointed to indicate the tube in his nostril—"will be gone." Will nodded again.

He took a final look at his father's face. Homer's eyes were open, looking, apparently, at nothing; his mouth opened and closed rhythmically, as if he were saying one syllable over and over again. But there was no sound.

This is the way you go, Will thought. In a glaze of hospital lights, among a swarm of bored attendants; the pain within you mocked by bright, bland decor, the unruffled efficiency of a fast-food joint. You wonder if your life has had meaning, and the nurse's aide considers her pastrami sandwich with anticipatory relish; your peacefully drooping life-functions are gauged calmly, as if you are garbage to be taken out. Garbage: to be thrown onto a smoldering landfill, while gulls wheel in the air, cry, dive and squabble over innards, while smoke rises and then disappears in the sky—while the nurse's aide slathers mustard on her pastrami, sighs, and picks an errant blue thread off her white, white sleeve.

Will patted his father's hand; soft flesh even there. He shivered. "I'll be back tomorrow," Will lied. He walked out, passing into the glare of the corridor—and for a second Will thought that he too had disappeared in the brightness of the light.

The front entrance was in shadow; the sun settled over the park. In a parking lot a man hobbled on a cane, making a long, crooked shadow. He put his cane under his arm and struggled into a bent black Pontiac; he turned the key, the car merely clicked—a series of rapid taps, Morse code for nothing. The man swore in Spanish.

Will walked over to Madison and headed downtown. A bald man was closing up a jewelry store. He yanked on a steel accordion; the curtain unfolded, rattling, and banged shut. The bald man pulled from his pocket a ring bristling with keys; plump fingers twisted them in a glittering array of locks, making loud, hollow snaps each time, like gunshots.

A wrecking crane hovered over a half-demolished building; its ball dangled motionless, suspended beside shattered walls. Will walked on downtown. He watched a crackle-faced old woman light-finger a tomato from a bin outside a corner store. She tottered off; she had a hump. A rubber ball rolled into the street, a car screeched to a stop; but no children pursued the ball, and indolently it too stopped. The smell of fried food came out of a restaurant door; a red-haired waitress slammed it. Will walked on. On a corner playground a basketball game went on. Half of the players had their shirts off, half of them shirts on, all of them were black, none of the shirts were. Mostly they played in silence, grunting and sweating. A tiny girl with pigtails paid attention to her ice-cream cone; still it ran down over her hand, pink driblets. Though it was not that hot. It was a strawberry. It was surprising; it was not that hot.

Will walked. A taxi's horn got stuck, and demonstrated the Doppler effect. Another cabbie, annoyed at the racket, protested the honking with his own. A siren shrieked uptown, a hugely fat woman spoke loudly as she passed: "I couldn't care that he's a pervert. He's the only one I've got and I want him to be happy."

A dog led a tiny man to a fire hydrant. The dog, crouching ashamedly, pissed and shat; the man rocked back and forth on his heels, whistling, looking away. The man had a small, thin moustache, and with one finger he teased the close-cropped edges in and out of place, sniffing continually. The dog rose and led him purposefully to the next lamppost.

The sun crouched in the west. Unlucky, it was held up behind more clouds; the golden light faded, long shadows vanished. It was time, Will thought, to go back to Howard's, back to bed. With a heavy heart he did that.

When Howard asked, Will answered that to him it seemed like a matter of charts with dropping figures and bedpans containing material of uncertain origin.

"He's lucid, anyway," Will said. "But suffering." He took a sip of Howard's gin. "I guess he's just dying," Will added mildly.

"Oh, is that all?" Howard asked.

"Unh-hunh," Will said.

7

Hubbub; over the clatter of silver pawing porcelain and waiters shouting in Italian, Howard and his mother chatted. Mrs. Bard asked that salad *follow* shellfish; the waiter flashed a solid-silver tooth, nodded sagely, and made his triumphal return proudly bearing a glass plate heaped with drab lettuce and strands of enervated onion. Mrs. Bard, smiling and blinking, tried to discreetly rectify the situation; she spoke slowly and made rapid, vague gestures in the air with her fluttering fingers. For a woman who shuddered involuntarily at the vulgar abbreviation of draperies to "drapes," this misunderstanding was trying. She smiled even more broadly and unhappily, blinked frenetically, even disinterred the remnants of her Italian. The waiter left, his smile apologetic now, and came back with three variations of commercially manufactured salad dressing. He placed these bright-labeled bottles before her, accompanying them with a grandiose gesture and an expression of futility. She smiled, hastily nodded her thanks—more and more Eunice Bard is disturbed by distur-bance, Howard remarked—and slid a dollop of chalky "blue cheese" dressing onto a lettuce leaf, a tale of misery inscribed on her drawn face.

"Why are you doing that?" Howard asked, afraid that he already knew the answer.

"So as not to offend him," she replied; yes, Howard had. Eunice chewed reluctantly. "How did you happen on this—" (her search conveyed distaste) "this—place?"

"The architecture correspondent recommended it."

"Architects," Mrs. Bard said, and shivered. "Modern archi-tecture. Dreadful."

"He said the pasta is fresh."

Mrs. Bard dabbed the corner of her mouth with a red and white cloth napkin. "You've never had an eye for these things, dear," she said. "You're content with your leftovers."

"Oh, I don't know about that," Howard said genially. "I like a good brandy."

"You may like one, but you don't know one."

"Mother, please don't let a monoglot waiter put you in a bad humor. An ill-timed salad is not the end of the world; it really needn't spoil our lunch."

"Nothing is spoiled, Howard," she said firmly; paused, then added, "Well, perhaps *I* am. I always have great expecta-tions. It's much more pleasant to have expectations."

Hopes, perhaps, but not expectations, Howard disputed silently. But he saw no use in upsetting his mother; disagree-ing was tantamount to that. Howard noticed a plump fly heading for the basket of bread before them; "I agree with you," he replied, nodding vigorously, hoping she wouldn't notice the fly.

Mrs. Bard was irritable because she had a question for Howard. It came out of her arid mouth just after that mouth had carefully chewed a crusty breadstick. "Well, what was it like?"

102

Howard feigned ignorance.

"How is your father, dear?" She tried to sound chatty.

My poor mother, Howard thought. "Not well," he answered, becoming grave.

Howard's visit had been different. He'd heard Will's depressing version, had fortified himself with a dose of pessimism. When he came away he decided that Will had overreacted. I'll reconsider. Perhaps the truth is, Will, that Howard's visit was formal, and Will's emotional. Will's attachment to his father was far stronger, after all, his need far greater; at nine one still has a father, Howard hypothesized, but by fourteen one is alone. Howard had already buried his father.

A more objective chronicler would probably stress the fact that Homer was in somewhat better condition when Howard arrived. Homer sat up in bed, sleek and clean-shaven, face rosy. He was still fat, of course—Howard was astonished at just how fat. Howard had inherited his father's round face, and in his late thirties had come to resemble the Homer he remembered. But this sick man was no mere double. Howard's vision of this older version of himself was a ghastly caricature. The same eyes gazed benevolently back at him, but all around these the features had been caught by some imp and pulled out of place. For the most part the imp pulled down: chins dangled, cheeks sagged, lips bulged, and even nose seemed to droop; this waxen visage had come too close to the flame. The thought that he beheld his own sordid future unsettled Howard—but to give him his due, he resettled himself rather nicely. He sat calmly in the bedside chair and read a bit of Henry James aloud in a strong, clear voice.

Homer seemed immensely pleased to see Howard; if he was similarly shocked by the treatment time had given his eldest son, he was kind enough not to show it. He did not, for example, remark how tall Howard had grown. Nor did he comment on his own transformation; he joked about the proportions of his nurses instead. Homer didn't seem possessed of any great desire to unburden his soul for Howard's benefit, much to Howard's relief. They chatted about the weather, the weather was fine; the longshoremen might strike again; Howard couldn't say who was leading the league, but he knew it wasn't the Red Sox. A nurse bustled in with a pill; watched Homer swallow it, and hustled out again. Now a silence fell across the room—a natural, easy silence that deepened into a difficult one, tense and gloomy. At last our father said, "Would you like to read something else?"

Howard chose *The Complete Adventures of Sherlock Holmes,* the book Homer had given Howard for his eleventh birthday. Howard read "The Speckled Band" aloud. And that was all, really. They shook hands good-bye.

They did not shake hands good-bye; that was not all. To his mother Howard neglected to mention the affection he found himself feeling for this pleasant, unassertive fat man. What happened to the bombastic patriarch who smugly patted his bow tie at the breakfast table? Age had blown up the balloon of his body and withered the corpus of his spirit; Homer in his hospital bed was meek and mild, a nice old man. If no longer our father.

One thing more Howard failed to tell our mother: he never finished reading "The Speckled Band." A short, chubby woman, plump-cheeked, drab and dowdy, walked confidently into the room carrying a black patent leather purse; she spied Howard, and stopped.

"Oh," she said.

Homer introduced Howard to Mrs. Constance Jesson. The name rang a faint, unfindable bell. Howard took one look at her, as she stood uncomfortably fingering the belt above her wide hips, her frizzled hair dyed a ridiculous shiny black, and he knew the answer wouldn't come from her.

Homer cleared his throat. "Constance and I have lived together for, uh, twenty—"

"Twenty-six," she filled in.

"Twenty-six years," Homer finished, neither proudly nor expectantly. He was stating a fact, and for him it was a very old fact.

Howard found it laughable. He had never known there was an Other Woman. He might have imagined one: tall and slinky, a lascivious smile curling around her wanton scarlet mouth. Howard stared at Mrs. Jesson's smudged lipstick. "That's a long time," he said.

"Yes," Homer said.

Howard rose. "It's about time I was going."

Mrs. Jesson moved quickly toward the door—in short, swaying steps. "You want to be left to yourselves, I'm sure. I'll just go powder my nose," she said politely, even kindly.

Howard put his hand on Homer's shoulder. His father looked up with a placid smile. "Very nice woman," Homer said. "Very nice."

Howard nodded. "So it seems." And it seemed, too, that his business was completed for the time being; that he could leave in good conscience and come back another time without dread; even, perhaps, that the years could proceed in an orderly if incomprehensible manner, and the business of being human be conducted delicately and decorously right up till the last minute. But out of Howard's mouth, much to his surprise, came Will's question: "Why did you leave?" he asked.

"Why did I leave what?" Homer responded, still smiling.

Will would have said, "Us." Howard said, "Cummington."

"Oh. Cummington. Well, I was in love." He winked. "Still am."

"Love?" Howard said, sounding as if he weren't acquainted with the word.

"Constance is a very sweet woman." After a pause Homer

105

added: "Very sweet." After another pause: "Eunice was not so sweet."

Howard nodded. No, our mother was not so sweet.

Much more quietly, our father said, "I never loved Eunice. She never loved me."

"Are you sorry you went?" Mrs. Bard asked, just as her clams and Howard's lasagne arrived, the fly jumped at last from the bread basket, and the waiter's tooth flashed.

"Not at all."

Mrs. Bard sighed. "Howard, you know that I'm not at all happy with Will. I'm convinced he's ruining his life. It's so dreadful."

Howard didn't disagree. "He's trying to do the opposite, you know. He's trying, however dimly, for regeneration."

Eunice, swallowing wine, had her mind in several places. She tilted her glass between two fingers and watched the liquid pale as light passed through it; at the same time she sat across the table, where Howard was, to watch herself lift the glass; and to that one movement she tried to impart all of her delicacy, her sensitivity. She felt the rosé slide against her tongue. At the same time Howard was speaking, and she listened, as she always listened to her sons, to the sound, trying to recognize the tone. How her children treated her mattered so much to Mrs. Bard—they would never know how much until they had their own. But Howard would never have any, she felt; Neal might not; and now Will had left his lovely little Sarah. It made her grandmotherly heart sick, to have that joy taken away, the last great joy she would ever—but Howard had said something to her.

He had said something about Will's generation. "I disapprove of his generation," Eunice said stoutly. "They don't have the willingness to stick things out. There are duties. One should just do them. Will does not yet have the stamina for life."

106

Will would always be Mrs. Bard's baby, there was no taking that image away from her. But there was no need to. "I agree with you," Howard said. He noticed that but for a red shred of noodle his plate was empty; he had just swallowed his last bite of lasagne. Apparently it had had no distinguishing characteristics. But then lasagne was always the same; not much different from spaghetti or manicotti. He was still hungry. He might grab a hot dog on his way home.

Eunice picked up a clam. When she raised it off her plate it dangled from one tine, and she set it down to spear it more firmly. With horror she recalled Howard's manner of eating spaghetti. He never bothered with a spoon, just sucked the strands to his mouth. . . . He started doing that while Homer was in Sicily, a medic for General—it was Clark, she thought, General Clark. She had to feed little Will, had to help Neal feed himself. She couldn't be bothered to tell Howard not to suck his spaghetti. Not that it hadn't crossed her mind; it pained her every time her chubby Howard slurped; she shuddered. Times had been difficult, Eunice told herself. One had to bear unpleasantness. Times had always been difficult. She smiled painfully. What's to become of us, she asked herself—plaintive, if rhetorical.

Howard was still talking about Will. He provided a happy ending for his mother: Will reunited with Lucy and Sarah, back at his teaching job, and more thankful for his blessings as a result of his follies. For his part, Howard believed everything but the last bit.

Howard signaled for coffee, and the waiter arrived promptly with the check. "Dreadful," Mrs. Bard said under her breath; a fly circled her head. In the opposite corner a glass smashed on the floor; in the ensuing confusion someone knocked over a chair. The waiter arrived at last: he brought tiny cups of frothy coffee, and his broad, silver-toothed smile. "Dreadful," Mrs. Bard said again, as she looked away.

107

"This is really good," Neal said.

"Really?" Delsey asked, conversationally.

"No, but it isn't too bad. You should tell the chef not to put sugar in it."

"Okay," said Delsey, who didn't tell the chef anything. The chef had been there about a hundred years. "But a lot of people like it that way."

"A lot of people put ketchup on their scrambled eggs."

She shrugged. "I put ketchup on my scrambled eggs."

"Oh yeah? It doesn't kill the taste of the eggs?"

"Well, maybe," she admitted. "But I don't much like scrambled eggs anyway."

"Ah. In that case you should just eat plain ketchup, and forget the eggs."

Delsey looked closely at Neal. "I do, sometimes. But you feel stupid drinking ketchup out of the bottle."

"You drink it?" Neal sounded delighted at the idea.

"Well, yeah," Delsey said reluctantly. "But I don't usually. I use a spoon. You've gotta promise not to tell the other girls."

"Sure. But how come you tell me?"

"Because you tell me a lot of stupid things," she said. "You probably won't get all excited about one more stupid thing."

"I think it's a wonderful thing. Have you got another one?"

"Oh no. No fair. You've gotta tell me one now."

Neal lied easily and with pleasure. "Okay. When I was little I used to eat shoelaces."

"That's nothing. Everybody did that."

"Everybody does that? All right, I've got another one. I still eat shoelaces."

"Lots of people still do. Come on, it's gotta be a good one. Quick, because I have to go."

"Here's something I don't tell everyone. I've eaten a Volkswagen." He looked proud of himself. It wasn't a bad lie.

"The whole thing?"

108

"Unh-hunh. Except for the manual."

Delsey put her hand on her hip. "I believe you," she said, and walked off. Neal gazed affectionately at her white shoes, like nurses'. Like all the women he admired, she was somewhat pigeon-toed. He didn't like her *because* she was pigeon-toed, he thought; he just liked her, and she was pigeon-toed. He admitted that the proportion of pigeon-toed women among the ones he liked was startling. He was a little pigeon-toed himself. But that wasn't connected with it either, he thought; nothing was connected.

When she brought Neal his check she said, "You forgot to ask me tonight."

"Ask you what?"

"If I fraternize."

Neal looked at her distrustfully. "If you say no this time, we're finished," he warned. She nodded. "Well, do you?"

"I work on the weekends. But I could fraternize on Monday night."

"Fine," Neal agreed, and as if the matter were closed he started to pay the check.

"Hey. Aren't you going to say what time? And what we're gonna do? And whether you'll pick me up, and where? I can see you're gonna be a terrific escort."

Neal had assumed that he would come to the Flo for dinner; she would take his order, talk to him. That would be the date. But he could tell that he hadn't considered it very carefully.

"What would you like to do?" he asked.

She became diffident. "Who knows?"

"We could go to a movie or something," he tried, without much hope.

"Great. You never get to go to the movies anymore. I love movies. What are we gonna see?"

"Whatever you like," he said, gratified. "I don't know what's in—"

"There's some old Humphrey Bogart movies playing at the Globe on Monday. You like that kinda stuff?"

She lived over in Easthampton, in an apartment just off Holyoke Street. He wrote the address on his wrist. Pick her up at seven thirty, a drink first, maybe?

"Make it seven, and we can have two," she said. This guy was really something. Next thing she'd have to teach him how to French kiss.

But Delsey figured that she didn't mind. He didn't have everything all fixed up. He didn't already know what record was going to be playing when he sat down next to her on the couch, and how he was going to get her blouse off without fumbling for the buttons. She wouldn't have to go any farther than she wanted with this one, even if he was—what was it again? A lawyer. That just meant he was smart with words, not with people. Delsey had been around a little; she guessed she knew what they'd be like. She wished she'd been around a little less so she wouldn't always think about how they were going to get her undressed. Maybe then she could just undress when she wanted to undress.

Neal was taking bills out of his wallet. For a second she thought he was going to leave a ten-buck tip or something, and she wasn't too pleased about it. She was ready to say: I'm sorry, but you can't buy fraternizing. See the look on him when she stuck the bill back into his face; this girl isn't for sale, Delsey said to herself. But when she brought his change he left about twenty percent, like always. Once she forgot his lamb chops and they weren't too warm when he got them, finally. He mentioned it, but he left the twenty. Delsey thought that maybe this guy would just watch the movie. There was plenty of time for messing around.

Neal went home to his apartment. He sat in his armchair, where he rarely sat, and tried to think of nothing, without much success. He lay down on his bed, where he always lay, and tried to read the funny book he had been reading—the

110

autobiography of the last court executioner of Britain. It wasn't quite as funny as he remembered. Maybe the beginning was the funny part. Finally he got up and paced around the room. He was accosted by his image in the mirror as he went by: a sharp-featured man with a cowlick looked at him with considerable surprise. Neal stopped and stood before the face. "You're not crazy if you talk to yourself," he said.

"Only if you answer yourself back."

"Okay," Neal said. "So you be quiet, hunh? I'll do the talking."

"Agreed."

"Don't answer this," Neal said. "But what is going on?"

"I won't. I'll just give him hints."

"No deal," Neal said, and sidled away. "I don't like your looks," he added, and suddenly weary he thought: Not funny.

He tried to write a letter. Dear Mr. President, he wrote,

I don't have an ounce of patience for your type. The Red Cross has been saying, and I think I agree, that your films are morally objectionable, that your shirts are rarely pressed, that you are lousy with chopsticks, that you use non-biodegradable tennis shoes,

but Neal's heart wasn't in it. He didn't even bother to finish. The President's heard it all before, he thought; let him rest in peace. Neal was unable to do the same. He twitched on the bed, twiddled a pair of inert thumbs, stared at the ceiling. In hopes of blessed relief he turned on the television set. Immediately he was confronted by a white-haired man kicking the air with his spats. The man held a straw boater in his hand, and shook it like a tambourine, waving good-bye. The applause rose as he left; and he returned, still singing, still waving good-bye. He sang:

I'm in love, I'm in love
with a beautiful gal:
That's what the matter with me.

"Oh, for Christ's sake," Neal muttered, and rose to turn off the set; while the white-haired man smiled at him, and waved good-bye with his boater.

Neal recalled that games had started well before sunset. Dark cars with rounded fenders began pulling up to the four diamonds just after five. They disgorged boys wearing oversized baseball uniforms: caps rested on ears, ends of belts drooped, dangled pendulous in midair. First names, inscribed in script, ran a rakish diagonal across the heart: Howard pawed soft strips of cloth that read "Howie"; Neal had to submit to a jaunty "Vic" running over his hurt heart. Gothic letters announced the team sponsors, Cardinal Hardware, in blocks too big for Neal's thin back; Howard's broad one, arranged in Yankee pinstripes, stretched three rows of Crane Letterpress—the letters seemed to ripple as he ran.

Howard used his father's old first-baseman's glove, a tiny hinge of soft leather with a few strands of loose webbing; in consequence of this and his height he played first base. Neal had a new Wilson, still beautifully blond and stiff, with a Ted Williams autograph; despite this he played right field. In his

113

first two seasons he touched the ball only when infielders threw it past each other.

Little League was new to Cummington. Some dads claimed it had been better before, when kids played pickup games without coaches or umpires; but Little League was here to stay. The eight merchants who chipped in for uniforms had something to say about that.

A coach dragged an olive green duffel bag out of the trunk of the car, opened it, and began to distribute baseballs to his team, counting the balls as he passed them out. Everyone started to play catch, including the coach, a hulking round-shouldered man who chewed tobacco, just like the major leaguers. He *had* been a minor-league ballplayer for a while, got as high as class Double-A—"which ain't that bad, lemme tell you. They got guys there what can hit." He was a pretty fair pitcher himself—fast, but wild. "Once I lost a no-hitter," he claimed, grinning. "Nobody believes me, but it's true." His name was Mr. Daw, Jack Daw; he always said, "Call me Coach, kids," and everybody called him Mr. Daw. Mr. Daw liked going out to talk to his pitcher ("You got this guy, I'm tellin ya"), but the part he liked best was having a catch with the rival coach before the game. He never used his best hummer, but sometimes he stung the guy a little; and every once in a while Mr. Daw threw his big overhand curve, so he could watch the guy run after it, right there in front of his team. Mr. Daw was a good coach, all right: it was Neal's ambition to be a minor-league baseball player when he grew up. After all, he wouldn't be good enough for the majors.

Howard's coach was Mr. Willet Finch, and Howard's ambition was still to be President, though he was wavering. Mr. Willet Finch worked at Crane Letterpress, the largest business in Cummington, and was anxious for promotion; although clean, honest, and hardworking, he wasn't a naturally friendly man, and there was something in his bony, pumped-jaw demeanor that his boss, the effusive Chat Crane, seemed

114

to take exception to. Younger, kindlier men quickly made their way past Mr. Finch on the company ladder. Casting about for a *deus ex machina,* Mr. Finch decided to take on what he called the "company team," hoping a Little League championship would bring his long-awaited promotion. Mr. Finch was a serious, even dour coach, who used his best nine players at all times: he sat tensely on the bench during games, pinching himself, as you might in the dentist's chair; when he shook hands after a win, his eyes blazed with martial joy.

Crane Letterpress took their infield drill first. Mr. Finch hit fungoes to his infielders. A sharp grounder at the feet of the third baseman jumped into left field; the shortstop overran a slow roller; the second sacker fielded a one-hopper cleanly and lobbed it high over Howard's head.

Infield practice was over. "Run it in, run it in," the coach said. Howard ran it in, wondering what "it" was. Mr. Finch tugged at the brim of his cap; clapped his hands idly. "We're up first, swing a few bats. Swing a few bats, now." Though a neophyte as a coach, Mr. Finch knew enough to say everything twice. "We're gonna hit tonight. Gonna hit tonight."

The Cardinal Hardware outfielders chucked it around. The sun was low and Neal lost a throw on its way up; he stood helplessly, squinting, waiting nervously for the sound of ball hitting ground. At the last second he covered his head with his arms; it was only then that the ball landed, yards in front of him. Neal picked it up and threw it halfway back. Piney Siskin was laughing at him. "Lost it in the sun," Neal yelled.

Siskin picked up the ball. "What?" he taunted.

"The sun."

"What?"

Jack Daw hit a few flies to his outfielders. He got good wood on the one to Neal. Neal didn't do such a bad job on it. As soon as he heard the crack of the bat he was off and running, his back turned to the plate. He almost caught up to it; for a second the ball, towering in the blue above, looked like it might drop down into his mitt. Neal ran faster, heart pounding in his chest; the ball fell just beyond his hands and bounced away in the grass. Neal got to it before it stopped rolling and wheeled quickly, ready to fire. When he looked back toward the diamond he saw his team leaving the field. Most of them had already left. Piney Siskin stepped on second base on his way in, as he always did. Neal straightened up, holding the ball loosely in his hand. He imagined an enemy runner tearing around second, heading for third. Neal reared back and let fire, putting everything into his throw. He saw his cut-off man handle it perfectly, swivel, and fire to the plate, where in a cloud of dust the runner was out, unquestionably out. Neal picked up the ball on the way in. When he got to the bench he dropped the ball into the duffel bag.

They all huddled around Mr. Daw. "All right, guys. I'll give ya the batting order when ya come back in. But the line-up stays the same. Okay, men? Everybody got his shoelaces tied tight? And throw strikes tonight, Jay boy. Lotsa strikes."

Mrs. Bard drove up with Will as the game began. She waved hello to Neal out in right field. He waved back, a little proud. He would've been real proud if he'd been in left; Peewee Bunting got some balls out there in left. With a distant whoosh a plane passed above, a jet: Neal followed the twin trails of white smoke all the way across the sky. He was roused from his admiration by the crack of bat against ball; he looked nervously, trying to catch the flight of the ball. But it was to left: a single. Neal turned back to the jet soaring by the edge of the sky. Maybe he didn't mind right field so much; he could watch jets, anyways. When he moved his foot he noticed the perfect imprint of his sneaker in the dewy grass.

Howard got up with two men out and a man on first base. The first pitch came bouncing in the dirt. The second one came in waist-high, and Howard lashed it between the short-

116

stop and the third baseman. Mr. Finch jumped up: *"At-tababy, 'way we go. At-a-bay-bee!"* The ball bounced twice, hit the left fielder on the wrist, rolled up his arm, and went over his shoulder. Mr. Finch started to wave his arms in circles. "Go for three, go for three," he shouted, veins standing out on his head. Howard reached third standing up and put his hands on his hips. I only deserved a single, he was thinking; Peewee Bunting should have stopped it. Mr. Finch exultèd: "Atty eye, baby, atty eye!"; he held up a bony clenched fist.

Howard stood on third wearing an air of indifference. He wasn't indifferent, but troubled; he wished his coach's face was less red. Howard didn't verbalize it yet, but he already believed in grace. He saw his mother waving to him from behind the bench; Howard touched the rounded bill of his cap in response, the way Granpacky Singer did when he passed ladies in the street.

Robin Linnet popped out to end the inning. When Neal loped past Howard he muttered, "Hit him in the head next time, and I get to play left." Howard only grunted; and Neal reminded himself, heading for his end of the bench, the far end, that he had just renounced his ambitions for left field in favor of the more peaceful pastimes of right.

The coach read off the batting order. Neal was seventh. He wasn't the worst hitter on the team, anyways. He walked a lot. If it was below his waist he never swung; he figured it might be a ball, and he knew he couldn't hit it. Neal's greatest virtue as a batter was a knowledge of his limitations.

A little towheaded girl came wandering up to his end of the bench. It was Piney Siskin's sister; her name was Phoebe, but everyone called her "Bags." She was only three or four. Bags was wearing a pair of shorts, and sneakers, but no shirt. She had big staring brown eyes and a dirty face; Neal guessed it had been vanilla.

Bags nestled on the bench next to Neal. Piney came up and

117

told her to get off the bench. Wordlessly she slipped off and sat in a heap on the ground beside Neal's feet. Piney started to stalk away, but then he had an idea, and bent over his sister. "Hey Bags. Sing your song."

Bags looked down coyly at her hands, which now contained three stalks of grass. "Come on," Piney insisted. "Just once."

"O-kay," Bags relented. She drew in breath, and then breathed out, in a soft monotone,

> Peek-a-boo
> I see you
> Hiding behind the chair.
> Peek-a-boo
> I see you
> Put on your underwear.
> Bum-bump. Have one? Nope.

"Who taught her that?" Neal asked, not entirely sure as to its significance. Bags glowed.

"I did," Piney said proudly. "Neat, hunh?"

Noddy Tern came back to the bench, swearing. "That guy is murder," he said. "Wicked sidearm."

Neal turned his attention to the game. Martin Vogel was pitching for Crane Letterpress. He was a lanky boy with steel-rimmed glasses, therefore considered bright. He was throwing with a sidearm delivery. It was even rumored that he had a curve.

Neal leaned nervously over toward Noddy. "Is he fast?" he asked.

"Wicked fast," Noddy said. "He comes out of third base with it, too."

Comes out of third base? Neal wondered what that could mean. Perhaps it had something to do with velocity.

A tall, pretty woman in a pleated skirt approached the bench, her hair wrapped in a blue silk scarf. She put her hand on Neal's shoulder. "You haven't seen Will, have you, dear? I've lost track of him again."

"Already?" Neal said.

"If you see him, tell him to report back to me, please."

How was Neal supposed to see him? Neal was *play*ing.

"Okay," Neal said. "Hey," he added. "Where's Dad?"

"He's working late again. He said he'd meet us for a hamburger at Doc's after the game."

"I'm starving," Neal said thoughtfully.

In among a bright clump of day lilies on the bank Will pulled off his shoes without untying them; peeled off his socks and stuck them inside the shoes; carefully rolled up the legs of his pants. He was looking for crayfish, though he had a fear of finding them. After the first step one of the pantslegs unrolled. Let it go, he thought. The water was cool and the bottom surprisingly sandy. After two more steps the water jumped up over his knees and soaked the other pantsleg; Will's lips tightened, and a foreboding feeling crept up over his knees. He was gonna get it. Grimly he plodded on. He had an objective: the sun-warmed rock right in the middle. Glassy water parted before the rock in quiet obeisance, as if knowing it was coming. That was the place, Will thought; nice and flat, nice and warm. The water was chilly; his ankles ached with cold. For a moment, as he trudged along in his wet, heavy trousers, Will had the feeling that he had been not only bad, but foolish. And then he reached his rock.

He clambered onto it and lay on his stomach. Yes, it was warm; it was perfect. He propped his chin on the back of his hands and stared into the stream. Two dragonflies, coupled one atop the other, darted before him, wings shining, bodies a glittering green; they landed on a small stone, flew off, were back, circled crazily, fluttered off. Now they were gone; no, the same stone. The copulating dragonflies danced in the air once more, and fled for good.

119

Will put his head sideways on the stone and listened to the slow murmur of the stream. He imagined that it was speaking in a foreign language no one understood—French, maybe. Maybe it was speaking of a treasure. Maybe it was just waiting for someone to come along who could understand.

From around the bend he heard a familiar rattle. He held his breath and waited. A small gray-blue bird, with oversized head and arching crest, came swooping low over the shallow water. Will had a good look at him; that's a neat color blue, he thought calmly. The kingfisher made a rapid circle around Will, and darted upstream. See, Will claimed: I'm in the middle of the world. The trees on the banks pointed their branches, bent with verdant weight, toward Will; the river was almost entirely in shadow, but the sun shone on him. He thought: There isn't anybody else in the whole river, except me.

But that made him think of crayfish. He always went looking with Neal; Neal wasn't afraid. Besides, they never found any. There was only the once: in the tiniest stream imaginable, trickling down through the pasture, Neal had lifted a flat rock off the muddy bottom, and a gray shape scuttled slowly under the lip of the overhanging bank. Neal cried out in triumph, and reached his hand right where the shape had gone; but that was the last they saw of the creature. Will had seen just enough to be afraid, and not enough not to be. But Neal wasn't afraid, so Will tried not to be. And the two lifted up every flat rock for miles around, never with as much success.

Soon the sun would go down, Will thought. The river murmured something to him, something he didn't catch. Will mumbled something back. A crow perched in a dead elm took sudden exception to some small movement Will made, and croaked a harsh warning; or perhaps it was trying to call attention to itself. Will turned onto his side and watched; the

120

crow hesitated; then jumped into the air, and flew down-stream.

It's time for me to be going too, Will thought, and didn't move.

Neal ran hard out to right field. He would be up next time. He couldn't say he liked to be up, particularly against Martin Vogel; but you weren't supposed to ask yourself if you liked to be up. It made him excited, that was certain. Once he had taken a swing, and the ball hit the bat, and went over the second baseman's head, for a double. It was always a double when it went into right field; because the right fielder was always the worst player on the— Neal stopped himself there. He put himself back on second base: he had waved happily to his mother, and seen Mr. Daw smiling and laughing on the bench. "Way to go," Mr. Daw had called out. "How we hit, Neal boy." To the next hitter Mr. Daw had called out: "Everybody hits tonight. Everybody hits." Neal had hitched up his trousers, looking for his father's wide face in the crowd—

With the loud crack of the bat Neal looked up worriedly from his sneakers. Only a foul ball. Hey, that was Howard again. How'd he get up so soon?

"That's a piece of it, that's a piece," Mr. Finch yelled through his cupped hands. Jay Swift, the Cardinal Hardware pitcher, threw his best fastball, right over the middle at shoulder height. As Howard watched the ball coming, he imagined that he could see the red threads in the seams spinning leisurely toward him; then, as he swung, there was that blank space, when he felt nothing, saw nothing; and then he felt the bat in his hands come against the ball. The fog disappeared; Howard dropped his bat and started for first, mechanically searching the field for the ball.

He had gotten under it a little; the result was a lazy fly ball a few steps in front of the left fielder. Peewee Bunting tip-toed in hesitantly, grimacing, and stopped; then he took a few more steps; and was starting forward again, when the ball came down behind him. He made a lunging stab with his glove, but it was too late. The ball dropped over his shoulder, landed with a thunk, and didn't bounce. Howard pulled reluctantly into second. There was something vaguely dissatisfying about baseball. Later Neal would charge that it came too easy for Howard; but that wasn't this matter's crux. Baseball was a game of imperfections—you took advantage of a fat pitch here or a lousy fielder there; you relied on other people's mistakes, that was how you won. Howard didn't love games. He liked sports where you could try to achieve a harmony, a rhythm, and no one would stop you, nothing would upset the balance you made. He mentioned crew, running, swimming, gymnastics; Neal sipped his drink, popped a handful of peanuts into his mouth, and answered that he liked balls, that was all.

Another fly ball dropped in the outfield. Howard trotted home. Mr. Finch slapped him on the back. The score was already five to nothing, and it was only the beginning of the third inning.

Crane Letterpress always wins, Neal remarked; Howard always wins. Neal's fighting spirit, not a frequent visitor to the Cummington Little League field, rose up in him. He would show Howard. He was first up next inning, and he was going to rap that apple, powder that pill.

Booby Turnstone, the fat redheaded catcher ("Carrottop"), struck out to end the top half of the inning. On the way to first Howard passed Neal and said pleasantly, "I almost got Peewee for you. Maybe next time." Neal didn't answer, smile, or even look up. He went right to the on-deck circle, which was just a bare patch of ground, and started swinging two bats purposefully.

When the infielders were ready Neal stepped into the batter's box; he crowded the plate more than usual, menacingly waggling the bat next to his ear. With one finger Martin

Vogel pushed his glasses up on the bridge of his nose, bent over, and wound up: twisting toward third, now turning to the plate, he threw, his arm extended at hip level.

Neal never saw the ball. He saw Martin Vogel's mouth open as he threw, eyes staring, face expressionless. Neal waited stubbornly for the ball to enter his line of sight; but all he saw was Martin following through, beginning to fall off toward first. Something made Neal jerk his head backwards. The ball cracked into the top of his spine, just below his neck, and ricocheted sharply toward the bench. Neal fell face-first onto the plate. Still clutching his bat, he rolled in the dirt, knees pulled up into his stomach. He rubbed the ground with the palm of his hand, swept circles in the dust, his face contorted.

Neal could remember the color red behind his closed eyes, a full field of stunning crimson; gradually it became rusty orange, and then pale yellow. He opened his eyes. There was a ring of faces, and past that the sky; he knew that the worst of the pain was gone. "I'm all right," he groaned, and tried to get up. The wide fleshy hands of Mr. Daw held him. "Just you stay still for a minute," Mr. Daw said. "Where did it get ya?" Neal, under the impression that he was not to speak, motioned to his back. He noticed the glassy face of Mr. Daw's watch, which reminded him of Martin Vogel's face, and the silver-colored coil of the watchband. "Ya want me to rub it?" Mr. Daw asked.

Neal didn't feel able to shake his head. "Unh-unh," he said. "What time is it, by the way?"

Mr. Daw checked his wrist. "A quarter after," he said.

Neal noticed Howard's face in the ring. Howard was speaking to him. "Why'd you ask that? You okay?"

"Just curious," Neal said weakly. He started to stagger to his feet, and to his surprise no one stopped him; the ring loosened as he rose. He saw his mother sitting on the bench with her handkerchief in her hand; he waved stiffly, and then trotted off to first with his head held carefully in place. Mr. Daw trotted beside him. "I'm fine," Neal said, though no one had asked.

"You all right?" Mr. Daw asked.

"I'm fine," Neal repeated. He wanted to put his hands in his pockets, for some reason; but his uniform didn't have pockets. He folded his arms tightly.

Martin Vogel called over from the mound. "Sorry, Bard."

"He didn't mean to," Howard chimed in. "He always has control problems. He hits somebody every game." Howard added, "Dad'll look at it later. He's got some ointment."

"You're gonna be fine, Neal kid," Mr. Daw said after a pause, sounding like a coach for the first time in several minutes. "You're gonna be *oh*-kay." He patted Neal on the rear end. Neal said to himself that he had a good coach. He leaned toward second.

It would be pleasant to report that Neal's presence on first made a momentous impression on the game; but Martin Vogel struck out the side. He made his way through the rest of the order with similar dispatch. By the bottom of the sixth the score was 11–0, and Neal reached the plate in considerably different spirits. He stood a more discreet distance from the plate and waved his bat politely at the first two deliveries. He was fully prepared to strike out on the next pitch, and head for the bench none the worse for wear. Martin Vogel, too, was set to strike Neal out; Mr. Daw expected it without rancor; Mr. Finch gleefully expected it. But events turned themselves around—on their own initiative, for there was no conflict of interest—and contrived a small disaster.

Perhaps Martin Vogel, having beaned Neal, was nervous in facing him again; perhaps there was even a streak of cruelty behind his blank face. Unaccountable, but the next pitch, a sidearm fastball, hit Neal in the back.

It struck flesh instead of bone, and didn't have the speed of Vogel's previous ball. It stung, all right, but the pain was momentary, and modulated. All the same, the psychic effects of this second shock were far more catastrophic, as if the pain of the second hurt began where the first left off: for this time Neal had imagined the event before it happened, and this time it was with horrifying clarity that he saw, despite his frantic contortions to escape, a grinning ball spinning toward him. No, he couldn't avoid it: here came his nightmare, true.

Will didn't bother to roll up his trousers a second time. He slipped off his rock, slipped into the deep blue of the water, and vanished from the waist down—like a sword disappearing in its scabbard. This time the water was cold, painfully so; it seemed deeper, too. Will was relieved when he saw his knees rise out of the river. He picked up his shoes and socks and ran barefoot up the slope toward the field, wet trousers slopping. His feet still ached with cold, but he was happy— as if he had just come down from giddy and dangerous heights, or crossed a raging river that he need never ford again. Will ran until he was exhausted; and then lay down under the tall trees beside his mother's car.

How you gonna keep 'em down on the farm, Will thought, pulling his lips back to examine his gums in the Petersens' mirror. Pink. In the pink. I pink, therefore I am. His hand twisted the faucet's cross and water came hissing down like a straight snake. Will nudged a worm of toothpaste onto his brush. Here's a man who squeezes his toothpaste tube in the middle, he thought; a man who burns his candle at neither end, but evinces a fatal attraction for his own image. A man who watches himself brush his teeth. A man who watches himself shit. A man who would like not to have to look. A man who. Vote for, elect.

He was thinking like Neal, he thought, and spat out. He

looked down. Someday he'd have to remember to buy cleaner for this sink. Grime like shadows. If Lucy saw that she'd shake her head. How he'd hate it: no reproach, just a shake of the head. Her capsule description of old Will in one motion, negation.

Will drew the knife toward him, slashing cubes of bright red beef into strips. He approached Harwood with eyes averted; even a casual glance could prevent the perverse hawk from eating. Will held out the red shreds in his glove and stared pointedly out the window. A stone wall, coming apart, edged the dirt road; blackberry bushes shoved up through the stones, bearing berries and cedar waxwings. Two crows descended, wings flapping heavily, and the waxwings darted away. Will felt a pull on the glove; Harwood was trying to eat his thumb. Gently Will moved his hand. No response. A crow wolfed a blackberry. Will flicked his eyes to the side; Harwood stood with head bent, back stooped—curiously submissive posture. Will moved the glove again: the meat was practically in Harwood's face. Eat, old man, Will thought; live a bit longer. For an instant there was an ounce of weight on Will's palm: Harwood had put out his foot for the meat. His talons touched, drew back. Slowly Will turned his hopeful head—but Harwood's head was down, and his talons empty.

Will would wait. He propped his elbow on the cage and gazed down the dirt road. Among the pines two twining birches flashed their skeletons.

On the way the locust tree, though fallen, was in flower; white flowers, continuously ransacked by bees in a state of high excitement. In the air was their fervent buzz, and the redolence of white locust flower, and in the high sky the sun was adrift among a few white carnations. It was not hot; it was just right. There are seasons within the seasons of the year, Will decided, spells when the weather seems bound to spell out the same credo as the day before, whether in sup-

126

posed repentance (the rascally schoolboy at blackboard after class) or firm avowal (the Bible-drunk lunatic on the corner) it was impossible to tell. On Will's walks the flora always blossomed under repetitions of the same dolphin blue Easter sky with silver-tinted sun. Beside the road Will saw various wildflowers, not bothering to name them, and in their half-dreamed state they remained touchingly unfinished, their petals indicated with an inarticulate dab of watercolor, fine at a distance but on a close inspection only a blur. Lucy walked beside him, wearing cut-offs, and eagles flew by, on the right.

Harwood did not eat. Will was getting weary. He had never been the patient one (that was Howard). But a hawk needed patience more than anything else.

And Lucy had too, Will decided; perhaps that was why he'd lost her. He dreamed her less and less, he was glad to say. But he had to admit that in his occasional dreams of bliss she was the only permanent resident. In these quiet ecstasies she was not the one who provided the dripping sweetness of honeyed loins; instead she was as indispensable, as unnoticed there on the table of his heart, as salt. Common salt. No wonder his wounds had taken so long to heal. Will hoped nowadays that he was better; he thought he'd given her up; but here she was, with thorny locusts blooming, and eagles on the right.

He looked in Harwood's eye, startling him. Harwood ruffled his feathers and rocked nervously on his perch. Will flipped the strips of meat into the dish, and Harwood jumped away angrily. "Christ, you're just like Homer," Will said loudly, angry in his turn; Harwood flapped his broken wing, dripping blood, and in dismay Will turned away, cursing his own impatience. His stubborn impatience.

He slid open the massive wooden door. A few cows looked up, mouths full of hay; but no sign of Pete. Where had he gone off to now? Oh well, Will would have to do it alone again. He took the milking machines, shaped like teakettles with tentacles, down from the shelves. As he began to attach them to anonymous udders Will abruptly wondered if he would be able to look back on this part of his life with satisfaction. Or with compassion, or with what. It's like writing a poem too many times, he thought: the more you considered, the less you could guess; the more times the words came back, like incumbent candidates for local election, the less they meant; until his own reflections caromed off each other as if caught between two mirrors, rebounding endlessly and trailing away, trailing away. Will looked down the row of black and white flanks, and did not know what to think.

When the sound of the machine-suck changed, it was important to take the hoses off quickly. Will didn't pretend that the mechanics of his daily life, the motions, gave him pleasure—dull eyes of cows, not bothering to regard him. He was doing no one any great good; he lugged full machines over to the cooler. He was doing no harm either; he emptied them. While he was no longer certain it was possible to do great good (milk spilled, slapping concrete), he was still quite sure that harm was possible. At least he was avoiding that, yes? And everything else in the cheap bargain? He snapped hose onto rubbery teat. Fly landed on nose.

He had never liked milking, perhaps because he had never liked milk. If there was satisfaction, it lay in soporific effect, gentle lulling. For Will had a lot of things he didn't want to think about; and it wouldn't be such a bad idea, he reasoned, to be a bit more like a cow. He rolled his jaw, champing the imaginary cud.

Macaroni and cheese; he could smell it. Stewed tomatoes too, he guessed.
"Want help, Edna?"
She never did. "Just you sit yourself down."
Right: they squirmed in their red juices.

128

"Seen Pete?"

She flinched. "Surely have."

Will put the casserole on the trivet. "Whereabouts?"

She shrugged, and Pete staggered in.

"I wanna apologize," Pete said, waving his hands and holding his forehead. He sat down heavily.

Will stared; it was early for this. "Uh, that's all right."

"I missed out the chores," Pete explained.

"I know. It's okay."

Pete gave Will a blank look. "I wanna apologize," he began again.

Edna approached with serving spoon held aloft. "You can just take the afternoon off, Will. Pete'll take care of chores."

Pete snapped out of it. "Edna! For the love of Jesus!"

"It's only fair," Edna said quietly, and gently ladled tomatoes onto Will's macaroni. He always forgot to tell her about stewed tomatoes. "Will did the A.M., you can do the P.M."

"I don't give a damn about A.M.s and B.M.s, Edna. I'm not up to it today. Not today."

"That's okay with me," Will commented.

"What's fair is fair," Edna said sharply.

"Come on, Edna. I apologized, didn't I? I said I would, and I did. But I can't do the goddamn chores by myself tonight. I can't even hardly walk straight."

"Don't worry about it," Will put in. "It doesn't bother me. I don't mind."

Edna glared fiercely at Will; a gaze like a hawk's. "What's fair is fair," she snapped. Will looked down, put his spoon down toward the tomatoes.

Will slashed the twine around the bale, admiring the pitchfork—like four knives, he thought. He pried into the bale, lifted half of it up on the forks with a grunt.

What was it, Will wanted to know, that caught in his craw

129

this time? Fuck, it was the whole situation, including this job. He blamed it on Lucy too; Homer too. Will blamed the ubiquitous dandelion of unhappiness on time itself. Oh hell, it was probably just his blood sugar or some damned thing; but the miracle he hankered for, Will admitted, was escape.

Wishes while you work. Will was in luck. It was a beautiful red.

One fork had gone right into his running shoe. A jolt of surprise went through Will's body. Had he really seen that?

It was a beautiful red—bright, then darkening as air mixed with it. He let go of the unfortunate pitchfork calmly, not very like him at all; wasn't that agreeable. The handle banged on the floorboards, the pitchfork rocked.

A distinguished red. Could he walk? No problem. Perhaps he ought to limp. His left foot left purple pools. Flies took an interest. When he walked toward the open door, a vague shadow trailed behind him on the wooden floor.

Strange; no pain. Blood oozed over the tongue of his running shoe; he was reminded of boysenberry fruit percolating through white yoghurt. He began to feel that he ought to worry, and sat down hurriedly on the stone step in front of the barn. He yanked the laces apart, wrenched the shoe off; but as soon as this preliminary step was accomplished, his urgency dissipated, and Will found himself admiring the shoe itself. Usually a phosphorescent green, its verdure had succumbed to sudden autumn, and was a dark, dead brown. Its innersole had lapped up cups of blood, and Will noted that the maker's name and logo, a striped three-leafed plant of unidentified species, had drowned in the flood. There was a pool perhaps an eighth of an inch deep in the heel. Will impulsively held the shoe to his lips, as if it were a baptismal vessel—but thought of germs, then of cannibals, and couldn't drink. Warily he looked down at his foot, worried at what he might see. A drenched, dripping athletic sock. He peeled it off his foot, closing his eyes in readiness for pain. No pain. He

130

looked again. The hole was in the top of the arch. Blood pushed out in rhythmic spurts, a pulsing river. *His* river, Will thought, taking uneasy pleasure in the idea, his river trickling its way to the ocean. There was no pain; Will held his running shoe beneath his foot to catch the drip, feeling lucky. But this was more than luck; this was Will's miracle. Blessings on all, daffodils and purple crocus in abundance, baskets laden with pastel-painted eggs, ladies in light, bright dresses, spring's full swoon in tender green, Will didn't feel a thing.

Well, old Pete Petersen took care of him all right. He wrapped that damn foot in a towel and took him down to emergency. Hot as hell in emergency; the nurse kept asking about Blue Cross numbers and Social Security numbers and some other damned-fool numbers; then of course he had to wait there, though he's gone all white and the towel's gone all red and is dripping right onto the tiles. But they got to him finally, and I guess Doc Bruce fixed him up pretty good. He give him a tetanus shot and a painkiller and sewed the bastard right up with that heavy thread. Quite the hole, too. Doc Bruce took good enough care of him, all right. Only funny thing is when Doc asked him, in the beginning, how he done it. Will says, "With a pitchfork." The Doc doesn't believe his ears, which is not too surprising. "You accidentally pitchforked yourself?" he says. And Will doesn't answer for a long time, as if it's a hard question or something. Then he finally says, very solemn-like, "I think so."

His foot healed rapidly; but Will's health seemed to undergo a period of instability. As Neal was fond of putting it (too fond. Neal's aphorisms paled with insistent use.), "Inside of every healthy man there's a sick man struggling to get out." Well, Will's was coming out now.

A fortnight after his pitchfork accident Will woke suddenly and thought: I've been shot.

131

That wasn't right. In the instant extremity of his state he had trouble recognizing the real. Let's see. He was lying in bed; this murky, half-lit retreat from bright dream was the world of the living; and this object, here, was pain. It came from the heart.

A moment later the pain had grown till his consciousness had no room for anything else; but some relentless child was still blowing into the balloon. A man's mind is a toy, not well made, and can't accommodate serious use: so kindly let go of me now. But the sick man kept expanding within him, as if he'd blossom rain or shine, ready or not here he came. Will was giving birth to his twisted double.

He doubled up with pain, but the doubling didn't help. He lay back and tried to think. Instead of thinking he put his right hand on his chest and listened with it. Nothing. Don't be ridiculous, he thought. You're thirty-five and you jog.

But Will drew his knee up to his chin and hugged legs, writhed in the labyrinth of his writhing sheets, alternated moans and gasps and even cried out, for pity's sake; all without slowing for an instant the sturdy, soundless ship, bound for disaster, on which he was helpless passenger.

In his suffering Will submitted to a confusion concerning his body and his pain; for the untenable moment it wasn't easy to tell them apart. Heedlessly he tried to abandon all ships. For there was nothing he wanted more than out, out of his own body, unless it was sweet nothing itself.

Another pang. All right, if it's a heart attack, what do you do? You go down and shake the Petersens awake, if you can make it that far, limping and coddling your twisted torso with two tender hands. He'd been in the Petersens' bedroom once or twice, remembered it now: portable TV winking, Kleenex and detective novels handy by bedside, Pete's underwear draped on doorknobs. Will couldn't violate that musky, alien sanctum, couldn't make Edna sit up straight in bed to meet her waking nightmares (don't shoot us all, mister), couldn't force old Pete to dissipate the last drops of dream and step right into his slippers. A lover was needed. Someone Will could hold on to, a life preserver; Lucy. Pang. He'd never loved her so much as this. After all, he was dying, maybe. He needed time, one more loving moment with Lucy and Sarah. His poem too, a few more minutes now and he was certain the words would come—the right, the true words (Death was knowledge, he summed up, grabbing a handful of stomach and twisting). Just one painless hour and he'd go quietly. He was nearly ready.

Pang. He was being melodramatic. But only because it hurt so much.

Pang. He'd have to wake up the Petersens, that was all. If he just moaned loudly enough, maybe. Then again, if it wasn't a heart attack?—how ridiculous he'd appear to Pete!

That was an absurd thought under the critical circumstances. What did it matter, how he looked to Pete? This might be death, Will.

Will remembered riding the bumper cars at Old Orchard Beach. He was only five, and scared. After a few turns he was sick to his stomach, and wanted to get off. He shouted to his parents, but in the noise of the crowd they couldn't hear. He held on to the little wheel with the powerful grip of terror and with his free hand frantically motioned for help. His parents waved back, grinning with pride. "Ride em, cowboy," his father's voice boomed out. Will never understood how he could hear his father's voice so perfectly when they were deaf to his shrill screams of fear.

Pang. Will tottered to his feet. It didn't feel much better to be upright, but it didn't feel worse either. That was true consolation for you. Then again he couldn't imagine worse pain. Couldn't imagine, in fact, anything: pain located him squarely in the miserable here and now.

He was making, he noticed, an effort. He was going into the bathroom. Why? he wondered. When you have a problem, he noted, you always go to the bathroom—you open the medicine chest or sit on the toilet, or both. You kill the pain, or evict it. But this pain wouldn't die out, and wouldn't leave the premises.

Let's talk about this, Will said. He was making desultory swabs at his chest with a wet washcloth. How about if *I* leave instead? He was sounding like Neal again. Pang. He was drawing a bath; and now he was sitting in the tub, not bothering to remove his boxer shorts, not bothering to refrain from moaning, not bothering about a damn thing—

"All right," Will said aloud. "I give up."

The water crawled up his chest. But the pain didn't stop.

Will woke around dawn. He touched his chest; he was all right. He was fine. Heartburn, he thought, almost disappointed; simple heartburn. The bathwater was freezing; Will shivered violently. His feet made lily pads of water on the linoleum. Where was that damn green towel? He dug into his laundry bag, dripping on it.

Finally he remembered that the towel had been washed. He strode to the bedroom, where it lay calmly coiled on a closet shelf; but upon entering the room he was immediately struck by a curious anxiety, and stopped short. He sensed a presence, or, as he later put it, an absence—as if an inordinate amount of time had suddenly passed, and he found himself out of place: in time, not space. Will looked carefully around the room, and found Harwood lying on the newspaper in the bottom of the cage. The hawk's eyes were open and his frozen stare was still full of bright power. He doesn't look very different, Will thought; death isn't much. And as the sun began to fire light into the window, Will stood wrapping the hawk carefully in newspaper, shivering like a creature who has just come ashore for the first time.

Later in the morning Will carried Harwood out to the trash cans. They were full, but Will pushed with his foot and made

134

a little space. A corn husk stuck to his shoe. Will left it there. He laid the newspaper in the space he'd made, and replaced the lid. It was a Monday; Bruce Benham came for the garbage on Monday. Harwood, garbage: they almost rhymed. Will stood staring at the trash cans under the catalpa tree. Harwood, garbage; above him a carrion crow cawed in what sounded to Will like triumph.

9

As regards the gentleman on the near bench: perhaps he came to dispense kindness to squirrels. This hypothesis was put to the test by a squirrel whose only desire lay in caressing Howard's trouser leg; but who came to his end on the pointed end of Howard's cane, or nearly. Or umbrella, or nearly, for Howard carried no cane. Since Howard hated squirrels and disdained to admire the lovely nearly-natural scenery of the park, one could ask his purpose. For Howard did not come to spy upon lovers, swooning under the hawthorne as twilight deepened. He didn't care to gander at the goose, or goose the gander. It could not be said that Howard came to gaze upon the excrement of leashed pets, a variety of excrement that abounds in that sector; for about excrement Howard feels the same as others, all others. Howard fears excrement. Muggers too Howard fears, though a man of Howard's extensive size will naturally fear them less than those of more economic construction. We abide by an inverse proportion: small fears for large people; large fears for small. The medium person's fears will be middling, unless otherwise noted. In the name of reason Howard feared muggers somewhat.

In the park I compose. At home, among my things, I'm not free to drift, to catch others' drifts. In my home there is always the puzzle to think about. What clue to the given solution, for instance. What about this corner, that cranny, for instance. The artificer in his workshop isn't free to merely be a man. Here, human among dogs' piles, surrounded by presumably rabid squirrels, I allow myself to adopt the pretense of presence.

Here, for example, are a male and a female. The male drags the sheet up to his chin, and folds it back; his sex has crept back into its accordion folds, I see it creeping there; he sighs; the light fades. We've seen many such scenes after the messy fact. As in most, the limp host smokes, his moistened paramour frets; the humming electric clock beside the bed marks time. Long silences; talk is small, and deliberately offhand. Toward sunset the female pushes aside the window shade to glance out; she could swear that thunderheads are gathering, marshaling flashes of gold in a blackened sky, could swear that it will rain ashes before final nightfall. But it's just a painted set, with crude clouds riven by crooked streaks of lemon-yellow; and tomorrow will be another, a similar, day. The shade is drawn down from its roll, drawing the scene to its muted close.

Beardsley's, a Northampton restaurant, was designed for intimate theatrics. Aubrey's own prints bless patrons from the walls; low, glowing light filters in through stained-glass windows; potted palms tower overhead; cut-glass fixtures swoop from the ceiling on graceful curves of bent wood; the wainscoting is oak, everything seems to be oak. Lucy sat on an oaken pew, across an oaken table from a lovely young woman in pigtails. Lucy was agitated. Brief smiles kept appearing on her face, to dissolve into chagrin, vanish altogether, and be replaced by the next one.

"You know what he said, Marty? The first time we slept together, and I don't think he'd even pulled out yet—and here I am, who hasn't slept with anybody but Will since I was twenty-seven or something ridiculous—and Donald says, 'I'm not sorry.' God. 'I'm not sorry.' Good old Donald."

Martha Hawkes was the pigtailed Smith poetess-in-residence. She was in fact young and lovely, which had always been difficult for her. She wrote, as she always said apologetically, *tons;* she wrote about men and women, and tried not to take sides. Martha claimed that it took twice as long to say nothing at all. She had been a Scientologist as a teen-ager, and now had trouble with the word *clear.* "Anybody can write *clear*ly," Martha was in the habit of saying, sometimes to herself, "but life isn't *clear* at all."

She held her espresso in her palm, as if she were weighing it, and said carefully to Lucy, "Well, what do you think Donald meant?"

"A lot of things," Lucy said. "I think he meant: 'I don't feel guilty'—though I think he does feel guilty. I think he meant: 'Well, if this is just a one-night stand for you, I promise not to feel hurt'—though I think he would feel hurt. I think he meant: 'You shouldn't feel guilty'—though he's *sure* I feel guilty. In fact, he thinks I *should* feel guilty."

"Do you feel guilty?" Martha asked, smiling.

"Of *course* I feel guilty," Lucy said, and laughed. "What good is sex without guilt? But at least I don't think that I *should* feel guilty."

They both laughed. "God, I'm getting a buzz from this coffee al*ready,*" Lucy said, and drained her tiny square cup.

"What good is coffee without guilt?" Martha mimicked. "Let's split a cognac," she added quickly.

"Jesus, yes."

138

"And then we'll split another cognac," Martha said, encouraged.

"Jesus, Marty. What would I do without you?" Lucy looked admiringly at Martha—who was lovely, and wanted to split two cognacs.

"Drink less," Martha said, and ordered the cognacs.

Lucy felt the back of her neck, where pigtails would be if she had them; but of course there were no pigtails. She wondered what she would look like if she had pigtails again. "You know what I love about you?" Lucy said suddenly. "When we get together, you wouldn't rather be somewhere else. With my old friends, every time we sit down together they have to jump up and go somewhere. They have to pick up the kids at the day-care center. They have to go jog with their husband or something. I love you because you just sit still."

"Not because I sit still. Because I'm still single."

"That's not it. I love you because you don't jog. God, I hate jogging."

"I thought you did jog, Luce."

"Oh, I jog. I jog. But I hate jogging." Lucy didn't laugh. "I don't know why I do it," she confessed. "I think it's because it's painful. That way I can forget the things that really hurt."

"Like Donald?"

"Oh no. Not Donald," Lucy said, shaking her head sadly. "You know what happened that night with Donald?"

"He was impotent."

"No."

"He hurt you."

"*Don*ald? Unh-unh, nothing like that. *He* was okay. It was me."

"Did he say that?" Martha asked quickly, her voice rising.

"No, he didn't even know. Good old Donald had a good old time. I think he did, anyway. I didn't come, but that didn't surprise me; but it was worse than that. I felt like I was watching us through the wrong end of a telescope. I was

139

totally objective, Marty. Totally. I watched him pawing for my clitoris. I watched him pry me open. He used his thumb and his index finger. Then he wiped it on the sheet—I think he must hate getting wet. Then I started to wonder, you know, when he was going to get around to putting himself inside me. I'll count to twenty-five, I said to myself, and then he'll put it in there. He didn't. Maybe fifty, I said. He still didn't; I kept counting, like a lunatic. I felt completely heartless. I felt like I was be*tray*ing him or something. It was like he was down, in a boxing match or something, and I was counting him out, like the umpire. Jesus."

"It was only the first time," Martha said softly. "You always feel weird the first time."

"It's not like I didn't tell myself to stop," Lucy went on. "But I kept thinking, What *is* the Lucky Number? Even when he put himself in, I didn't stop. He had his orgasm, and you know what I thought, right then? I thought, Coming is such sweet sorrow. And I laughed, right in the middle. And he stopped. I didn't come. But I kept counting. I think I got up to a thousand. Poor Donald lay there with his big soft eyes and his poor soft cock and his hurt look, and all I could do was count." Lucy laughed nervously. "Isn't that the most disgusting thing you've ever heard of, practically?"

"Don't be hard on yourself," Martha said. "Sex is impossible anyway. Drink your cognac."

Lucy took a gulp, and coughed. "You know what I'd like to know, Marty? Could you kindly tell me, when did everything get so hard? My God, even pleasure is rough these days."

Martha's hand dove into the bag beside her, wriggled, and yanked out a bent legal pad. "Can I use that, Lucy?" she asked.

Lucy looked puzzled. "Use what?" she said.

Martha's hand dove again for a pen. She found it, uncou-

140

pled it, and jammed the silver top between her teeth. The pen danced quickly along the pale lines of the paper:

Lucy: rough pleasure

Martha considered for a second. Then she wrote:

(Heard it somewhere before? Ask Judy)

Lucy had always slept with her hands to her throat; but lately they had begun to tighten. In the steamy mirror (her mother showered early and long) she made out the red fingermarks, edged by the curve of her nails.

Lucy had been dreaming, lately, about eggs; about pools of water; about anonymous lovers; about relatives long dead.

The eggs, maneuvered by an unseen stooge, found their way to precarious perches, and fell, and smashed utterly: humpty and dumpty. Their crunch hurt her in her sleep, as if it were her own bones breaking up. Who had been careless with all the eggs?

The pools of water that Lucy dreamed were green and murky, steamed under the sun, sprouted palmettos and moss-draped cypresses; alligators threatened her toes, her feet, the stumps of her legs. Someone forced her to stagger all the way around the swelling circumference of that ever-widening pond, while her legs sank ankle-deep in mud. Overhead, monkeys screamed.

The lovers were men she had never even seen. Awake, she could not quite reassemble the mirage of their faces; she wasn't sure they had any. I'm just repressing their faces, Lucy announced, annoying herself. But annoyance did not alter the arrival of these men, who came to her, now, every night, sometimes alone and sometimes in small groups, twos and threes, to tease her, starve her with unattainable presence and then pour down her a flood of sex. Her moistened timbers shivered.

The colors of the room were cold. Lucy's long-dead relatives appeared in groups; they discussed her under their breath. Her grandmother, rocking calmly in a chair not for rocking, unnerved Lucy. This woman sported her late husband's moustache; the rubbery features of the face, though properly wrinkled, did not seem real. Lucy had attended her funeral, had wept in the stifling heat, had stabbed her wet cheeks with a shaking wrist; and she was not easily fooled. *What I am dreaming could not happen,* Lucy affirmed, and as if she had swallowed a quantum of air Lucy rose to the surface. She woke exhausted; eyelids collated, encrusted; fingers digging into her soft white throat. Well, it was morning, it was past time, she had things to do, so many things. She'd better get a move on. Lucy did not move.

Her poor throat. She patted it, rubbed it gently, standing in front of the fogged mirror. The late sun finally made its appearance at the clouded horizon of the bathroom window. Lucy looked at that ball of fire rising in the wet windowpane, and then turned to her drawn face drawn in watercolors in the mirror: looked from one to the other, feeling sick and sorry; from one to the other, sick and sorry.

You cut right through the garbage, Lucy told herself. You get right to the bottom of the pail.

Elizabeth Burnham, Lucy's mother and Sarah's grandmother, put her hands on her knees and bent over: "Would Sa-rah like Grandmommy to get her a sody? A Cokey?"

"Mom. For Christ's sake. Can you go easy on the Coke? That stuff's poison."

"I was just going to get her a *little* one," Mrs. Burnham said, sounding hurt. "And I wish you wouldn't use so much foul language in front of her."

"That's her fourth *lit*tle one today. That's a lot of Coke for a kid."

"But she likes it so much. She really drinks it. She'll feel

142

badly if we have something to drink and she doesn't have anything at all."

"Give her Mister Duckie. Just because you're an alcoholic doesn't mean the kid has to be addicted to Coke."

"I wish you wouldn't keep telling me I'm an alco*hol*ic, Lucy. I just like a little drink, that's all. Like most people."

Sarah waved her pudgy arms. "Cokey," she said, laughing at something.

"There, you see?"

"Cokey, Grammy!" Something was really funny. Sarah laughed as if being tickled.

"Does Sarah want a Cokey? Just a little Cokey? Aw, let her have one, Lucy; she *wants* it. Does you want her Cokey, Sarah? Does you?"

"For Christ's *sake.*"

"Aw, there's a whole big bottle in the fridge, Lucy. Why don't you give her some?"

Shaking her head, Lucy climbed slowly out of the lawn chair. "Another goddamn Coke coming *up,*" she said, and went inside. Mrs. Burnham watched her leave the patio, then turned to Sarah. "Yes, you gets a Cokey. Grammy gets you. Not Mommy. Grammy."

Lucy reached into the cupboard for a glass. She knew that the glasses on the left were the little ones with maps of states on them; souvenirs from the forty states Mr. and Mrs. Burnham had visited with their silvery Airstream trailer and their golden Thermos jug. Without looking Lucy pulled a glass out: South Carolina. It was all right for Sarah to use these glasses —because they were cheap, sturdy, and because there were so many of them; and because Lucy loved to see them broken. Lucy wanted to smash everything in this house. Her baby things—most of all—the album, her little toys and her little shoes, all the cute mementos of Lucy's distant past, when she had been helpless and Mrs. Burnham loved her to pieces. She was still helpless, Lucy thought. She had no way

143

to avoid the past: it had happened. But I don't *want* it, she nearly cried out, and clenched her teeth ferociously. More and more Lucy was murderously unhappy at the thought that she couldn't go backwards, couldn't rehabilitate the past. She poured Coke into the South Carolina glass. The fizz was settling near the northern border as she opened the screen door.

Mrs. Burnham, who moved slowly now (she was sixty-something, but wouldn't tell), had maneuvered herself back into her green and yellow lawn chair and taken up her book again. She was reading—wistfully, one would guess—a paperback copy of *The Sensuous Woman.* She looked up, shaking her head reprovingly: "It is well-written, though"; she read on.

Lucy carried the drink over to Sarah, shading her eyes with her free hand. Her sandals slapped the flagstone. "It's darling of you to be so sweet," her mother said. She added, "The temperature is absolutely perfect today. It's perfect out here."

"Yes, it's lovely," Lucy replied absently. "Here's the Coke, Sarah. You know very well you have to put down Mister Duckie. Hold the glass with two hands."

"O-kay," Sarah said. Mister Duckie went down face-first on the patio. He smiled as lugubriously as ever despite this turn of events; Lucy often had the feeling that Mister Duckie was laughing at her.

Sarah held the glass securely and tilted it against her lower lip, with her mouth wide open, in case soda came running out quickly. It didn't: a low ridge of liquid sloped smoothly into Sarah's mouth. She made a loud swallowing noise, and smacked her lips. She wiped them with the back of her wrist.

"Two hands, please, Sarah," Lucy said, frowning.

"Yup," Sarah said, and again wrapped her second hand around the curve of South Carolina. "Two hands."

144

Will might ruefully comment that Lucy did everything with two hands, a litany Sarah learned well.

"What a lovely temperature," Mrs. Burnham marveled again. As if in response, a black and brown head poked out from under her chair, smiled (it seemed), and emitted a gangling pink tongue.

"Oh, look, Sarah! It's Barky," Mrs. Burnham said, patting him.

"Would you please stop calling him *Barky*, Mom? He's been Satchel for about a hundred years, and then Sarah comes along and you start calling him *Barky.*"

"Barky, come," Sarah ordered, striding up to the head, which disappeared under Mrs. Burnham's chair.

"Yes, dear," said Mrs. Burnham icily, now patting Sarah. "Does you like your puppydog to be called Satchel, honey? Hunh? Does you?"

"Satchel," Sarah said. She showed her empty glass to Mrs. Burnham. "All gone," Sarah commented, and handed it over.

"Yes it is, isn't it, Sarah? All goney-gone. Did you hear that, Lucy?: all gone. She's talking in *ideas* now. She's so smart. I've never seen a brighter child."

"Unh-hunh," Lucy said, peering out from under her shading palm. The rays of the sun made bright, mother-of-pearl shapes like wings in her vision; she thought, perhaps, of wings—of crows passing like shadows under the sun; of Will, perhaps.

Mrs. Burnham put the glass down beside her own on the flagstone and held her book in front of her. Presently she looked up. She glanced all around her, as though she were seeing everything for the first time: their green and yellow lawn chairs standing awkwardly on flagstones knit by cement; the square of beaten grass, shorn of wildness, dying in the sun; the triangle of rhododendrons, the bed of tulips, morning glory curling up the white gutter; and then the endless line of neighboring houses, shrinking toward the

145

horizon as if pressed down by the sky; all that was there.

"So lovely," Mrs. Burnham said, and took a sip of her drink. "My ice has melted again. But this is still my very favorite temperature; for my money, September has the best range of temperature of any month. The best *range.*"

"Unh-hunh."

"Wouldn't you say so?"

"Unh-hunh. I'm trying to read, okay, Mom? This is the first week, and already I'm not pre*pared.*"

"Well, that's all *I'm* doing, after all. I'm reading too. You don't have a monopoly on all the books in the world, young lady, I'll have you know."

"I'm not a lady," Lucy said mechanically.

"Well, I don't know about that. I just don't know. But you don't have a mo*nop*oly on all the books in the world."

"Okay, okay. I heard you the first time. You're right. Let's just drop it."

Lucy looked around unhappily, propping *Middlemarch* on her knee. Sarah sat on the flagstone patiently trying to make a bow with the lace of her miniature sneaker. "You're just like your father," Lucy snapped. "Always tying your goddamn shoes."

"Lucy! She's only *two.*"

Sarah, having looked up briefly, went back to her laces, now intricately tangled; she stuck her tongue out of the side of her mouth in a sign of concentration. From the corner of his eye Mister Duckie regarded her with a circumspect glance.

The afternoon wore on, slow, Sunday; Sarah's laces stayed untied, tangled; conversation was sparse. On a few occasions Mrs. Burnham further remarked the joys of the weather. It must have been on one of these occasions—after Mrs. Burnham noted that "the temperature is absolute perfection," and sipped her drink; and after Lucy responded, "Yes. Yes it is"—that Lucy thought for the first time: someday she would

146

go back to Will. This idea came to her with increasing frequency throughout the rest of the afternoon; and by nightfall she permitted its presence without rancor or unhappiness, as if it were an established fact, an invited guest.

In New York the rare sun shone that day with similar success: with less humidity Howard too would have judged it perfect. He sat on a park bench with the seeds of a puzzle sowing themselves just in back of his consciousness. For a change Howard wasn't entirely sure what to make of what was past, passing, and coming to pass; he was too busy, he told himself then, to care. He was wrong. Thus this.

Well, shit. She thought *she* liked to sleep late; but this was just ridiculous, this guy. Delsey left him lying on his stomach with his head tucked into the crook of his arm, like a kid. When she went into the bathroom she had a sort of shock: blue tiles. Usually she was right on about colors. Well, that was a mistake anybody could make.

She sat on the toilet, staring: robin's egg blue. You never knew, Delsey said to herself. She flushed. You never knew.

Delsey used his toothbrush, the only toothbrush, a shitty-looking green one. Maybe that's where she got the green for the tiles. She always put a lot of toothpaste on the brush, really loaded it up and scrubbed hard. She had such lousy teeth, she figured she might as well *try*. She knew she didn't look exactly attractive, with gobs of spit and toothpaste always kind of coming out of her mouth. She poked the brush all over the place, and her face got twisted up. Yeah, she was a little self-conscious about it. Some guys liked to watch when you went to the toilet; that was weird, sure, but they couldn't *see* anything, and Delsey didn't care, go ahead and look if it does your little hearts good. But she drew the line at tooth-brushing. Locked the door. One guy gave her nine kinds of hell, because he worried she was going in there to mastur-bate—because maybe he didn't *satisfy* her, or some stupid *Playboy* magazine idea. He used to pound on the door. Well, shit, that affair didn't last long. It's tricky enough getting along without complicating it with all these *com*plexes. Del-sey was as understanding as the next person, but when some-one keeps banging on the door when you're trying to brush your teeth. . . .

After she brushed she got right into the shower. She always rinsed with cold, so she was shivering when she stepped out and grabbed a towel—any old towel hanging up. That was green, too. Anybody could have made that mistake. She brushed her hair out, getting right to the roots, and she was done.

It didn't matter to Delsey which year it was, or how ad*van*ced everyone was, she still liked a little mystery be-tween another person and herself. She didn't feel like pranc-ing back into the bedroom with nothing on, not right off, and especially not in the morning, when he could see where she could drop a couple pounds. She knew the way it went. Pretty soon she could walk around naked and it would be like she was wearing an old housecoat. Delsey wanted him to be *excit*ed when he saw her. Passionate and all. She was old-fashioned, was all, she said to herself; so she opened the linen closet and found a dry towel to wrap herself in. Another green one. Everyone said that green went nicely with her red highlights. She tucked the towel in in back and went back in.

"Hey. Hey, would you kindly wake up?" she said, sitting on the edge of the bed and shaking Neal's foot.

149

He moved his mouth and swallowed a couple of times without opening his eyes.

"I mean, would you kindly? It's *eleven*." She yanked his arm out from under his head.

He opened his eyes and turned onto his side. "What's going on?"

"I'm here," she said. "I'm special, remember?"

"Who told you that, lady?"

"Nobody told me that. You *should* have, but you didn't." She lay beside him, letting her hair fall on his arm.

"What's special about you, lady? You're local talent, right?"

"Hey. Don't play rough. I may be local, but I'm good. And don't call me talent, I don't like that. Call me Sweetie-Pie."

"Sweetie-Pie," Neal snorted. He put his hand on her neck and rubbed the nape lightly.

She smiled. "Rough guy," she said. "Rough, tough, cynical bastard. Pushover, is what you are." Neal was looking past her shoulder. "Hey, wake up. What are you doing now?"

"Nothing."

Delsey threw her hair back. "So are you gonna fuck me, or what?"

Half of his mouth smiled. He touched her leg.

"God, she's crude," Delsey said. She drew his hand into her crotch; his fingers spread, as if to stop themselves. "Right? Crude, but good. Right?"

"Sorry, Sweetie-Pie. Goodness is not your particular virtue."

"And might I ask what is? Since you're handing out merit badges and all?"

Neal, head on pillow, had on this big, broad smile. Now what's so funny, Delsey thought to herself; he always looks at me as if some secret joke was going on, or something. Neal reached out and stroked Delsey's cheek.

He was still smiling. It wasn't the jokes; she knew that. It was her. Well, Delsey said to herself, he was pretty cute too.

Her finger pressed the end of his little nose, like a button; but it just stayed there, the finger, stuck, almost.

You had to be careful, that was all, Delsey warned herself. No matter how much you liked a guy, you still had to be careful. The *more* you liked them, the more careful you had to be: let a guy know, and he treats you like wall-to-wall carpeting. As if, Delsey thought, looking at her finger and Neal's nose together, they think you're a fool *because* you like them. Because they don't even like themselves.

Well, they're right not to, mostly. But Neal wasn't, she was thinking, as she watched him decide whether to make a joke or kiss her. He was weirdly serious, because he was just learning about skyrockets—about the way the whole room vibrated when sex went on, and how just fucking suddenly got important, and touched you all the way in. Delsey knew about that part.

It's good, Delsey thought. I don't think he even knows that. She pressed his nose again, and told herself again that it was the smart guys who always learn last, the poor babes.

"Well," Neal started—he's finally thought of a joke, Delsey said to herself—"you certainly get the Knock-Kneed Merit Badge. Order of the Pigeon-Toed, First Class."

"Hey. You're pigeon-toed too, you know."

"Oh, I know. I absolutely know. I'm awarer of that than anybody. As far as pigeon-toehood is concerned, I'm the expert." Not funny, Neal thought. "I'm the goddamn expert," he added.

"Yeah, you know practically everything, sweet baby," Delsey said; and kissed him, and meant it.

Neal got himself a new car in October. He bought one of those Volvos, a sensible kind of car to buy because they last. They never do last, so they're not sensible, but sensible people buy them. They always start in the wintertime, except that they don't. They're not fancy, but they cost a lot of money. Neal bought his because it would start in the winter and because it had rear-window wipers and a rear-window de-icer. He liked the light on the dash that glowed a soft, warm red when he turned on the rear-window de-icer. He figured he'd take her out for a little spin. Neal didn't cruise around very much these days; oh, once in a while he drove up to Mount Tom, where the couples went parking. He sat there with his lights out, his motor purring and his radio on, just like everybody else; the red lights of the radio tower blinking on and off. Neal liked it there. On the night end of dusk, after everyone had been parking for a while, the amorous heat began to rise; Neal turned on his heater, wiggling his toes.

He didn't mind love, in a proper context: there, for example, where the road looped underneath the radio towers. Love was something you did in high school; it was marked by bright eyes, pimples, and uncertainty, and entailed confusion, an automobile, and blushing. Though it seemed impossible, love was not difficult. Wiggling his toes, Neal experienced an adult pleasure akin to attendance at a children's birthday party.

It had been a while since he went up there. If you buy a new car, though, you've got to take her out for a little spin. Neal thought he might do that; might just do that, take her out for a spin. Might go on up to New Hampshire, where Will was apple-picking. Spin on up there.

Neal grimaced: he was lying to himself. He caught sight of himself in the rearview mirror, and saw his wry, sage, sad semblance nod. "What are *you* looking so superior about?" Neal asked him.

At the edge of his vision Keene, Dublin, Peterborough flickered unevenly by, unrolling like a moving-picture backdrop for a film—while a stationary actor sits, false breeze

152

ruffling a few strands of hair, gliding his hand calmly back and forth along the arc of the steering wheel. Neal hummed something to himself, trying to be jaunty; new car, bright October afternoon, carefree bachelor. But he had the persistent feeling that the winding road was trying to get away from him.

He pulled into an apple cider stand, got out and picked up a gallon, climbed back in, talking to himself. He told himself that he would try to tell Will everything. Not easy to, not after years not. But what (in the name of blank) was going on? A waitress liked him, Neal's reflection remarked ruefully: why such a stir from such a paltry stimulus?

"Hey! Hey you!"

Neal turned in his seat. A bulky young man was shouting at him; Neal looked up at a square, crimson face. "You figure on paying for that cider, or do I haul you outta there?"

"Sorry," Neal said, forcing a smile. "Just forgot. Absentminded." He touched his forehead and stretched out the smile. "Tetched in head. You betcha." He nodded at the crimson square. "Not native speaker, too. Seventeen years in western Hungary."

"You Massachusetts people go crazy when you get up here. Think you can get away with murder."

"Absent-minded. Hungarian. How much?"

"I got half a mind to haul you out."

"How much for these apple juice? Sorry. Not native speaker."

"I got half a mind, I tell ya."

"Two dollars? Here. One and one."

"You know that? I got about half a mind—"

"Here." Neal shoved bills in the man's meaty palm and put the car in first gear. "Not native," he said unhappily. "Seventeen years in Hungary." The Volvo crept out in little jumps while a voice came out of the faint plume of his exhaust:

"Go home, robbing Massachusetts cocksucker!"

153

Neal had to talk to Will. It really didn't seem as if he could afford to wait much longer.

Avoid all entangling alliances, George Washington told America; and for the past dozen years (a long dozen, a baker's), Neal had taken him at his word. Though Neal never perceived his activity to be systematic, at roughly equal intervals he reviewed his list of female acquaintances—never a long list—and went through it, ticking off each woman. One declined to shave her armpits; one had a taste for loud, dreary music; one wore spangled platform shoes; one used a cigarette holder; one was outdoorsy. It was a pleasant exercise, no less pleasant for being easy. And Neal found it exceedingly easy to avoid entanglement; it was no longer possible, he estimated, to fall in love. Even at the outset of his affairs he couldn't care. This was the sort of information that paramours seemed to be able to ferret out—quickly and without apparent effort, but with dramatic and terminal effect. These days Neal admitted it. Lover A asked if he loved A, and Neal replied that he wasn't sure. But you can't stop progress, and a year later, when lover B unaccountably came up with the same question, Neal managed to ignore the intimate contortions his person was at that moment engaged in forming with B's; he told the simple, deflating truth. But here the vacancy in Neal's emotions created a vacuum. Against all odds (Neal claimed), and for whatever misguided reason, B wanted to love him. In fact, she said she'd done it already; she told him, baring her teeth, that she was hurt. Neal apologized remorsefully, but in the end he had no choice in the matter. These things choose themselves, he commented to himself in a comforting sort of way.

Neal remembered the features of B's face only with difficulty. With Delsey he encountered a different problem, the coin's other face. A few weeks of blameless hanky-panky agitated him past its due. It *was* hanky-panky, he insisted; the face in the rearview mirror demurred. Though he tried, Neal couldn't avoid a certain dreamy pleasure when he thought of Delsey. It was a false pleasure, he reckoned; false to himself. He was right to distrust it—how many men had he seen, fools nearly forty, who chased pretty young things and were caught themselves? That was Let's Play Pretend. Pretend you're young, handsome, virile. And pretend you care.

Delsey reached a part that was a long way in, a part Neal hadn't known he had. He recognized it; he'd seen it on billboards. It was the part that played tennis and tanned nut brown, wore tight white trousers and dreamed about the jugs on movie stars (or wanted to).

No, he'd never played tennis. It wasn't just that part. He liked her; she saw things from the other side. She was a relief, he told himself; she was like goddamn aspirin, for a headache he'd always had.

Delsey had fun, and forgot the rest. That went against Neal's nature. A pleasant universe, feathery and tickling, was closing in, smiling a vacant grin. And Neal didn't have the slightest idea of how he might escape it, how he might regain control of his senses, and of his life. Neal was at a loss. He'd never been ticklish before.

He wanted to ask Will; undoubtedly this thing had happened to Will, probably several times. Neal wanted to ask—not ingenuously, may blank forbid, and not bluntly—but he wanted to ask Will what to do.

Will would probably say that this was the wrong woman for Neal. But that was just the point; the right woman had never gotten a pretty foot in the door, the right woman would never cause an agreeable thought to flicker across Neal's mind. Instead the right woman would read the Sunday *New York Times* in bed with him, swapping sections; she would buy him yellow underwear; she would laugh at his jokes. He had the feeling that with the right woman he'd always have a longing to go out for a cold-cut grinder on the sly. No, come on, Will, Neal wasn't equating simplicity and goodness: Delsey wasn't simple. Alien, but complicated. Will might understand that, or he might not.

Oh hell, there was no harm in taking her out for a spin, anyway. She sounded fine, even if Neal didn't know a thing about automobiles, beyond an unqualified admiration for universal joints, for rear-window de-icers, for car radios. And for rolling, as he was rolling now, at sixty, moving hardly a finger—as the loop of film unrolled, and images fell on the screen in back of him.

Will's orchard was called Sammy Brack's, and wasn't hard to find; there were signs for miles. Neal had nursed the notion that Brack's would be like Petersen's, that he'd find Will picking apples out back of an old clapboard farmhouse, with Sammy and Mrs. Brack watching the World Series inside. Instead he found a rambling warehouse, a huge green-and-white-striped tent in front, paved parking lot complete with abundant New York license plates. Fruits and vegetables were on sale outside—apples, peaches still, winter squash, pumpkins. October: of course, pumpkins. As a child Will loved to labor over his jack-o'-lanterns, carving elaborate, grotesque faces, and at twelve he loved to smash pumpkins on Halloween night, so they'd spew their seedy insides on moonlit asphalt; Neal, on the other hand, was interested in pumpkins mainly for their appearance in pie form, and it was pie that he thought of now, fondly, as he stood beside a pyramid of pumpkins—and patted the nearest one.

The barefoot, long-skirted girl selling pumpkins didn't think she'd heard of Will. "Is he a seller or a picker?"

"Picker."

"I only know sellers. You can ask inside, though." She gave Neal a smile like those he'd seen in California.

The warehouse was filled with apples: bins of green, red, and yellow in such proliferation that Neal had the feeling it might be impossible to eat one apple, period. In an apple world, could matter be picked apart, broken down to its basic mystery?

Neal walked unsteadily along apples toward the cash register. No, he wasn't moving; he passed the same apples over and over; he walked in place, while a loop of apples flickered on the screen behind him. Neal set his sights on the cash register, where a little man wearing a beret and smoking a cigar stood beside a stool; squinting, Neal promised himself he was getting closer.

"Don't know the name. This his first year or something like that?"

"Something like that."

The man jammed the cigar between his teeth and pulled a clipboard from below the cash register. He flipped through some mimeographed forms.

"He's not Jamaican, is he?"

Neal was pleased. He couldn't think of a reason in the world why this officious little man should thrust a cigar into his mouth and ask if Will was Jamaican.

"No, he's not," Neal admitted. Somewhat reluctantly he added: "Why do you ask?"

"For Cripe's sake. So I won't go through all the lists and then find out he's a Jamaican. How do I know? You never know. He might be."

"You're right," Neal agreed quickly. "He might. Actually he was raised as an Episcopalian. But he's not a believer."

"So what do I care?" the man responded, and his cigar wiggled spasmodically.

"Oh, you don't," Neal said. "Just in case you did. You never know."

The man started to flip faster through his forms. "Awright, here he is. Willie Bard, right? He's on C Crew. You didn't tell me he was on the C Crew. Could have saved us some time here."

"What's the C Crew?"

157

"C Crew is the hippies. This guy a hippie, this Bard guy?"

"I don't think so."

"He's on C Crew," the man explained, feigning patience. "That means he's a hippie. I already told you that. They're out the Tamworth Road. Left here, first right, then right again at the crossroads. You'll see the trucks. The Jamaicans are out there too."

Neal blinked. "So it didn't make any difference, then," he said.

"What didn't?"

"If he was a Jamaican. Because the Jamaicans are out there too."

"Of course it makes a difference. Who the hell wants to be Jamaican?" The man shook his beret with his head. "Boy, you must be crazy. 'Doesn't make any difference.' You liberal types gotta be crazy."

Neal shrugged. "Been a long day, I guess," he said. "Lotta driving."

The man nodded almost sympathetically. "Feeling your oats, hunh? Where'd you come from?"

"Jamaica," Neal said without thinking. The man's cigar jerked violently. "Queens," Neal added. "Long Island. Jamaica, Queens."

Easy, Neal boy (he recommended). Bring yourself back alive. Where was Will?

The orchard was bursting with brilliantly ripe fruit; its trees laden with ladders and pickers. Neal noted its plainly symmetrical arrangement: the pickers on one side were black men, and on the other white; a game of chess about to begin, perhaps.

The pickers wore metal-framed green canvas bags that opened below the chin, like backwards backpacks. Magic: a string was pulled, apples dumped out—a flash of color at the bottom, flow of scarlet below drab olive, like silver escaping a slot machine.

Neal, who had a great admiration for physical work as

158

performed by others, watched as though hypnotized. He woke with a start. Will was one of these pickers.

There he was. He was standing a few rungs from the top of his ladder, wearing a woolen shirt and corduroy jeans. Neal heard Irish folk music, brimming with penny whistles and fiddles, coming from a cassette tape-recorder lodged in a crotch of Will's tree. The tune was a reel, a brisk joy that swooped around Will's apple tree like a swallow darting among rafters; but Will managed to whistle right along. Neal wished he could; he stood with hands on hips, listening with oddly paternal pride. As he listened, gazing up admiringly at Will—there among shining green leaves, blazingly red apples, a dazzling blue beyond—Neal suddenly felt a sense of relief.

Neal shouted up: "Hey. Is this Purple Marauder Headquarters?"

Will turned, apple in hand. He saw Neal and laughed, perhaps silently. Neal cupped his hands again: "Am I too old to join?"

Will tossed the apple to Neal and clambered down. His shoelaces were loose; like always, Neal thought. Careful you don't break your neck, he said, not aloud.

Will's hand extended. "What the hell you doing here?" he said pleasantly, and they shook. Will always pumped a few more times than Neal. "Howard send you after me again? So I'd go work for Citibank?"

"Nah, nothing like that. I got a new car, thought I'd take her out for a spin. Come up and see the old sports fan. A Volvo."

"Volvo, hunh? Well, I'm glad you came," Will said, looking into Neal's face to see what he could find there.

I suppose he found something bothering Neal; but my guess is he wouldn't know quite what. Within the family Neal was considered to be the one not obsessed with himself, beyond concern about his cowlick.

"Yeah, she's pretty nice, seems to run fine," Neal said,

159

absently. "How's it going up here? Got nice weather, at least."

Will looked doubtful. "Well, today. Quite a little rain last week; and cold as hell. But it feels good to do some real work for a change."

"Yeah? That wasn't real work at the Petersens'?"

"Oh. The Petersens'. Yeah, that was too," Will said quietly, and looked around for something to rest his gaze on. "Did you see the Jamaicans?" he asked, half pointing.

"Unh-hunh. How come they're up here?"

"I don't know; they don't talk much to the whites. They've got fantastic accents, though. They say 'mon' all the time. One guy asked me about my fiddle music—'What kind of music be dot, mon?' I said it was music from Ireland. Now they call me 'Ire-mon.' "

"Pretty acute."

Will looked at his feet. "I guess so," he said. "I'm trying to change my ways, though. I'm attempting to be halfway human."

Just great, Neal thought: True Confessions. Neal put on a grin and said: "Don't you think that's kind of a tall order? Maybe you should just try to be one-third human. Or All-Orangutan, maybe." Will too smiled a little, not much amused. "I'll support you in your efforts, champ," Neal went on, listening to his nasal voice with petty dislike; "I'll start a Bard/Orangutan Fan Club. I'll marshal the troops. Together we'll storm the zoo: 'Let our ape in,' we'll shout."

"Yeah, we'll storm the zoo," Will said listlessly. "Hey, listen, let me get this thing off me." He started to pull the bag off his shoulder when he glanced at the half-full wooden bin beside him. "Uh, I'll just finish up this bin, okay? I'll just be another fifteen or twenty minutes, then we'll go back to the cabins. You can take a walk in those woods"—he pointed—"down there. There's a really perfect little pond. It's leaf season, too."

Neal did as he was told. Neal was never carried away by nature worship in the way Will was; esthetic bliss didn't come naturally to him. He didn't mind a bit of pretty country, but wasn't altogether enthralled, as he thought he was supposed to be.

He remembered (or I remember; but Neal might've, if he'd given it a second) a night spent camping out in the pine forest in back of the house with Howard and Will. This is some twenty-seven years before: three boys. Howard narrated a patently unbelievable ghost story about Lucky Pierre, the terrible one-legged Canadian lumberjack. He succeeded in terrifying both his audience and himself. When the fire was low (a lapping pool of fierce red), little Will stumbled into the bushes to relieve himself a final time before again attempting to sleep—despite the pounding of his heart and the noisy drone of mosquitoes. When Will didn't make a prompt return, his brothers assumed that the little rascal was attempting to heighten the gothic mood, that any minute now Lucky Pierre would haunt the campsite with his rhythmic thumping. But Lucky Pierre didn't show. Howard took the flashlight and went in reluctant search. In a while his prey answered Howard's echoing shouts: Will was found lying in a field not far away, gazing at falling stars. Even under the uneven beam of the flashlight, rapture could be discerned on his small face. He'd never seen a shooting star, he said. He'd been lost; been terrified. But this dark, immense, churning world, after wrapping little Will in its black clutches, gradually turned to blue, became warm, became soft, showed him falling stars; and with a breath of breeze his terror passed on into the miles of surrounding woods. There, where stars left hints of their traces always at the very edge of his sight, Will swapped fear for ecstasy; and when a grown Will thought of his past, it was as this dark, immense, churning world that he had come out of just then, to stand aloof, or to lie down beneath the stars.

Neal didn't get quite this feeling when he took his walk in the woods. He did admire the pleasant colors of the autumnal leaves. The little pond was nice. He used to sail little boats on ponds on fall afternoons like this one; so he hitched a crackly leaf to a forked stick and set it afloat. Neal's ship sailed dutifully out to the center, where a sudden gust capsized it. And with that he shrugged, and turned back to Will's apple tree.

A crow flew out, whirled in the wind. Will too came down, and dumped his last apples.

The cabins perched at the edge of a round lake. Beside a patch of imported-looking sand a white rowboat keeled over on its side, paint peeling.

"I play the banjo now," Will said as he held the door open.

"Really?"

"Well, I don't *really*. But I'm learning. I've got one, and I'm learning."

A smell between must and mold—clothes that never quite dried—joined something like cooked cabbage. Bunk beds in each corner. Refrigerator—"Electricity, hunh?" Neal said. "No," Will replied, "just for keeping things in. You know. Food you don't want to stink up the place with. Cheese." Wood-slab table on concrete block, an old painted desk, a trunk. It was Will's trunk. He unlocked it and sheepishly pulled out his banjo.

Neal held out his hands for it. He turned it over carefully, impressed. A circle of gleaming chrome (Neal guessed it was chrome) around the head; the neck inlaid with crescent moons.

"Mother-of-pearl," Will said, tapping a moon.

"I see."

"This head is real skin. Most of them are plastic now."

"Terrific, champ. Play something for me, will you?"

"Nah. I'm not good yet."

"Play the old tunes. Play 'As Time Goes By.' "

"On the *ban*jo? Knock it off, will you? I stink, so far. But I'm gonna be good. I really am."

"I know you are, champ," Neal said, not kidding.

"Knock it off."

Neal took hold of Will's elbow. "I've got a great idea, boss. You grab the banjo. We'll take the car and drive all night. We'll get drunk. We'll go fishing. We'll watch the sun come up."

"Come on, Neal, I mean it. I'm just trying to learn how to play. It's plenty hard enough to just *do* the damn thing, without you making me more self-conscious than I already am."

Neal, lounging in the doorframe, spread his hands; a slouching innocent.

"I'm not kidding," Will continued, heating up. "Can't you see what I'm trying to do? Seriously, can't you? I *know* all the assholes in the world pick apples and play the banjo. Or maybe the guitar. I know that; I live with them." He banged the trunk lid open, laid his banjo inside. "I'm not doing *an*ything different from the assholes of the world. I *know* that." He turned to Neal as if he were turning on him. "It's like you said: I want to be an orangutan; a nice, decent orangutan. I want to be a part of the world, the orangutan world, and stop picking my psychic scabs. So if I have to learn to play three chords on the fucking banjo to do it, I will." He locked his trunk, banging. "That's what I'm trying to do, and that's all I'm trying to do. And you can quote me to Howard."

"Yeah?"

"No. But that's the only answer I'm going to give you."

"I didn't ask anything," Neal said patiently. "I just said, let's take the car and drive all night. Champ, I was serious."

"What do you mean, serious?" Will shot back. "You're *never* serious."

"Of course I am, sometimes. Just because I'm trying to be

163

funny doesn't mean I'm not *serious*. Come on, you're supposed to know that." He shook his head. "That's a goddamn
orangutan *ground* rule. You're going to be about the crudest,
most unlettered orangutan I ever saw."

"I do know that—theoretically, anyway. But you *were*
quoting from *Casablanca,* right? When Bogart says 'Out of
all the gin joints in all the towns in the world, she has to walk
into mine'?"

"Not bad," Neal said. "Glad to see you weren't educated
entirely in vain. What else can you do?"

Will persisted. "So what do you mean, you were serious?"

Neal shrugged. "You wanta?"

"Wanta what?"

"Take the car. Drive all night. Get drunk. Go fishing."

Will sat down on his trunk. "You don't have to drive all
night. You can go fishing right in the lake here."

"Nobody said we *had* to. You want to?"

"Why? Do you?"

"Unh-hunh. Yeah, I do."

"Why?"

"I thought you'd know why." Neal shrugged again.

"Well, I don't," Will said, stubborn.

Neal paused.

"Just to do it, I guess."

"Why, what's wrong with right here?" Will's voice was
shrill.

"Nothing's wrong with right here. You don't have to get
de*fen*sive about it. I just mean that you live here. It's not off,
you know?"

"Off? Off somewhere?"

"Yeah."

"Neal. What do *you* want to be away from? You mean that
you—"

A group of people appeared in the doorway. They were
young men, generally bearded, wearing loose jeans and big

boots. The type of people, Neal judged, you'd expect to find in a vegetarian restaurant; they'd eat with chopsticks, and smile condescendingly when Neal asked for knife and fork. Will introduced them to Neal.

"Are you staying to supper, Neal?" someone asked.

Will answered yes for him.

"Want to see how it works?" the tallest applepicker asked Neal.

Neal didn't seem to be able to understand anybody today. "Sure," he chirped. "I'm a sport."

The tallest picker promptly pulled a yellow sheet down from the cork bulletin board, spraying tacks about the room. "Every day, see, someone stays behind to cook dinner—that's this column here—and someone else is assigned to cleanup—over here. Once a season every person has to do the shopping in Concord—so somebody shops twice a week, which works out, as you see, to once a season per person. Now, the menu is chosen—"

"I think it's about dinnertime now," Will interrupted hopefully, hovering. "Let's check, okay?"

He ushered Neal into the kitchen cabin. Other pickers slowly drifted in, and gathered in cocktail-party groups, twos and threes. Gossip centered around the number of bins that each person had filled that day. A dark-haired woman "got just three" due to sore hands; a blond-bearded man boasted "six today"; someone else laconically remarked, "Picked five and a half." Neal, standing on the rim of the conversation, felt an absurd sense of deprivation—because he couldn't chime in, sum up his day with a number.

A bell made tinny tintinnabulations; immediately everyone sat down. The steaming pot—spaghetti, twining through its sauce—was already seated in the middle. The largest man ladled out ponderous portions, small volcanoes. Wordlessly the first eruption was placed in front of Neal. The spaghetti sauce was pinky orange. Neal regarded it with some interest:

165

for a second he was sure he saw something moving on his plate.

He felt a hand on his forearm. "Bread?" asked a braided woman seated beside him, holding out a wicker basket. She pointed at his plate. "Go ahead, don't let it get cold. You're Will's brother, hunh?" Neal nodded assent, and put his fork tentatively in among the pasta. "He's going to be good," she said. "For a beginner he's very good."

"At picking?"

"Picking? Frailing, even, someday. Old-timey. You know."

Neal didn't have the slightest idea. He moved his fork uncomfortably and said, "Yeah, he's a champ."

"Has he played for you yet?"

Neal thought for a second. "You mean banjo?"

She gave him an uncomprehending look in return. "Yeah, banjo. What did you think I meant?"

Neal gave himself up. "Confidentially," he said, "out front and all, I thought you were talking about apple-picking."

"*Apple*-picking. Oh, apple-*picking*. I see. That's funny," she said, nudging Neal. "Funny, hunh?"

"Yes, it is funny," he said.

"Don't let it get cold," she said again. "Dig in."

Neal nodded, twirled his fork. His spaghetti made a cylinder around the fork, and he held it up to his mouth, gingerly, testing, it seemed, the heat.

Dessert, plunked in the middle of the table, was Jell-O with apples. Will shook his head: apples again: damn. The original sin held very little temptation for Will these days.

He looked across the table to Neal, whose eyes were moving quickly back and forth in their sockets. Will looked at the faces all around the table, and it suddenly seemed to him that he was a long way away; that touching any one of these faces with his hand would require an arduous journey. A suffocating warmth ascended from his stomach, lodged in his craw.

Will closed his eyes. When he opened them again he rose from his chair. He said to Neal, "Let's skip dessert."

"Don't you want coffee?"

"I want a drink." Neal looked at him with mild surprise. "Let's drive all night," Will added. "Let's go fishing."

Neal ground the Volvo's gears once, got her into reverse, and backed out. "Where do you go for a drink around here?" he asked.

"I really don't know," Will said.

In the end they drove to Concord, some twenty miles. Neal was used to the Northampton bars, overrun with college kids. Here at the Crow's Nest the clientele was of less tender years. At one end of the bar a gentleman crowned with a delicate horseshoe of gray hair cradled his head with his arm, apparently passed out. After a few minutes he roused himself, or roused himself enough to light a cigarette, order a double whiskey, puff twice on the cigarette, and down the whiskey. His head dropped back onto his arms with an audible thump.

"That's what I want to be like when I grow up," Neal said admiringly; but it was Will who ordered a double Old Crow. Neal asked for a bottle of stout and was given instead a cold stare by the bartender, a stout man wearing an apron that read "Pittsburgh Steelers." Neal settled for a draft; and when the bartender brought the drinks, Neal tried to make amends. "Your boys won the big one again last year, hunh? They absolutely deserved it, too."

"Hunh?"

"The Steelers," Neal said, pointing quickly to the apron. "The Super Bowl," he added.

"It's the wife's," the bartender growled. He lumbered toward the other end of the bar and set up a drink for his unconscious customer, just on spec.

"There's the place to get your free orangutan lessons," Neal muttered. "One guess who's the bouncer," he added. Turning, Neal saw the pool table for the first time. "Hey,

Will, you wanna shoot some pool?" Without waiting for an answer, Neal started rolling up his sleeves. He was an enthusiastic pool player, but Will (like Howard) was a good one, to whom the angles came naturally, from internal rhythms. Neal dropped a quarter in the slot, racked the balls, selected his cue, chalked it, and accidentally got chalk (blue, azure) on the tip of his nose—all in the time it took Will to abandon his barstool. Will ordered another Old Crow and picked out a cue at random. He gazed at Neal.

"You've got chalk on your nose."

"Yeah? Here you go." Neal tossed the chalk to Will. "Don't say I ever give myself unfair advantages. You wear just as much chalk as you want. It won't help you one bit. I'm gonna run this old rack." He broke the rack with that smudge still on his nose. It wasn't until Will gave him a handkerchief—Will's wedding date embroidered by a maiden aunt in the corner—and the start of a scowl—you could almost spot the marks of Will's wedding on that too—that Neal removed the clownish mark from his face. The bartender stared.

They played a couple of racks of straight pool; Will was far ahead, and not interested. "Let's quit," he said. "I want to sit at the bar and be morose, just like everybody else."

"Everybody else is exactly one guy; and he's dead, anyway. C'mon, I've only got three in so far."

"Play by yourself, then. I want to get good and drunk. This place is going to close soon."

"No, you've got to play too. I don't want to just play; I want to beat you."

"The hell you do. You don't care any more than I do."

That was that; Will had his mind made up. They put their cues back in the case and sat at the bar. Neal got another Michelob, and some peanuts; Will ordered another bourbon. He was getting pretty glassy. Neal realized that soon there wouldn't be a brother left to talk to.

"How's Lucy?" Neal started.

Will waved his hand in the air, as though throwing something over his shoulder, and out. "Haven't been in touch."

"Well, she's okay, anyway," Neal said, feeling ridiculous. "I see her every once in a while. Usually I ask her if she wants to go to the movies."

Will looked at Neal with a vague perplexity—as if Neal had his shirt on backwards or something, Neal thought. "She went to the movies with *me* about three times in the last four years," Will said.

"She didn't go with me either," Neal said quickly. "Anyway, I knew it was safe to ask."

"How is my child?" Will sounded formal.

"Good. Great. She does sentences now." Will smiled, and Neal added, "Beautiful sentences."

Will's smile was wistful. "What does she say?"

"What does she say? She says lots of things."

"Like what?"

"Lots of things. Like she walks around the house carrying stuffed animals, and she says, 'I like bears. I like the red rabbit. I have Mister Duckie.'"

"Mister Duckie? Where'd she get a Mister Duckie?"

"Oh, I don't know. Maybe it's a Mister Potato. But things like that. Real sentences."

"I never gave her a Mister Duckie."

"Oh for God's sake. I was just making that one up. Never mind."

"Mister *Duck*ie," Will said scornfully. "Goddamn mysterious Mister Duckie. Who is this fucking Mister Duckie?"

"Hey. Hey, Will. I was just making that one up. I don't *know* exactly what the hell Sarah says, you know?"

Will polished off his bourbon, sucking in his chest, and got another. He frowned at it. "Neal, would you tell me something?"

"Sure, boss."

"Who is fucking with Lucy these days?"

169

"Champion. I really don't know."

"I mean, what kind of guy? That's all. Not *who*. What kind of guy, I mean."

"Probably Mister Duckie himself, champ. Listen, I don't know anything about that. I've got my own fucking problems, champ."

Will raised his eyebrows ironically. "That right? You have fucking problems? Who have you been fucking lately?"

Neal shook his head—he hadn't meant the adjective seriously, he told himself. He had just used Will's kind of adjective, that was all. But Neal grabbed onto the chance. "I'm—fucking—someone these days," he said. "Yes."

Will was startled, he moved his hands (thin, steady as a rule, a rule with occasional exceptions) quickly and unsteadily enough to topple his small, broad-bottomed glass. Half a whiskey slid along the counter. Will cursed his luck; the bartender moved in with a wet cloth.

"Problems, hunh?" Will said.

"Yes," Neal answered, opening his palms on the bar top in supplication.

You could see, if you watched, the thought occur to Will, as he stared at the bartender wiping up bourbon; the processes were slowed enough to be discernible, there on his slightly numb face. He looked at Neal with a small, malicious light gleaming in his fine brown eyes.

"Who's the lucky fucking orangutan?" he asked Neal.

Neal smirked—at himself, really—without pleasure. "Unh-hunh," he said. "Yes, you get three points for that one. From way downtown."

"No, seriously, Neal; who's the lucky subhuman?"

The bartender had his hands on his hips. It looked like closing time to Neal. It seemed (why hadn't he thought of it before?) a long way back to Northampton.

"Her name Guinevere? Beatrice? Mary Magdalene? Mary Magdalene Orangutan, is that it?" Will taunted.

170

"It's Miss Rheingold," Neal said. "My very own Miss Rhein-gold."

"Time to close," the bartender said. He took their empty glasses.

Will paid for the drinks—out of guilt, Neal affirmed. Every time Will did something that was ordinary, that was friendly, that was *nor*mal, for God's sake, it was only because he thought he should.

Howard would like to come out and disagree, here. But Neal thought: Well, to hell with it.

Will put the folding change in his wallet, coins in his pocket, and touched Neal on the wrist. "I was only kidding," Will said. "You know that, hunh?"

"Sure, I know that," said Neal, indifferent now.

"No hard feelings, right? I'd like to know what's going on in your life. I really would."

Neal gave him a hard look. "She makes me happy, I make her happy. Simple as that. Hearts and flowers."

"Great. That's terrific, Neal. What's her name?"

"Bob," Neal said, looking away. "Bob Rheingold."

While Neal ground the gears again, a placid, immovable smile on his face, Will went on. "All right, I wasn't kidding. But I'm sorry, Neal. Hey, hear what I said? Sorry. I just couldn't resist—after all these years, when I had problems and you made jokes. It kind of serves you right, you know?"

"Unh-hunh."

"Look, you know what we could still do? Go fishing. We can take that dinghy by the cabins out on the lake. There's supposed to be bass and perch. I'll row, you fish. I can still quote 'Le Bateau Ivre.' You can get your line tangled up, like always. I got a bottle of Scotch in my trunk—it's not good Scotch, but it works. We can jack bass out of that old lake no trouble at all. We'll probably get a shitload of fish out of there, I hear it's got—hey, listen, you still angry?"

171

"No," Neal said. "Just sleepy."

"Wanta go fishing?"

"No, I want to drop you off and drive back to Northampton."

"Come on, Neal. Don't isolate yourself, okay?" Will said, and a second later he added: "Don't isolate *me.*" Neal stared at the yellow stripes of the road, didn't answer. "I just don't want you to leave all pissed off," Will tried. "I wasn't trying to—"

"I'm not pissed off. It's my bedtime. We orangutans have to get our beauty sleep."

"All right," Will said, warily. "If you're sure you don't hate me. Because if you hate me, I'm not gonna get out of the car."

"You might as well get out, champ. This car just isn't going anywhere you want to go."

II

They were just sitting around in their underwear with the football game on in front of them. Neal was pretending not to pay attention; he was keeping it secret that he cared. Or so he believed. At least, he thought, he was disgusted with himself for caring. The New England *Pa*triots, for Chrissakes. They weren't a *real* team, like the Red Sox, who wore leather belts and who your grandfather used to boo; they were the invention of an advertising man with a couple of hours to kill before a three-martini lunch.

Delsey was kind of reading. It was one of those cold, bright, blazing, sun-glazed New England days. Neal had just pulled down the second of the three window shades in the room; now he began to painstakingly pare the nail on his largest toe. He managed a graceful, curving crescent around the pink, held the foot in the air for his own admiration, and dropped it: the foot, the scissors, the process. Someone kicked the football, and for a second that was the only object on the

173

screen—lazily turning over itself, autumn sky behind.

"I was just thinking," Delsey said. She pivoted her head; she found Neal gazing at his small stomach as it rose and fell in time with his breathing. "Hey," Delsey said. "Would you mind listening up for a minute, please? Pretend that I'm a quarterback or something."

Neal looked over. "So where'd you get the fancy chest pads?"

Delsey ignored him. "Are you gonna listen, Neal? I'm serious."

Neal laid the scissors on the night table and sat up, his back slumped against the headboard. "All present and done for," he said, and added "Aye, aye" for no apparent reason.

"I hate to be blunt and stuff." Delsey watched as a big guy threw a little guy onto the ground. "But I think we should talk about opening up the relationship."

Neal gave her an incredulous look. "To *what?*" he asked.

"Well, shit, Neal, what do you *think?*"

Neal's mouth turned down, sour. He spent the next ten seconds silently trying to control his immediate, careening despair. The television set spontaneously erupted in a sympathetic fit of crackling madness, its picture gone completely out of joint. Cubist distortions gave way to an image of Neal himself, twenty-one years earlier. He sat there on a folding chair. His bladder was bursting with beer; his hair soused and shirt soaked; the dance floor before him slick and sloppy; his sixteen-year-old mind reeling at a considerable distance from his limbs—his entire environment, in short, drowning in beer. Beside him primly, prettily, sat the girl he had just spent seven weeks trying to get the nerve up to wrap his arm around: Cary Blake, a blossom. He could still hear her quiet, angry voice; she said, "You're drunk. You don't mean a word of it. Will you take me home, please?" The party was instantly over. Howard drove, whistling.

Hands outstretched, a man with inflated shoulders and

hips bent for a ball. He lay down on it, cradled it to him. Neal turned to Delsey.

She wore her green terrycloth bathrobe; underneath that, just the striped panties. Funny, Neal thought, that she tells me when she's naked. Didn't even bother to tie the belt. A bobbing boob, a nipple cherry-bright; tra la, tra la, he added grimly.

Down there was her belly: a home for his head, and slightly fat. He cherished that belly. He admired her forthright nipple. He delighted in the kitten-pocket in her upper lip, in the red highlights of her warm hair. He watched her kneel on the bed, as calm, he thought, as an egg.

Nausea came to Neal as he projected loss. He recognized love: what was making him sick. Love, he repeated wonderingly. Love, which includes despair.

Delsey was waiting for an answer. "An open relationship?" he echoed.

"Well, yeah. Sort of."

"I think I have a better idea," Neal said, and exhaled. Apparently he had been holding his breath for quite some time.

It was around that time of year, early November, with the apple harvest over, when Will moved into his apartment in Brattleboro. I need to be around people, he said to himself; I need some *roots.* From this perspective one instantly notices that he tried to pronounce *roots* like a Vermonter—and thus made it sound short, flat, and shallow, more like *ruts* than *roots.* Well, he needed his ruts; and I imagine him energetically nudging a white chest of drawers snug against an off-white wall when Neal called.

For his part, Neal was reluctant to speak to Will at all. They hadn't been in touch for a while, not since Neal had that bright idea to visit Will among the apples. Neal didn't have a lot to say. But you have to *tell* him, for Chrissakes; you get married without mentioning it to your family and it looks like you're trying to hide it. That was probably because he *would* like to hide it, Neal told himself. Marrying Delsey was for *him* —for everything in Neal that made him different from his family. But he owed them the news, at least.

Will had to hold in a laugh when Neal told him. "Seriously?" he asked.

"Seriously. Even legally."

"Great," Will said, wary.

"Yup."

"You have to tell me the name this time. No jokes."

"Adele. Delsey, sometimes," Neal told him grimly.

"Great," Will said again. "Happy hearts and flowers."

Neal tried to explain himself. "You probably won't understand," he said to Will, "but these days it seems to me that there is more to life than can be despaired of."

Will was quiet for a second. "You make that up?" he asked.

"I think so," Neal said, truthfully.

Will paused again. At last he said, "Neal, do you remember the day Lucy and I got married?"

"Sure. There was a lot to drink. It was great."

"You remember the talk we had at the reception at the Burnhams'? You explained to me the idea of an 'attractive nuisance.' You said that love was an attractive nuisance. Remember that?"

"Well," Neal said, smiling, "there was a hell of a lot to drink." He added quickly, "Do I get to apologize for it now?"

Will went on—if Neal could have seen him, he would have watched Will leaning against an off-white wall, rubbing his forehead, shaking his head over and over—"You don't remember that conversation?" Will asked excitedly. "You don't remember the secret I told you?"

"Lemme in on it," Neal grinned.

"I was really happy that day. Hopeful as hell, you know? So I put my arm around you and I said, 'I'll let you in on a

176

secret. There's more to life than can be despaired of.' "

"No kidding," Neal said. "In those words?"

"In those words."

Neal thought about it. "What did I say to that?"

"You said, 'Just watch me, champ.' Then you took a big swig of champagne."

Neal shrugged. "Guess I was wrong," he said regretfully.

"Unh-unh. No, you weren't wrong. You were just you." Will waited; and it was as if he were talking to himself when he added softly, "Just you, champ."

"Chet," Mr. Bowen said, as he shook their hands. "Nobody calls me Chester. Nobody calls me mister, either," he added, and wiped his nearly bare head with the palm of his hand, as if stroking back into place remembered hair. This habit was so constant that Neal noticed Mr. Bowen running a palm over his head even during the ceremony.

"Ain't that right, Mildred? Can't get nobody to call me mister. Ticularly the people who work for me. They seem to think I should call them mister; they seem to think I'm working for *them.*" When Mr. Bowen grinned he showed his gums. "Welp," he said, "I think they're about right. I *am* working for them, by God."

Delsey laughed. Neal didn't think it was funny. He laughed too.

Neal told him why they were there, and Mr. Bowen grinned again. Mildred offered her own sticky smile, and even a man buying shotgun shells chuckled knowingly. "Welp, you two go right on through to my office," Mr. Bowen told them. "I'll be right with you, soon's I finish up Wally here."

Neal held the door to Mr. Bowen's cubicle for Delsey. "So this is what it's going to be like," she said. "Not bad. What else can you do?"

"Sweat," Neal said, and held his palms out to show her.

"Well, shit. I'm nervous too, you know," Delsey claimed, and sat down to read *People* magazine. Neal paced. He stared at the walls, where aphorisms resided in plastic frames —the customer was always right; one should Plan Ahead. Neal grunted, like a dog as it lies down.

"Hey," Delsey said. "It says Carla Thayer is married to Dave Naughton now. They really go for it, don't they?"

"Who's Carla Thayer?" Neal asked.

"You know. On TV. In *The Cucamonga People.*"

"Oh. Then who's Dave Naughton?"

"Well, shit, Neal. You don't know *an*ything."

"Not anything?" Neal teased. "Is this our first argument, dear?"

"Not by a long—" Delsey started, but Mr. Bowen appeared in the door. He mumbled apologies, fumbled with glasses in the breast pocket of his gray clerk's jacket; finally arranged half-bifocals on his nose. He hung the clerk's jacket in a metal closet, and pulled out a three-piece suit on a hanger. "Welp, I guess you got to look the part," he said. "Just a teensy bit, anyways." He donned vest and jacket. "You got a license?"

Neal gave it to him. "I see here this is one of Sally's licenses," Mr. Bowen commented. "She refer you down?"

"Unh-hunh."

"I get most of my customers from old Sal. Wedding ones, that is. Not hardware." He showed his gums again; his hand went over his head. "Nope, the old hardware takes care of itself," he said. He poked his head into the closet to inspect himself in the mirror; his voice came out with its echo. "The old hardware takes care of itself," he repeated softly, as if he were speaking of a good friend who had just died. He straightened his tie, and patted his own head.

"You look fine," Neal said involuntarily.

"Hey," Delsey said to Neal. "You're supposed to say that to *me*. Only the right word is *beautiful.*" Delsey took Neal's hand. "He's really a very smart man," she said to the justice. "He just gets a little confused sometimes."

"Oh, I'm sure he is," Mr. Bowen replied evenly. "I always get nice couples. I got a prett darn good record, too. Only five divorces, leastways that I know of. Lemme tell you, these days that's a prett darn good record. I got one couple that sends me a card every year to tell me how good I stuck em together." He wiped his skull. "Welpsir, I stick em together real good."

"Terrific," Delsey said. "Stick *us.*"

Neal looked at Delsey, intending to find pleasure. But the sight of her gave him sudden shock—not because it was a surprise, but because he'd known what he was going to see: had known explicitly, as if he'd seen her strike just that pose before. She was turned a shade more than full profile, white wall behind her, magazine dangling loosely from her hand, dark desk stacked high with black ledger books beside her. Her four freckles, her pale skin. Delsey had done that to Neal before—shaken images loose from moorings. As Neal stared at her, little jolts were still going off like tiny firecrackers in his memory: even the minute red veins on the inside of her nostrils, the strangely stout hairs there. He imagined (at that moment, at least; as she stood beside him, holding *People* magazine, about to marry him) that he loved her on account of that connection—as if she'd entered his inner life first, and it was only much later, years later, that she'd poised pencil against pad and told him the chicken à la king was on special.

Delsey turned to Neal, as he'd known she would. "Stick us good," she said to the justice, as she stared at Neal's face. "Like Crazy Glue."

"Welp, I'll do my best," Mr. Bowen said, and chuckled softly through his nose. "By the way, would you folks like a little pep talk? I got a little pep talk I use. It's about what marriage means to the persons. How you best be careful and all. Sometimes I talk about Lily and me: thirty-eight years now, and goin strong. Course, I always ask the persons if they want it. Some don't, you know. Some just want to get straight through." He paused. "Welp, folks?"

Neal slouched against the desk. "Sure," he said.

"No," Delsey said, frowning. "I don't think so."

"Right," Neal said. "I don't think so."

"Welp, it's perfectly up to you," Mr. Bowen said quickly, and touched the top of his head gingerly. "I'll just get some witnesses, then."

Mr. Bowen returned with Mildred Phelps, who wore a gray clerk's jacket like the one in the closet (perfect match for her hair, Delsey noted), and Al Tyler, a policeman who happened to be buying light bulbs. "I love these," Mildred said to Al. "I just love happy people."

Mr. Bowen took a book from his desk and opened it. "Join hands, please," he said to Neal and Delsey, who were already holding hands. Mr. Bowen began reading out of his book; it was a Bible. That's funny, Neal said to himself. Craning his neck, he saw that Mr. Bowen was reading from a sheet of paper pasted over Revelations. This struck Neal as ridiculous. Al Tyler blew his nose; Mr. Bowen paused; Al finished, and with both hands solemnly held his handkerchief over his crotch.

Neal laughed out loud. Delsey stared, squeezed his hand hard, and Mr. Bowen paused again—as if Neal too were blowing his nose, Neal thought, and again he started to laugh.

He'd have to stop. What's so funny, he said soberly; everybody does this. It's *nor*mal. Like graduating from high school or something. (Though Neal had certainly laughed then.) Mr. Bowen droned peacefully on: that same speech. You hear those words God knows how many times, Neal thought, and then suddenly someone is saying them about you. Neal recalled the laughter he suppressed his first time in court, when the court recorder actually went ahead and said, "Do you swear to tell the truth, the whole truth, and nothing but the truth?"

"I do," Neal said.

"By the power invested in me by the state of Massachusetts, I now pronounce you man and wife." Mr. Bowen wiped his head. "Welp, don'tcha want to kiss her?"

Mildred applauded, beaming. Al Tyler blew his nose, and shook their hands still holding onto his sodden handkerchief. They stood around in a nervous circle, until it occurred to Neal to take out his wallet.

"Is there a set fee?" he asked. Mildred scurried out the door.

"Whatever you feel comfortable with," Mr. Bowen replied, looking very comfortable, grinning and rocking back and forth on his heels. Here came his vested stomach, as he rocked this way.

"Well, isn't there a going rate?" Neal asked—a little sharply, he realized.

"*Ne*-al," Delsey whispered angrily. "Just pay the man."

"Is it Dutch treat again?" Neal asked her, loudly.

Delsey gave a sigh. "Oh golly," Mr. Bowen said, his gummy grin gone.

"It's okay," Neal said, and wanted to add: it's just her time of the month. But I didn't, he congratulated himself; at least I still have *some* control.

Finally he gave Mr. Bowen twenty dollars, with a quizzical look. Maybe he'll give me change if it's too much, he thought.

"Oh, this is fine," Mr. Bowen beamed, and Neal said to himself: Too much.

"Yessirree, anytime you get married you come right to me," the justice said.

"Come on now," Delsey complained. "You *stuck* us, remember?"

"Sure I did. You bet. Say, did I give you one of my cards?" Neal shook his head. Mr. Bowen slipped one out of his wallet. "That's not just regular printing there," he commented, pointing. "That's embossed, there. Feel it? Little bumps?"

"Sure can," said Neal. "Little bumps. Yup."

Delsey started to edge toward the door. "Thank you so much, Mr. Bowen," she said, and pulled on Neal's arm.

The justice reached out his hand for shakes. "Thank *you*," he grinned. "Chet," he added. "Nobody calls me Chester. Nobody calls me mister, either."

They didn't have what you could really call a honeymoon. Neal booked a room in a local hotel on principle, and they had the best and most self-indulgent dinner they could think of, lobster, with lobster for dessert. The next morning Neal wanted to hang the bloody sheets out, which was his idea of a joke, since the sheets weren't bloody. At first Delsey thought, Why not go along with it? Then she realized that white sheets were dirtier than bloody ones. The joke was at her expense, after all.

In the end they let nothing hang out. They stole sheepishly back upstairs after breakfast, to linger between spanking-white sheets. Marital sex was an oddly different kind of toy, not entirely the same gimmick they'd been playing with. Orgasm, according to Delsey, felt like opening a can of grape soda that had been shook up too much beforehand.

"Are you the soda?" Neal asked.

"Not exactly. It's like someone uses you to have the orgasm in, so she can get out. You know what I mean?"

"Nope." Neal smiled.

"Yes you do."

"No. I really don't." He smiled wider.

Delsey tried again. "Well, it's like waking up when you've been sleepwalking. And there you are, standing on the stairs with the nail polish and an onion in your hand. You know?"

"No idea, honey."

No, Neal was no sleepwalker. When he crept between the covers he shifted the way a dog circles the place where it will lie: then adopted his spot, curled there like a child, and was

182

motionless till morning. He slept soundly, and believed that he didn't dream. Delsey, maternal and affectionate, watched him sleep: What a cute little man, she decided suddenly, and curled up against him, like spoons in a drawer. A morning moon descended, hung in the window frame—watching, wearing white, in the blue distance.

It was noon. It was Neal's turn to wake and watch his partner doze. He found his hand in seemingly natural repose on her stomach, as if it belonged there, and for the first time Neal decided that their love, which existed, was possible.

He invented a motto for them: Against all odds, the normal.

He was a changed man, they said. They said he was what Will used to be. For my part, I wonder how much Neal had changed. Look at him. He wore the same tiresome suit—one for summer, one for winter, other seasons left in eternal quandary—all the vest buttons done up, as if no one had told him to leave one undone (Howard certainly had), the jacket pockets still crammed with chewing-gum wrappers, weary handkerchiefs, used paper napkins. In conversation he continued to lean on larger structures, divert his gaze from his audience, and make continual jokes. He still gnawed erasers off every pencil for miles, and used the side of his fork to cut his food. It may be that he whistled a bit more frequently, unattractively thrusting forth his lower jaw, squeezing air through varying gaps among his incisors to produce a toneless drone—does this mean that he was happy?

Neal was always potentially pleased. It's true, his smile is an exceedingly thin one, usually including only half his mouth, one side of his face, and never exposing teeth, gums, tongue—never exposing Neal himself, Will would add, perhaps unfairly. Perhaps Neal just didn't think that anything was *that* funny, Will.

Which leaves me—beyond these disgusting park pigeons,

these rabid squirrels, these loose-boweled dogs, shoo, get away—with the problem of a happy man, who made jokes and thought nothing really funny: my brother Neal, the pleased cynic. He's gone back to sleep. In bed with his wide, nearly blond Delsey, he's experiencing at a hopelessly advanced age the skyrockets of puppy love. I'll let the old dog lie.

No, I don't know if it's a lie. I suppose Neal's been coming to this scene for a long time. And if it's a delusion, it's one that Neal chose—a deliberate one, chosen deliberately.

At some point Neal and Delsey must have woken up. They probably rang for room service, probably drank champagne in bed. And possibly giggled, and if possible made love again. And the next day they went back to work—Delsey to be plagued by bunions, Neal by a sinus headache. But for the moment, among sheets humped up like a relief map of dangerous country, hard climbing, they're asleep. Let's don't wake them quite yet.

12

Will's new car cost him a hundred bucks: a '63 Ford Fairlane, okra-colored, with bashed-in trunk and a rectangular hole just this side of the accelerator pedal, through which you could glimpse the highway passing relentlessly below. That asphalt vista whizzing underfoot marks with a blur the matter's heart: the highway did pass. "Christ yes, she runs. If it's not too cold she runs good," the portly owner, cracking his knuckles, twanging his suspenders, told Will. "If she goes over fifty she starts to shimmy maybe a little; but if you're not meaning to travel too fast she's fine and dandy."

"I'm not traveling fast," Will said, and bought the car. He was proud of its lumbering, elephantine gait—it was more beast of burden than car. He had now owned it for five weeks without spotting even the phantasm of trouble. But on this December morning it was six degrees out. Will woke in the shape of a question mark, shivering.

Will crossed the yard, crunched crusted snow; he approached his car warily, an expression of pain already fixed on his face. After wrestling the hood open, he unscrewed a creaking wing nut and spun off the tarnished air filter; taking premature revenge, he grimaced balefully at the carburetor and squirted something from a pressurized can. He ran around, jumped in, and grimly twisted the ignition key; but there was no trouble, the engine made an impressively leonine noise and then sat idling, bubbling away. No trouble: the car was no trouble. On principle Will distrusted anything with moving parts, and he didn't believe it for a second.

The Ford quietly effervesced; Will clambered out to scrape the windshield with a plastic triangle, compliments of the Brattleboro Supply. One of these days I have to remember gloves, he noted, remarking with perverse pleasure the livid color of his knuckles. His breath came in short-lived clouds, mirroring the car's panting exhaust, and filmed over the windshield even as he rubbed it free of frost. He massaged the glass with the side of his aching fist, replaced the air filter with fumbling crimson fingers, and slammed the hood. The car's heater didn't work; hell, it had only been a hundred bucks.

After apple-picking, Will had meant to work full-time on his writing. On a few occasions he sat down to it, but the blank page could outstare him. He found himself actually embarrassed as he sat there, mocked by silence. What had he hoped to say? "Writing requires limitless pretension," Will wrote; "the assumption that *your* words, among all the words in the world, make some kind of" . . . What word did he want there? *Sense? Difference?* His toes were cold. He fidgeted for a while in his chair, put down the pen, looked out the window. A jay posed on a bare bough; a crow stroked by. It looked as if the birdfeeder was empty. Will stood up; he went to the shed to get his seeds.

These days Will was trying to make pots. This morning there was no one at Brearly's pottery; Will flicked the switch, and after a pause the fixtures shed a peculiar yellow fluorescent light. The room was white and spattered with white, with gray, clay dust and clay, and here or there a dot of color, pale blue or brown, where glaze had splashed from its bucket and speckled the wooden stool, cement floor, plaster wall. Broken cones lay scattered by the kiln door, and shards of pottery on the floor. Two wheels, a bench, cupboards; buckets and stools. In these bare but intimate ruins Will found what almost amounted to solace. He came here at night, when he could be alone, and sometimes he came just to stare.

In a literary way, Will liked the idea of throwing pots—of wheels, of centering, of closing in on the circle. But hand-building better suited his temperament, and the pots that resulted better suited his taste: his lopsided, pockmarked, humpbacked taste. With hand-building you were not attempting a set perfection, a given task, but expressing yourself. At the same time Will wasn't sure exactly *how* he was expressing himself by making pots; and after a while Will decided he was just keeping quiet. Renounce pretension; in the end he answered that, oh, he was just keeping busy. No, no one had asked.

He was about to travel to Northampton for Christmas; he was going home, going back, and he might as well have been traveling in time. The prospect gnawed his nerves: he envisioned uncomfortable conversations, or difficult questions, or even more uncomfortable silences; he had formulated answers to the questions, and questions for the conversations, but had nothing figured out for the silences.

At least he'd made his own gifts: plates, cups, bowls, a teapot for Lucy. He guessed he was proud of them.

Some of his work, the new stuff, had just been fired. Will found it on a lift in the corner, beside Brearly's kick wheel. Despite a maze of faceless vases, his eyes went straight to his pots, as if there were still some connection, an umbilical. He fondled a stoneware jar he had made with cordlike coils of

187

clay. His thumbs went around the rim—stroked a cold circle. It was his, and not too bad. Then Will noticed how much thicker it was in some places than others; when he set it on the workbench so he could step back and admire it, it seemed to keel over to one side. He had the distinct feeling that soon this pot would fall of its own weight.

He put it in the cupboard: he wanted to look at his teapot without anything else on the bench. Gently Will cradled the red pot in his palm. Here was its fat, almost soft belly; here was the round handle just big enough for two fingers, and the short curving spout; here the narrow, graceful foot. It's fine, Will said to himself, not quite believing. It was red clay, unglazed. Oh, it was fine: his first good pot. He left it on the table while he packed up his other things; left it for last. From time to time he gave the thing a fond, intimate glance.

Will's first pottery was software, using raku glazes. The nighttime firing was like fireworks. Brearly and Will drank warm saké while they waited for the glazes to become glossy, almost liquid, in the kiln; then with long tongs Brearly took out the first pot. They rushed out into the star-speckled autumn night; the pot glowed a winking orange, emitted small, musical, popping noises as it cooled and its glaze crackled. Brearly rolled the pot in sand, then plunged it into a barrel of water. A roar of steam hissed up into the cold night.

When they had cooled the last pot they drank again. They heated the saké on top of the kiln, and drank it out of small porcelain bowls. Brearly was a quiet, paunchy, bloodshot, melancholy man. His ways were dull and incurious; his stare sullen; his talk was about baseball, and he wore a Yankees cap when he threw on the wheel. For some reason Will took personally Brearly's habit of speaking disrespectfully to his own pots. Will remembered Brearly leaning his broad back against the wall, and slowly rubbing his cheeks with both hands. "Raku means 'happiness' in Japanese," Brearly had said, with a derisive snort.

Will loaded his pots into the trunk of his car carefully, wrapping them with newspaper and laying them side by side in a bed of crumpled news. Around the world there had been small wars: a question of religion was answered with theological spatterings from machine guns; a division of opinion as to the ownership of a certain territory was resolved by the destruction of same (Solomon's justice); humans of one tint made colorful messes on the street with those of another; these all chronicled by black markings on soft white paper. On top of it all (against it, he thought) Will laid his pots— though soya production was down due to drought, though quints were born to a luckless couple in a low-lying country, though books were endlessly written and written about, though people pleaded in small boxes full of abbreviations for an assortment of salvations, though violent death kept occurring around the misshapen world—Will cushioned his pots with the news, and banged the trunk shut. You could say that you make pots against the atrocity, Will thought. He wasn't, however, perfectly at ease with the thought. He locked up the pottery. He drove away.

At the entrance to the great highway Will was confronted with the specter of a bundle, perhaps female, squatting in the sunlight—the brazen, frozen sunlight. Yes, female, her arm outstretched, perhaps her thumb too; no, not squatting, she sat on an object, knees up and body hunched over. Will decided that that thumb was out, and pulled up beside her forlorn, crumpled form.

The object was a suitcase; the female a young, chattering one. Not a sociable chatterer, merely a cold one. She got in silently, and sat without speaking, chilly teeth clicking. Will apologized for the climatic conditions inside his car; for his useless heater; and had to stop himself from apologizing for the weather—even, perhaps, for whatever had caused his passenger to occupy her solitary arctic station by Highway

189

91. Will was generous today with sympathy, with anonymous tenderness.

"Where are you headed?"

"New York."

"Tough day to travel, no?" Will asked, chummy and solicitous.

"Well, you know, I had to get to New York."

"Unh-hunh." Will felt an unaccountable desire to kid his passenger out of her blues: "What's your grail, lady?"

"Hunh?"

"What's the attraction?"

"What, about New York?"

"Yes, New York. The Big Apple. Baghdad-on-the-Hudson."

"Oh, nothing, I guess. You know."

"The bright lights of the big city, hunh?"

"I guess so. You know."

"Is it love?" Will teased. "A great amour that beckons?"

She turned her tired eyes, with their torpid lids, toward Will for the first time. "Sure," she said. "Whatever you like."

Will was bound and determined: he would make light of it, and it would float away. "The trials of the heart, scourge of the senses," he tried. "Young girl led astray by desire. Pursuit of a romantic destiny in the great metropolis. The stuff fat novels are made of. Something like that?"

"Something like that," she mumbled, and turned away— and as she turned Will saw, in a white world, the sparkle of a teardrop, glinting in the sun, rolling from puffy eye down placid face.

Will flowed with remorse. "Hey, what's the powerful trouble, champ?"

She shook her smallish head. Several more tears tracked the traces of the first. On the other side of the poor girl's nose the crooked trickle of more tears completed a wretched symmetry.

"Come on," Will said, with an avuncular grin. "Come on, now. What's your name, then?"

190

The small head shook again, and a drop spilled from the point of her chin.

"Nothing will come of nothing," Will chided. "What's that name, champ?"

"Eileen."

"Eileen. Eileen McSpleen, I presume?"

"Maybe," Eileen said, with a wobbly frown. "Look, I'll just get out here. I don't feel too hot."

"Oh no you don't," Will said, as genially as he could. "You don't have to talk if you don't feel like it, but I'm not letting you play in interstate traffic."

"Don't care about traffic."

"Maybe not. But they got some fairly good-sized trucks roaming around out there, and if you've a mind to stay in three dimensions you might wait for the next entrance ramp."

"I don't *care,*" she repeated, rubbing her wet, rubbery cheeks with the back of a frozen hand. Her paw looked raw, and she still shivered; Will finally remembered the woolen blanket folded on the back seat, and offered it. "It doesn't matter," she claimed, looking away.

"If it doesn't matter, you might just as well take it," Will said, "just to make me feel better." He reached for it himself, regarding the slippery road out of the corner of his eye. "Here you go," tossing it onto her lap, where it sat untouched. "You'll catch your death of cold, champ. Eileen McSpleen's untimely end: Scandal in a '63 Ford." She averted her face. "Did you ever read a story called 'To Build a Fire'? Jack London?"

"Unh-unh."

"It's about a girl who doesn't dress warmly enough. She ends up a fallen woman. So you wrap yourself up in that old blanket, stay pure in heart and firm in mind, obey the teachings of the wise men, remember that policemen are your friends, and all will be right with the world, or your money back. Come on. What you haven't tried won't hurt you." Will

191

heard the words tumbling out of his mouth with a certain lack of connection; he sounded, he thought ruefully, just like Neal.

Eileen did not seem to register his jokes; instead she bent her head, sighed deeply—a fat person's sigh, but for all the weight of her troubles Eileen was petite—and sobbed.

Northern Massachusetts, slathered with ice, provided only a slender, tricky chute in clear asphalt to sled southward, and Will's concentration was required. It was all he could do to joke and drive at the same time; but to bend over, pat her back, provide earnest solace, and steer the car, all at once: this was not possible. And in the meantime Eileen sat sobbing into the crystalline cold, shedding buckets, her face a watery concourse shining amid drab surroundings of brown scarf and olive fatigue jacket. Will felt helpless, and a fool.

He chattered blithely. He was navigating toward home. "You should know," he blithered, "that the Miss Niobe contest doesn't start for another fortnight. All Opheliacs please note. Dry 'em and sleep." A sudden swerve was necessary. "Whoops. This boat may be headed for the last corral. The metaphor is mixed, but the spirit is willing. Doom down the highway in a sixty-three Ford. I'm legally liable for your safety, so I better take good care; even if you don't care a sue."

Eileen's quiet sobbing interrupted her breathing; she choked, emitted a series of raking coughs punctuated by curt hiccups. Will reached out. His hand hovered, as always; finally thumped tentatively on the blade of her shoulder. She redoubled her coughing. At last she hacked her last, sighed exhaustedly, and dipped her head to allow a measure of gray, diaphanous vomit to drizzle onto the heap of blanket.

Distracted, shocked, Will pulled over, easing the car gingerly onto the iced shoulders of the narrow-necked road. This is not pleasant, he said to himself in a burst of simpleminded lucidity. When he managed to slither to an uneasy halt, Eileen suddenly roused herself from her lethargy; she burst from the car, flinging the blanket onto the bare ground, and ran away, hands sideways at her hips and knees nearly knocking together. Haste laid waste. Her feet went sliding out from under her, and in a comic-book jumble of misplaced limbs she tumbled, landing with an audible thump on the ice—the hard ice, as Will redundantly thought of it, tottering quickly after her.

"I'm all right, I'm all right," she moaned.

"No, you're not, champ," he answered coolly, doctor and father. But she was all right; her ankle had turned more than it was made to, but the fall itself was bruising, painful, inconsequential. In a jiffy she was back on her feet—though she distrusted them, now.

Will seemed to have gained that trust. I'm not sure how. Eileen had used up her generous portion of tears, given out the tiny entirety of her breakfast, and on falling flat she had only two choices—to continue to lie low, frigid and dumb, until numbed by December, or to allow Will to help her up. At the end of her tether, I guess, she gave Will a limp arm.

Together they limped back to the car. Will tried to rub the vomit off the blanket with a chunk of ice, but the results were not satisfactory; when held up to the sunlight it looked whistle-clean, but his olfactory sense overruled his vision; and he left the blanket, folded, on the road's shoulder.

Eileen's hands were folded quietly on her lap, miming propriety. "Better?" Will asked, at once expansive and wary. To his relief she replied, "Much."

"Great. Still want out at the next ramp?"

"Guess I'll go as far as you can take me."

Will apologized again. "That's not very far, I'm afraid. Just Northampton. Home," he added, with sudden, gratuitous sentiment.

"That's what I just left," she said. "For good," she added meaningfully.

Will shrugged. "There's no place like home," he said. "Hell, there's no such place *as* home."

Will swung the car back onto the freeway. It immediately fishtailed wildly, swerved like a swallow. Then it steadied; but Will was suddenly certain that he was no longer in control of the car. This was no road, this was a river: the car was like a canoe in white water, a plaything for the waves. Will gripped the wheel as if it were his lifesaver; blood came roaring into his head like another river. Fear was translated into heat, and Will began to sweat profusely from every cranny in his long body, soaking several layers of clothing. The blinding winter sun blazed before him; Will squinted, clutched the wheel. He felt strangely exhausted, tired as a man in a long dream.

No dream, Will. They approached a knoll with a long descent on the other side. The other side of the mountain, the other side of the mountain, Will sang, a soundless song that never quite emerged from his crazed mask of fixed, distorted features. He tapped the brakes lightly just at the hillock's rounded summit, to limit the inertia. Oh yes, his prophetic soul: as if he were a conductor tapping with his baton, he tapped the brakes, the car lurched, and then launched into a waltz: a slow, graceful slide. The rear end of the car caught up quickly, swooped ahead, and proceeded on down the hill —while Will and Eileen watched, rooted to the still center of a turning world. A field went around them; then a red barn glazed with ice; a stand of firs, black and white; here was their road again, and they were facing the direction from which they'd come. But this was not all. The slow-motion merry-go-round went on describing a circle. For what seemed a long time Will kept telling himself: stop braking and turn the wheel in the direction of the skid. But what did that mean, as the world danced a slow turn around them?

Eileen gasped—a long, drawn-out cry much like the one you utter as you slowly enter water that is cold, too cold. The

194

water crept up over her chest; Eileen gasped, and lost her breath.

Will lost his mind, for the moment. He found that time slowed quickly as the car waltzed him down the hill. He heard with some distinctness an ancient sound—his jar of yellow paint falling onto the kindergarten floor. Falling, and breaking. That sound meant: uh-oh; you're gonna get it. The angry, puckered face of the teacher came toward him.

Will now found time to pick through the postcards in his memory's full box. Here was one: Will, though the littlest, had his own project. He liked cherry pie, and it was with consternation that he noticed the frequent, rustling presence of black birds among the bright red fruit, heavily tipping the boughs up and down as they scrambled for cherries. Little Will went with characteristic directness to the need for a scarecrow; engaging Homer's ample help, he embarked, blithe and determined, on its construction. The scarecrow they made was a ramshackle thing, listing and listless, Homer's old clothes stuffed with newspaper and topped with a square cardboard head—they painted a pleasant smile on one side and an expression of rage glowering from the other. Despite the all-embracing duality, the scarecrow didn't work. The day after Will proudly poked its pole-back into the ground it was already an old acquaintance to the birds; Will, gazing out the kitchen window, found crows in residence on both shoulders of his self-portrait. The birds took one look at the real Will's fierce features, at the beebee gun he toted (Howard's gun), and fled with indignant squawks. Will shot instead at the scarecrow's square head, freckling his double's smiling visage with round spatterings, mementos of his rage.

There had been times when Will had been happy, but never content. Instead his moments of revelation uncovered a lucid despair. He thought of his father's bloated face, dotted with bristling white grizzle, floating atop the ballooning body —the marks and distortions of time.

195

In this postcard he was dancing with Lucy. It looked like fun; but Will recalled himself surrounded by frenetic music and swirling red lights, unable to dance and enjoy it, or even to dance as if he enjoyed it. It was hard to lose yourself among a multitude of mirrors, and no amount of liquor could get him out of being Will.

Here they were, on the day Lucy brought Sarah home— this barely human creature, red and bawling, constantly bawling. They gave it love, and then (now! Will thought, skidding downhill) it was walking about making sentences, posing with a wrinkle of the nose for a portrait of Lucy as a little girl, or demonstrating with a choleric demand how Will had refused his vegetables. Somehow she got it just right; it was uncanny. Soon Sarah would be burying her own parents; it was intolerable. It was an outrage; a heartache.

They were picnicking in this postcard. The blackberries were ripe. Their tongues were purple with the juice; they stuck them out at each other, like children. And now the blackberries were past ripe, they were rotting on the vines; and the tongues had blackened; and the wind came up, blowing hard, under a freezing sun.

These pictures went way back. Will began to flip through them: the crocodile smile of his grandmother; then his frayed stuffed cow; his black galoshes with buckles, sloshing through the relentless spring rains; the soft cave of his bed, a warm island of the senses. He was flooded; he was up to his neck in memory.

Will had two aches: that time had passed, and that it was passing. He felt strung between past and present, hung like clothes that would never dry. If only I could start *now,* he thought; but the word *now* echoed from ear to ear, becoming more and more faint—like music streaming from a passing car; like a joke he'd heard long before, and was hearing again; and again. Each *now* was a stick tossed from a bridge; passing away, carrying him back into the past. Time is a river, he thought, but it flows backward.

Time was a river, it flowed backward. Will, falling, called his mother; Howard came and picked him up, skinned knees and all. Howard casually wiped the blood off with his palm. Now Howard wore a purple bathrobe and patted down his bald spot. Now Howard sucked his pipe as Will said, "Reality is insufficient," and Howard replied calmly, "Well, what is it you need?"

Will reached for the last postcard. He couldn't seem to focus on it—as if dazzled by the brilliance of the winter light streaming through the windshield, or fogged in by the persistent haze in the city of memory. At last the smell of coffee, from the plant on the Brooklyn side, cut through: he saw the spiderweb spanning the East River, its traces marked by beads of light. One windless, cold night in their first fall Lucy and he walked out to the middle. They hadn't been in love long, didn't need to talk. Instead they stood, holding each other more tightly than they had to, and gazed over the edge. The water below was a velvety black, and rustled like crows in a cherry tree. Will remembered (it was foggy) thinking, as his eyes lingered on what seemed a soft way down, that some deaths might be simple.

The car was still whirling a slow circle as Will said to himself: There is nothing simple about it. He took his foot off the brake at last; at the bottom of the hill the car completed its circle and just stopped, facing forward in the middle of the road.

"Jeeze. Oh Jeeze," Eileen cried, and hugged the seat.

Will's shoulders were shaking, but he gave himself instructions in a calm, lucid voice: pull over to the side of the road; pull yourself together. Instead he concentrated on the quiver of his arms and shoulders, with the amused detachment of someone watching his knee jump to the call of the doctor's rubber mallet. Is that really my knee? Are my shoulders

shaking, or are they shaking me? Or am I just someone ob-
serving these shoulders shake? And the world is shaking, and
only the shoulders are still? Or—

Eileen loosened her hold on the seat and looked up. She
brushed a strand of hair away from her eyes. She sat up.
"Jeeze," she summed up.

She looked around her, as if she'd just waked. She looked
to Will. "Is the car still running?" she asked.

"Hear it?" Will said.

"Oh, yeah." She waited. "Aren't you gonna start going and
stuff? Are we stuck or something?"

"No," Will said, "we're not stuck." He looked at his hands.
The fingers crawled in the air like arachnids. *"I'm* stuck,"
Will added. His eyebrows went up and he gave Eileen a smile
—a wistful, plaintive, helpless smile.

Will's crow passed overhead, in front of the white sun.
"Come on, quit kidding around," Eileen said, beginning to
worry again. "Let's go, awright?"

"Yeah," Will said. His hands reached out shakily for the
wheel. "Yeah," he repeated steadily, to himself. He held the
wheel in his two hands. "Yeah," he said, aloud again. "Let's
go."

"Right," Eileen affirmed.

"Right."

He was navigating toward home. Here was his exit.

Eileen hopped out. "Thanks for the lift, okay? Have a nice
day," Eileen chirped.

Will waved his hands. "Nothing," he mumbled.

Eileen was suddenly confidential. "You know," she said,
holding the car door with both hands, "you're the first one
who didn't try to talk me out of leaving home. Thanks."

"Nothing," Will repeated, a foreigner who knew only one
phrase.

"People are always giving you a hard time," Eileen went

on. "And you really pulled us out of that skid, too."

Will shook his head.

Eileen had one more thought: "Hey, what's your name, anyway? I'm Eileen Branch."

Will looked perplexed. Finally he said, "Bard. Neal Bard."

"Nice to meet you," Eileen said. "Have a nice day." She whammed the door shut.

It was midmorning when Will pulled up to Neal's house. Nobody home—Neal still at work, Mother and Howard not up from the city yet—a note on the door.

> Will—
>   the French who is under a reversible tam, not o'-
> shanter. Make yourself to home.
>
>   Yours,
>   Robert Burns
>
> P.S. Wouldn't Puzzlin' Howard be proud of me now?

> Big Howie,
>   if you get here first, the key's under the mat. Now
> don't get upset, Howie. The gin's under a reversible tam in
> the liquor cabinet.
>
>   Love and kisses,
>   Carry Nation

Will went in. He put the teakettle on; remembered his pots, and returned to fetch them. The task required only mild effort, but Will found himself gulping for air; he panted evanescent dandelion puffs into the blue day.

He had thought that he might make tea in his teapot; his best, his good pot. Yes, he might. He hid the other pots on the floor in Neal's long closet, among a sea of boots and galoshes; but the teapot he held securely between his hands.

199

He paced till the teakettle pursed its lips, sputtered, and whistled.

One high note, held for an impossibly long time. The note seemed to get louder, more strident; but perhaps it did not, perhaps Will alone thought it so, perhaps another person in Will's place, pacing before the whistling kettle, might have disagreed.

Will's choppy strides carried him into Neal's bedroom, where he faced the full-length mirror, and his tense image faced him. He caught sight of the teapot in the mirror: it was hideously warped, a blunt, graceless shape, a blurry color like wet rust. He spoke to it.

"Know what I'm about to do?"

He was silent, as if waiting for a reply. At last he provided one: "Smash you in the mirror."

He didn't. Instead he looked up from the pot to the place where his face was reflected, and there noticed the blurry beginnings of a tear in his eye. As soon as it felt that it was being watched, the drop dried; Will found himself willing a tear, and unable to produce it. Instead he imagined with horrifying clarity the crash of pottery hurled fiercely against the mirror: splinters of silvered glass flew everywhere, splintering the air, drawing blood; a cloud of broken reflection, mixed with broken red earth, hovered in the imagination. Will went back into the kitchen and stiffly lifted the kettle off the burner; the whistle drooped, and stopped.

13

Howard, eldest brother, began to regret. He was a premature curmudgeon, he admitted, a puckered and sour puss; but penitent, penitent. This well-dressed flagellant was nodding with memory, the most primitive anesthesia, under the surgical knife of his mother's chiseled voice. Mrs. Bard was recounting distasteful doings with a Puerto Rican maid in her East Side apartment—rank thievery, our mother claimed, enumerating vast quantities of vanished silverware.

Let it go, Howard thought, calm with weariness. He drowsily retreated to his childhood, where he found Gertrude. Gertrude was our first cleaning woman, and only somewhat coincidentally the first "colored" person Howard had ever seen. It was a beautiful, lustrous color—a shining purple-black, with a silvery sheen when Gertrude perspired. Howard's fancy flew to her *culottes,* a word permanently linked in his mind to tall glasses of cherry Kool-Aid—

Eunice was saying: "She's a brazen, nervy girl. They *certainly* don't act as they once did—"

Gertrude baked a great cake, a banana cake, and sang as she pushed the carpet sweeper across the living room with swoops of her gangling arms. In the meantime the honeysuckle was out, and at the end of its stamen each pastel blossom yielded a brimming drop of sweetness. The weather was fine, all that spring and summer, but Gertrude's housecleaning was a ramshackle business; and she gave way, finally, to a mannish Teuton who believed the Advent was nigh—that, in short, God was gonna get us kids if we didn't eat the crusts too. The honeysuckle wilted, and our father went out the door, where a taxi waited.

Eunice was going on: "They're keenly aware of the difficulty of getting help, and they exploit that difficulty—"

Neal was always reading comic books upstairs then; Superman, bless his invincible heart, was new. The varicolored dots on the cheap newsprint did not even pretend to simulate real shades, any more than the world they portrayed presented an immaculate reflection of things as they are. But Neal found this distorted planet a cozy nest; and there he dreamed, occasionally passing a hand through his hair, twirling his cowlick.

Eunice had gone on to Will. Now she said: "I'm dreadfully anxious about him. Can you honestly tell me he's all right?"

"I think he's fine. Confused, as ever, but no more so than ever." The speaker was recognizably Howard, but only his public voice; still, the façade was the one Eunice found comforting—according to Howard.

Eunice adjusted her seat—lifted one side of herself and smoothed her dress under with a smooth hand; then the other side, with the other hand. And she *was* comforted, if only slightly, by Howard's calm intonation, his intimation of normalcy. But he is not right, she thought: he is only speaking about himself, as always. Howard's brow wrinkled, as it did

202

when he was serious, or intending to convey the impression of seriousness. And yet even I can see through him, she thought: I, who tries never to see through, for looking is indiscreet. But Howard parades his secrets, Eunice thought as she finished her tea, by the transparency of his manners; his mannered manners, she phrased it, pursing her lips, putting down her teacup.

"Will merely wants to be irrepressible," Howard said. "But he is bound by temperament to his good judgment. He is sane despite himself."

The word troubled Eunice. "Sane? Well, we're all *sane*, aren't we?"

"Yes, of course. I just meant that Will would like to be fashionably crazy."

"Oh, dear. Will is too bright for that."

"Yes, of course," Howard said again, and wrinkled his brow again, and Eunice thought: He is humoring me. But at once Eunice admitted that she preferred Howard's charade to the brutal truth. Perhaps it was age, an older person's wish not to be disturbed; but there were, she knew, lies that she approved of. One always pretended, for that matter. The truth was so unpleasant that one made sham, sham civilities. One had a duty to do that: to be false to a false world. It was a matter of being kind to people. Howard, at least, was kind to his old mother, Eunice thought, jangling her two silver bracelets and pitying herself. It was extraordinary to think of Howard as a kind person.

She knew she was straying from the subject; but she was his mother, and she had the right to do that. "Howard," she asked, "why did you never marry?"

"No doubt I was too much in love with you," Howard answered quickly, too quickly, smiling with apparent indulgence.

She would ignore him. "Were you never tempted?"

"Oh, I suppose so. Too busy, perhaps . . . perhaps one of

203

these days . . ." He fidgeted, fussed with his napkin; with hers Eunice dabbed at her mouth. Howard always said "perhaps"; but he never would.

"At present I'm still shocked about Neal," she said. "If you marry, Howard, you must give me time to recuperate."

"Wasn't it peculiar? After so many years of chaste proclamations. . . ."

She thought out loud: "Neal avowed bachelorhood; but you're the real one, Howard: you practice it."

"Oh, I don't know about that," Howard groused, and looked away.

Well, all right. She would drop the subject; just as he wished. And here the waiter came, besides. There were always waiters coming; always dishes being taken away, or else meals being placed before them; and sometimes Eunice thought that a waiter who appeared before them to remove the plates had come to bring the meal. Not that she was still hungry (she was never hungry anymore), just that she forgot; she forgot what had happened, or confused it with what would happen; a meal appeared that she could swear she had just eaten, forced down, and here it would be again, so vile, so vulgar—she was just raising it to her mouth, that dreadful food, when the waiter would bring the food—the vile, the dreadful food. Fortunately she had her diet; she didn't have to eat it all. No, not anymore.

Well, shit. Delsey kind of wondered what she was getting into. She hadn't even met them yet—maybe that was weird, but what the hell, Neal was a little weird. That's why she liked him, right?

She got off at two thirty and went straight home. This guy was standing in the living room, just standing there like he was floating, with a crookedy mouth and floppy hair; he was sort of bigger than she expected, but she knew who it was: he looked all serious in a spacey sort of way.

"Are you—?" he said, leaving it blank.

"Unh-hunh," Delsey said, slipping her bag off her shoulder and letting it drop onto the sofa. "Well, did you have a good trip down? Roads kind of slippery today, hunh?" She dropped herself down beside her bag. "I've been *stand*ing since ten thirty," she explained. "I'm not used to working lunch."

He didn't say anything. Funny expression he had—like he was shocked. Or in shock. "Did you get yourself something? There's chicken in the fridge." Will didn't answer. "I hope you don't think you have to stand on *cer*emony or something. You're not a vegetarian, are you?"

"No."

"You want some chicken? Neither of us like dark meat, so we always have drumsticks sort of hanging around."

"No thanks," Will said absently. He stood there, kind of wobbling and looking. When his eyes came back to Delsey he seemed surprised to see her still sitting there. He smiled with faint recognition. "Sounds good," he said softly. "A little chicken."

She looked dubiously at him. "Drumstick okay?"

"Sounds good. Chicken sounds good."

"Hey, you all right? You don't look too hot. Wanta sit down?"

"Not too hot," he confessed. He tottered over to an arm-chair and dropped into it, like a ship sinking.

Delsey made up a nice platter of chicken, sliced tomato (a pinky one, a December one), lettuce, mayonnaise. It felt just like work. "You want bread with it?" she asked as she carried it into the living room; but there he was, asleep, his mouth open, delivering a good little snore. "Hey, you want this now?" Delsey tried, loud. Will swallowed in his sleep. Well, shit, she could use a nap herself. She put the platter on the coffee table; unclenched the fists she found dangling at his side. What had she gotten herself into?

Neal arrived home to find his brother and his wife sleeping. "Great," he said. "I could watch this stuff for hours. Just go back and forth from one room to the other." He spied the plate in front of Will, and latched onto a drumstick. "Hey champ," he said, and dipped into the mayonnaise. "Hey, Sleeping Whatchamacallit. Awaken."

Groggily Will did. Neal sat himself down on the sofa. "You kids forgot your graham crackers and milk," Neal said. "You go to jail, directly to jail, do not pass go, do not collect two hundred dollars."

Will rubbed his face. "I feel better," he mumbled. "I'm sorry."

"Better sorry than safe, right? Sorry about what?"

Will grunted, and rubbed again. "I thought—never mind. I'm sorry."

"You often apologize when you wake up? Big Howie'd stand on line to hear that." Neal dangled a slice of tomato into his mouth. "Mmm, didja meet the wife? The little woman?"

"Yeah. She brought me this"—Will looked dully at the empty platter—"chicken."

Neal crunched into the lettuce. "Nice of her," he said. "By the way, Mr. van Winkle, how long have you been gracing us with your presence?"

Delsey's voice came out. "Neal?"

"Yes, dearest?"

"Can you come on in here a sec?"

"Whatever you wish, light of my life."

She motioned him to the bed with a twitch of her index finger, kissed him briefly on the mouth, and whispered at his ear: "You forgot to tell me something, Neal. You forgot to tell me he's crazy."

"Not crazy. Just dramatic."

"Okay," she said. "He's not crazy. He's just a normal zombie."

206

Neal smiled with one side of his mouth. He bounced off the bed, stalked back into the living room, and put the chicken bones in a neat row on the barren plate. He gave Will a mock-furtive look. "What's the matter, you don't carry drumsticks around with you? It cures arthritis left and right. By the way, my lovely wife says you've been acting like a zombie. Any comment, champ?"

Delsey's voice came out again. *"Ne*-al! For Christ's *sake."*

"Okay, I'm sorry. I was just trying to ruin an absolutely nonexistent relationship. By the way, champ," he went on, arranging and rearranging the chicken bones with his pinky, "a frozen chicken was used as a murder weapon in Tacoma last week. That kind of news item makes you understand progress."

Will was feeling better. Much better now. He'd gotten hold of himself again. Hold. For some reason he hadn't been able to tell Neal about the accident. But Will remembered now: there had been no accident. The car was out of control, he was out of control, but nothing had happened. In such a case, you just drive on.

The teapot had not been smashed. Everything was intact. Just drive on.

If that's so, Will wondered, what is the shadow that's crossed my sight? And what is the cloud that's come down, like fog, like sleep?

But he was awake now: wide awake, he claimed, examining Neal's small mouth as it opened, closed against itself. Winter light came through the window, and Will fastened on to it. Not possible to dream the light, soft light like that, he pronounced. He knew he was wrong; his dreams were accurate. His dream self had made countless proofs of verity, long ago revealed an intimacy with the real world. His sleeper knew how to let light filter into a room; knew how to reconstruct Neal's open mouth, Neal's closed mouth. For Will knew these things by his heart. Now he tried shifting in his chair—to touch and feel touch, make tactile proof of wakefulness.

Yes, he felt. He was seated, he felt, in a soft chair; the air was warm, dry. He heard the sound of pipes knocking in the old house, knocking out the heat, pings, pangs. Will made a quick check of his surroundings before emerging. On the low coffee table, three chicken bones lay on a plate, next to a tomato-rouged dab of mayonnaise. Bones. A magazine, an ashtray. Ashes. Pangs. Will heard the clock tick, and much later tock; it was an old clock, from the days when time went slower. Now snow was falling again. Now Will would come out.

Will's image first slipped into Lucy's daydreams one quietly storming morning two weeks before. She looked out her mother's window, if only to avoid looking around her mother's house, and she saw, walking between the snowflakes, a multiplicity of Wills. Will was clad in plaids, had flecks of snow in his dark hair. He looked like an illustration in one of her first books, a picture of a prince traveling by sleigh, on his way to take the curse, the chill, from the heart of his beloved. Lucy thought of the compound word *heart-warming;* we all hear about heart failure, she thought, but no one notices when it works.

Perhaps she was just being hopeful, but she thought she wished. Was there any reason not to go back to him? When she gazed around her mother's dimly lit sitting room that morning she felt a tickle of happiness, and of relief.

The first emotions wore off, eroded under the interrogative push of time. She'd left Will for *positive* reasons, she told herself: trying to accomplish change, after their static state. That *had* changed, she felt. Even if she couldn't say how. She wanted to come to him of her own free will; to know that the rest of her life wasn't a given. Will might be more conscious, now; and more careful, and more comfortable (grimly she watched the list run down toward the distasteful), more managable—more afraid—more resentful. Lucy had to question her intent. After all this time, was she just trying to win? Now, after two weeks, she thought she'd come to a decision. She gave herself the chance to back out, lingering at the telephone, receiver in hand. She wanted to be sure that what she would say was true. For Will was more than just antisocial; he was an impossibility. He willed his own discontent, disruption, eruption. Lucy just couldn't understand that; for she had the need to put things together: to put her life in order, to try to accomplish . . . (she left it blank). Will tried to stand outside himself, at some imagined crux, like a tragic hero at a crossroads. It was always Act IV for Will. You weren't married to me, Lucy thought; you were wedded to your unhappiness. As if the difficulties of living were Will's invention, and death his greatest brainchild: Will loved to talk about the idea of death. He didn't act, didn't do anything about the senseless, violent deaths, about poverty or slavery, about the poor world—just talked about the idea of death, and let it make him angry. Even the thought of what day in the week it was made Will angry; because of death. Living with Will was like having mementos of the atrocity strewn about the living room—bones on the coffee table, matted hair stuck to the rug, dried blood smeared on the walls. Will exhausted her. She didn't want to fight anymore; it wasn't in her nature. No. She wanted to achieve: to change something in the world, if only herself.

Will, if you were asked why I left, what would you answer? A shrug, perhaps. You might say, "Well, we didn't get along very well." No, we didn't.

But she missed him; her mind was made up; Lucy's finger snagged an eight.

Now she had to wonder (she was dialing: a six, a three) why she was going back. Was it her weakness, a cursed womanly weakness, that finally she could never let go—or her strength, that it was important to her, worth troubling over? It was worth taking the trouble, Lucy decided (a two, a nine); Will was an impossibility, but a necessary one. Well, that was being human. Damn it, bless it, in the end she'd have to accept it: her tender spot for the trouble of Will.

It was a matter of time, now, she thought; not time to come, but time been and gone. And that much, our long and difficult past, is yours, Will. Despite my shaky hold (a three, a two) on what I think I want, and my dubious ability to get it, we have that. (A seven. She was finished. She heard a ring.) Do you think we'll make it, Will?

It was ringing. Snow began drifting up around her mother's house, smothering it; the weak milk-white sun dipped down under the ground; the growing darkness oppressed Lucy, and made her heart sore.

Delsey loved wearing black. I'd be *right on* at a funeral, she said to herself. She'd never been to a funeral.

She was about to pull it on. "You wearing a slip?" Neal said, admiring her.

"Cute, hunh?"

Neal nodded. "Sure. Never seen you in a slip."

"Course you have. I wear one at work all the time."

"Oh no you don't. I noticed."

"Well, shit, it's your *fam*ily. I haven't met your mother, remember? I don't want her to get the wrong impression."

"You don't want her to get the right impression, you mean."

"*Ne*-all!"

He put his hand on her knee. "Don't get me wrong," he said. "I'm in favor of the right impression."

Well, he wasn't gonna get away with it that easy. "You've got cold *hands,*" Delsey said. "Would you mind?"

"I've always got cold hands," Neal admitted. "So you better not start using that as an—I'll get it." He picked it up. "Hello? Unh-hunh. Oh, hi! He sure is, just hang on a sec."

Lucy planned to say very simply: she felt the separation hadn't worked out. Perhaps they couldn't live together, but they couldn't live separately either. But with the slightly flattened electronic reproduction of Will's voice in her ear, she lost her sense of the dramatic, and perhaps part of her nerve as well.

"I was just thinking it would be nice to get together." No matter: he would know what she meant.

Will hesitated. Finally the flattened voice was in her ear again: "Yeah. That would be great."

"Neal told me you'd be down. I thought I would break the silence." It was her silence, she remembered; she had imposed it. She hurried on. "I thought it would be good to see you."

"Sure, Lucy," Will said; and then, though she thought she heard him sigh, he did echo: "It'll be good to see you."

Will stood beside the telephone and rubbed his skull. Hearing Lucy brought back too much of the too-recent past. Lucy walked with a cornflower in her hand; it was the one he had given her. She always walked slowly, with grave steps. In a library she put on her horn-rimmed glasses; now she took them off and chewed on them reflectively, her forehead furrowed. Now she peered at the soufflé through the tiny oven window; a tiny smile pulled the corners of her mouth. When she counted on her fingers she started with her thumb; when she argued her eyebrows met; when they visited friends with children she fell in love with precocious little girls. She wore a long skirt; she danced the jitterbug. She read the newspaper at her desk; now she snapped the newspaper shut.

There was no question that he would take her back. "Take her back"—as if he were the manager of the complaints department of the Deerfield Woolworth's: yes, of course he would take that percolator back if it didn't work, had never worked, but why did you wait six months to bring it in, ma'am? Why did you wait, Lucy? Will would come back; but it felt like failure to him, as if they'd tried to make separate lives, and had come back, now, to find the same crutch. The same old crutch, the percolator both of them knew didn't work. . . . He would come back. He couldn't pretend he'd left.

Time binds, Will thought. Time fixes in place—the way a photograph, once taken, can only be retouched with the brush of artifice. If only he could leave time. If only he could station himself in the inviolable future, and live in retrospect, he'd be safe—safe from the dangerous present, protected by the secret knowledge that time, that most private history, never repeats itself. Except in memory, where the repetitions never stop: Lucy's cornflower. It matched her eyes, her slow steps were grave. The soufflé was rising beautifully; it would always be rising. This constant business exhausted Will, and he sat in Neal's armchair. Underneath a crime novel on the shelf beside him, he spied a battered bunch of Superman comics, and ancient baseball cards surrounded by a rubber band. Neal was riding his bicycle, the cards making machine-gun noises in the spokes: here he came now.

Neal opened, saw them, and smiled. There was Mother: a Bizarro version of herself, now, her bony face all angles; a regal witch. He kissed her cheek at the doorstep; Howard pumped his hand. Neal helped them to take off their snowy coats. Here's Howard, overdressed as usual, with his damn ascot. What is Delsey going to make of that?: one brother a zombie, the other in his ascot, as if he'd just been boating in the snow.

It would be no use to try to explain them to Delsey, or Delsey to them: different planets. As for me, Neal thought brushing snow vigorously from his mother's fur, I'm every-

212

body's favorite alien. The thought pleased him. He looked around the faces and smiled at each one in turn: a quirky, amused smile. He clapped his hands; "Who's for a drink?" he said.

"Aren't you going to ask us if we'd like to sit down, Neal?" his mother said, wearing her brief, joyless smile, blinking her eyes rapidly.

"Oh, of course," Neal replied, showing her a seat; and Delsey thought: Oh well, shit.

Here we were: Howard closed his hand and bounced it against the door. Eunice made a pained face and attached her thin forefinger to the buzzer. A harsh, short noise gave out inside. Neal, answering, saw us and smiled quickly, crookedly, as if amused. Eunice (is something wrong?) touched her face with her hand, patted it; Howard bent down to regard his fly. He gave it a stern look, scolding, but it was closed. We scraped our shoes and went in, kissing and shaking; already unbundling, for the snow was already melting; and Howard wondered, as he sometimes did, what Neal was laughing about. Howard didn't see what was funny.

"So: this must be your Adele," Eunice said to Neal, looking her right in the eye. Adele was attractive, unquestionably, if wide-faced, and a bit sizable, generally. Mothers-in-law disapprove of size in daughters-in-law, Howard postulated. Adele was younger than Howard had imagined, though he'd been told; she was alert, wary, and in the vicinity of a blonde. Eunice kissed her cheek, and would have kissed the other one, had it stayed stationary. But Adele was already looking toward Howard, extending her hand; she had a firm, warm grip. She shakes like a man, praised Howard. He tried to say he was glad to meet her; but his bass voice came out distant and distorted, as if conducted by a megaphone pointed away.

Now it was Will's turn to kiss (both cheeks) and shake. This seemed to amuse Neal further. He put his hands in his pock-

213

ets, under the floppy ears of his gray houndstooth jacket, and rocked back and forth on his heels, chuckling lightly. His eyes kindled at each of us in turn. The thought struck Howard— this particular one had never come to him before, so it struck —that Neal might always have been crazy.

He wasn't sure what had brought it on, apart from Neal's lunatic chuckle, his amusement in a situation that everyone else found constraining. His young wife, for example, had the good taste to be displeased. Neal rocked back and forth, and tittered. It was *not* amusing. Howard bit the inside of his cheek.

Neal took his hands out and clapped them. "Who's for a drink?" he announced. "Hot toddy, sports fans? Warm your guggles?"

Howard thought: Now Eunice will be wondering where in the vulgar universe one's guggle is. Howard would try to smooth things over. "Perhaps Mother would prefer tea," he said soothingly.

"A toddy will do nicely," Eunice claimed, putting forth her brave smile.

"Tea sounds good to me. I'll get it," Will said, and hopped up. Anything to take him out of reach, Howard carped silently.

Neal turned to Howard. "Big Howie? What's your pleasure, if you've got one?"

Howard did not deserve this treatment; Howard had no bad words, ill wishes, for anyone. Howard, for all his ponderous wealth of self-possession, did no harm; meant, in fact, well. It is perhaps the fate of older, larger brothers to be looked down upon by their youngers and lessers. Topographically it makes no sense, but I hold that . . .

"Well, what'll it be? Gin?"

"Whatever is easiest," Howard told Neal. He offered help, which was, of course, refused.

Eunice had turned to Adele. "What are your plans, dear?"

214

Eunice asked. Mrs. Bard was already talking about grandchildren. She couldn't bear how Sarah spilled, splashed, dirtied (Mrs. Bard was far too old for diapers); but the child refreshed her. Mrs. Bard, who sat in her straight chair as stiffly and precariously as a china cup in its thin saucer, bounced Sarah on her breakable knee, and laughed delightedly.

Adele gave her a blank look, then said: "Well, I'm not going to stop working, anyway. I don't want to just kind of sit around while Neal hangs out with Bert." Eunice fluttered her eyelashes drastically, and Adele went on: "We've got vacation in February, did Neal tell you?"

"Not yet," Eunice said, her tone tinged with bitterness; then she brightened. "Do you intend to take a belated honeymoon then?"

"I guess you could call it that."

"Where will you go?"

Adele took on a dreaming expression. "We haven't decided yet," she said. "Officially, I mean. But I want to go to Brazil."

"Brazil!" Mrs. Bard said, startled.

It seemed that Adele hadn't heard her. "I think we're going to Brazil," she said; then, more firmly, "Yeah, I really think so."

Howard leaned into the conversation. "How did you come to pick Brazil?"

She smiled at him. "I like the sound of the name," she answered. "I always have."

Eunice let out a small gasp. Howard, giving it reflection, considered that Neal had probably married Adele to broaden his view. To Howard it didn't seem like a bad idea. "Bra-zil," he murmured.

"I think it's the z that makes it nice," Adele said, still smiling.

When Howard had first asked Neal what his new wife was like, what had Neal told him? "She's my tawdry Miss Rheingold," Neal had said: "She likes things that are orange. She sticks to genuine plastic." He summed up: "We have nothing in common but common itself."

If Howard was falsely dignified, he sometimes used his pomposity to ignore a joke and bore in on a matter's crux. "But what can you expect out of a wife like that?" Howard had asked, exasperated.

"Everything," Neal had answered. It had been some seconds before he added: "Everything and his brother, Bobby."

In Neal's tired, comfortable, tawny overstuffed chair Howard regarded Adele as the zoo-goer does a faintly unreal tropical bird. It was remarkable, Howard thought, the way people choose their lives: how one goes about trying to be happy. That is, Howard added to himself—Howard spoke to himself in complete sentences, one plodding after another— how strangely oblique the correct solutions sometimes are. . . .

Foolishly Howard always looked for the correct solutions —as if he expected them to be displayed in tomorrow's editions, so he could say, "There, do you see that?"

Eunice was pressing in on Adele now. Howard couldn't quite bear it. He wondered where Will and Neal had gone off to. He went chasing after them, like shepherd for miscreant flock. No, Howard was never discreet. I apologize, now, for his nature; for his shut-eyed vision, close-eared comprehension, clamped-mouth communication. I regret; hope to make redress here.

In the kitchen Howard bumped into an odd remnant of conversation. Will warmed his hands on a small red teapot; Neal juggled one lemon, and was talking:

". . . goes along with what I always say. You have to give up on something to get it."

"Give up on what?" Howard asked pleasantly, broad-shouldering his way into the small room.

216

Neal shrugged, and passed to Will. "Oh," Will said (he seemed sleepy). "Lucy called. She, um, wants to get together."

"How does she mean that?" Howard asked carefully, fatuously.

Will shrugged, evasive and uncomfortable. "Who knows?"

Oafish Howard jumped in. "Well, *I* think it means she wants to live with you again. I think she wants to forget this separation business."

Will looked out through a thin trail of stream rising from his round teapot. "Maybe," he said. "We'll see."

"What if that *is* the case?" Howard went on. "Are you willing to go back to her?"

Will looked blank. "I guess so, Howard."

"You mean you're not sure."

"I mean maybe it doesn't make much difference."

Howard pulled his pipe from his jacket pocket and eagerly thumbed its comforting bowl. "Explain yourself, my friend."

Will seemed to be fogged in by the vapors of his tea.

"Something has happened," he said. He raised his eyebrows and nodded sagely, as if he were revealing mysteries. "There's been an accident," he added.

"Accident? What kind of accident?" Howard asked, baffled.

"An interior accident," Will said reflectively. "I can't explain it, Howard. It's just the way I feel. Forgive me."

Howard tried to be jocular, though he noted with a tick of irritation that Neal was still juggling the single lemon. "Analysis fails again, eh?"

Will's eyes followed a particularly curly wisp of steam as it ascended, evaporated. "That's about the size of it," he said blandly, and turned his gaze down to the teapot itself.

"Well, you've come to the right century for it, at least. These days we've substituted revelation for articulation. Join the parade, my friend."

Will tried to pay no attention; he appeared to be considering the teapot, as if it were a problem rather than an object. But Neal couldn't resist. "I don't think we're too big on revelation these days, Big Howie. I think comfort is the name of the game."

"Comfort?"

"You know, Howie: pleasure. Like a warm house, a soft bed, a bottle of booze, and not having to get out of the car to go to the bank. Someday soon, we'll have drive-in schools, offices, houses. If you can't drive into it, you'll be able to dial it. You'll never have to be separated from your gadget."

"Regrettable, isn't it?" Howard concurred, and went on, lungs swelling, to add, "The domination of the automobile over our society—"

"No, it's great. Want gin and tonic, toddy, or tea, Howard? They're all equally easy. The world is getting easy. I think that's terrific. You don't have to do anything you don't want to."

"I don't think you believe that," Howard said, and added, "Gin, please."

"Some things never change, Howard," Neal said, thumbing the cap of the bottle.

"What do *you* think, Will?" Howard said. "About the world at large, and the future of mankind?" Howard chuckled soothingly to himself.

Will lifted the lid of his teapot and peered inside. The tea was done; its fragrance drifted up from amber depths, revealing distant continents, silent lives, unspoken history.

Will looked up. He gazed at Howard. "I think this is a ridiculous discussion," he said. "And I wish you would stop baiting me, Howard. I don't feel that great today, to tell you the truth."

In the long silence Howard slowly reddened. Neal looked away, flipped his lemon into the air. It bounced off his wrist and rolled bumpily along the brick-red linoleum, waddling

218

like a duck. Neal gave chase; the lemon found a nesting space between stove and dishwasher. Neal went down on his hands and knees; he too moved like a duck. "Listen, sports fans," he said, plunging his arm in after the lemon, "what do you say we end the internecine strife before it begins, hey? The ladies are waiting for their drinks. God knows what atrocities have been going on in there."

The atrocities had come to silence. Adele was emptying a cellophane bag of potato chips into a wooden bowl; Eunice flipped through a *National Geographic.*

"Here you go, kids. Two gins, two toddies, one man with a mug of tea and a heart of gold."

Mrs. Bard swallowed, and her face contorted. "My, but that's awfully strong, Neal. What did you put in it, rum?"

"Rum for your money, lady. What else would you put in a hot toddy?"

"Oh," Mrs. Bard said. "I wouldn't honestly know."

It was "drifting up," as we used to say, outside; inside too, and Howard imagined that Will was drifting away. The thick talk, and then the lack of it: up to your neck in snow. Will had never been in a drift that deep, but he was convinced that in his small-town youth it snowed more than nowadays— ankle-deep, knee-deep, thigh-high. They all flopped onto their sleds and skidded down the hill into town, heedless of the few prowling cars that wallowed along, gliding freely out of control. The beagle puppy, ears flapping, lolloped in and out of the snow, chasing after them with arching leaps; he was out of his depth. His name was Hercules; Howard had named him. He was supposed to be Howard's dog, but pre- ferred Homer's slippers. Hercules made a citron yellow pool in the snow, and was hit by a truck the next summer. But in the meantime, that is to say now, while Adele passed around the potato chips and Neal the soft cheese and stale crackers, Hercules bounded after their sleds; through the drifting snow.

219

Will wasn't going crazy, he was just drifting. For the moment he preferred the past to the immutable, mute present. He looked around him; Howard bit down on a Triscuit. Yes, immutable. There was only one path, and it was beaten, all its most minute twists and turns were marked out—Will thought of the transparent inset in an encyclopedia, manifesting in lurid red and purply-blue lines on clear plastic the tracks and traces of Man's Circulatory System—down to the finest capillaries. Will saw himself sitting across the round table from Lucy; she dug seeds out of a grapefruit half with the serrated edge of a spoon. He looked more closely: there were four seeds on her plate, her face was red. Across the table he was scowling; he was waving his arms. Will turned away from the sight. Oh, gradually the hostilities would cease; bones stiffen, feelings ebb; gradually their flames would calm to a candle-flicker.

Here they are. Two ancients, fixed in their places like bolts rusted into a shut door. They sit quietly. Lucy slowly creases a page of her newspaper, gnarled hands shaking; Will's remain folded in his chilly lap. At last Lucy has finished the newspaper, and there is no movement at all. Then the first crack appears in the patina; noiselessly the shells shatter, and with a breath of wind they fall. Will took a piece of cheddar and a Ritz cracker, gave a wry, melancholy smile to no one in particular, and grimly began to chew. Above the house his crow flew.

"It is due, I believe" (Howard was speaking, a rich drone) "to their mastery of light. The best indication of a painter's craftsmanship is facility with light—note, for instance, the way it pours through Vermeer's window, and dapples the scene from left to right." Howard tamped the tobacco in the bowl of his pipe.

Will watched Howard with the nervous, disdainful eye of the ex-smoker. That was like Howard, Will thought, to be interested in light: how it falls, and not what it falls upon.

220

Howard liked the Dutch painters because they painted the surface of things: the immaculate, unbroken surface. Life to Howard (Will proposed) was like a locked house—Howard doesn't give a thought to unlocking it, but contents himself with a careful description of the front door. God, no, he doesn't give a thought to tearing it down: because it is, finally, the door he is interested in. Howard *cares* about the damn door, Will said to himself.

Howard was still speaking: "They painted with fine brushes, building up layer upon layer. They made pyramids; and today we have cars that are guaranteed for three minutes, or six yards, whichever comes first. We've made a cheap matchbox toy out of life." He snorted, and settled in his chair.

Howard lit, puffed. Howard's pipe made small fog; Howard's gin made him tipsy. Eunice touched her temple with her index finger, then rested it on two other fingers. Will, recognizing his hunger at last, reached out with a long dark arm for another triangle of cheddar: it was dry, but agreeably sharp, causing the back of his jaws to ache slightly as he bit. Crumbs of cracker spattered his sweater. Adele propped up her chin with her two hands, watched Howard's smoke and Howard's mouth—bored, Howard guessed. Neal sat beside her, legs crossed, his trousers too short and his reedy ankles showing; both arms spread out on the sofa's back, behind the bent backs of mother and wife.

"I don't suppose," Howard said now, "there'll be much more great painting to look forward to."

No one would reply to this, Howard thought. No one was interested. No one cared about what he said; he did, but that wasn't enough.

Silence. Howard was right. Howard was often right, but this was paltry satisfaction. Howard gave it a slow measure of thought, as he puffed on his pipe, and he thought that perhaps he could see their point. He could see that there was no use in talking about light. There wasn't even pleasure in it. Howard, in fact, never gave pleasure, he said to himself—a little stricken.

Howard suddenly decided that he was a bore.

But was this why his family lounged in silence, swishing their drinks in their glasses, while the snow built walls all around and between them? Howard was no more boring than anyone else. Why should there be this silence, this distance between Howard and his kind? Howard glanced at Neal. Neal was musingly contemplating the top of Adele's left buttock. Howard glanced at Will. Will was now seven years old, playing with a stray dog on a deserted Cape Cod beach, popping the kelp under his toes. Howard looked at his mother. She was stretching her fingers, trying to marshal some arthritic pain and have cause to pity herself. He looked at Adele. Adele was kind of wondering what kind of family has to have the *ice* broken when they get together at *Christ*mas, for Chrissakes.

At last I looked at myself, as best I could: I had to acknowledge that perhaps my stomach puffed more than I had thought; that perhaps I puffed more than I had thought; that I was losing hair; that I was losing; that perhaps this distance was something that I had imposed, for safety's sake, to keep the world at large at length.

Looking again, I realized that they were all unhappy. No, that might not be true. I was unhappy. And I was alone. Howard put out his pipe, and tapped the ashes down in the ashtray before him.

I tapped the ashes down. Will finished crumbling crackers in his mouth; he leaned back, farther back into memory, into a dark grove of firs beside a swamp, where he bent to touch a newborn spring spring, and put one finger in the water. Cold, so cold.

I cleaned the bowl of my pipe and oiled it with a blackened, reflective thumb. I too remembered something: a distant July Fourth just after the war, when it seemed unaccountably good luck to be an American. That morning, a fine breezy one, Granpacky Singer stiffly raised the flag; Homer watched with huge, goofy straw hat held over his swelling heart. Then we all trooped out into the field to do some berry-picking. Wild strawberries—"for jam," Granpacky asserted, though of course we would never get enough for jam. Neal, for instance, was more interested in chasing crickets, and then got involved with an inordinately devout praying mantis. Will picked away, slowly, erratically, and ate as fast as he picked—turning his greedy mouth a brazen red. Well, I would show them. I didn't eat a one: the sweet sound of fat berry plunking into tin pot was meal enough for not-so-hungry me. I crawled through the strawberry bushes as eagerly and relentlessly as a sniffing spaniel. When my pot was boiling with berries I waltzed contentedly toward Will—who sat sucking on the aftertaste of a particularly sweet strawberry, dreamily gazing at a space where a white butterfly would muse in a minute. There it is: one butterfly, one dreamy boy, and my own ten-year-old face, complete with ten-year-old's sneer, as I proudly shoved my brimming pot beneath Will's amazed nose. Will blinked. He looked at me with his steady, liquid eyes. He said, "Don't you like 'em, Howard?"

For years I was proud of my restraint. Now I'm not. It occurred to me then, as I loaded up my pipe again, that Will might still think I didn't like wild strawberries. Or anything else. I wanted to tell him (he sat a short, impenetrable distance away): I love wild strawberries, Will. I always have.

In my way I loved a lot, and still do. You believe me, Will? At the very least I loved the language: the chance to pass matters through that sieve, pan out something solid, something luminous. I've stored up all my tiny feelings, egged them on, hatched them and nursed them in the warm nest of my solitude; in short, tried to understand what that Howard was doing, at long last. I tried to understand you, Will. Can you hear me, Will?

But Will wasn't talking to me, couldn't be expected to talk.

Will ebbed away, melancholy in his teacups; at the edge of his sight distant days glimmered, glossy and touching as the morning star. At dawn Will walked alone the long dusty way to the swimming hole. And in the end the sun came misting down, the fog rolling up, but the faint pattering rain fell warm. Here today what was gone yesterday: the extraordinary red-, white-, spectral heat that pulsed in him as his hardened lips flattened Jocelyn Stevens's plump ones; and she drew back, never for a second suspecting the depth of his need, saying, "Hey. Go a little easy, okay?"

Okay. Will began to test himself, to spy as deeply as he could into the tiny glittering keyhole of his memories; and I shifted uncomfortably in my comfortable chair, watching him keenly and unhappily, promising myself that someday I'd find some way to—

"Another drink?" Neal said to the general public.

"That would be lovely," our mother said brightly, and held her glass out; her charming air of expectancy.

Neal had already rounded up Howard's and Adele's glasses and carried them off by their throats, poor lambs. Will smiled mysteriously over his tea, unnerving me. I went to help Neal in the kitchen.

"Neal," I began solemnly, stirring with two fingers the drink he gave me, "what's wrong with Will?"

Neal looked at me suspiciously. "Maybe he's tired," he tried.

"Perhaps, perhaps," I said. "But he seems depressed."

Neal shrugged, and drank from an empty glass. He rattled his ice cubes. "Maybe he's come around to my view of life," Neal said.

"Which is?"

"You get born; root for the Red Sox; they don't win; you die."

"But what if you root for the Yankees, or Baltimore?" I asked.

Neal sighed. "Big Howie: you don't."

I had to try once more. "I thought the Red Sox won something last year."

"Almost," Neal said. "But Will doesn't know that."

"Neal, I'm afraid I don't understand," I persisted.

"And you never will," he smiled, squirting lemon. "By the way, Howard, did you hear about the murders in Paris this spring?" He went on without waiting for a response. "There was a guy running around there who did only Yugoslav girls. And why do you think that was?"

"Perhaps he was a Yugoslav himself?"

"Nope. He was a short Parisian. They asked: 'Why Yugoslav girls?' and you know what he said? He shrugged his shoulders and said, 'Just an idea that came to me one day.'"

Neal was finished. "What do you mean by that story?" I asked.

"Just that there's never any telling. And that's my final statement, sports fans."

Neal poured gin into a last glass and lifted the tray of drinks. With his eyebrows he indicated the door. I held it, and he advanced ceremoniously into the living room, the tray held aloft, whistling "Here Comes the Bride"—and only Adele laughed. I distributed glasses; we looked at each other, and at Will, who didn't take notice. There was a silence while we waited for someone to make a toast. At least that's what I thought we were waiting for.

Howard loved to toast. All rites pleased him. He often proposed "Confusion to the enemies of the Queen," and boomed his own laughter. Tonight, more hoarse than grandiose, I said, "To Will."

But where was Will just now? Absent: and small. His mother's hand came down to take him across the street.

Will could do better than that. The bars imprisoned him in the crib; on the kitchen counter the radio crackled. His mother's hand made loud sounds on the counter, rhythmic, thump, thump, thump. Her back was to him; her long brown back. Doing this was too difficult, and Will couldn't hold on any longer. The world came up to him from below, knocking the back of his head with the bars.

Will tried to summon it up, but he'd forgotten the pain. You forget what plagues you, he thought.

No, he couldn't recreate even one. He had tripped, fallen on his head—but how had he broken the ankle? He remembered that he'd rolled in the crackling, cold leaves, howling with it, holding on to the other leg because he didn't want to touch it. He had rolled right in the dogshit. He remembered the dogshit: moist. But he couldn't remember the ankle.

The best days still sparkled, candles still glowed: but was it true that the best moments were merely sexual, pulsing spasms of pleasure tinged now with defeat; or else just pastoral, pastel hues, pretty leaves, light thrown on a landscape, confessions of a recidivist romantic? Will wanted to leave sex out of this, delete love of nature: wanted to get past the stock, commonplace joys and remember the ones that had been his, Will's, his alone. It couldn't be that his mind was a common place. He'd always had a wild heart. He'd always been at an irreducible distance from the rest. When he looked at his family, he was gazing at them from the other side. There—there was the distance.

Baby Sarah had Will's eyes. Lucy said that, and she was right, as usual: he might feel apart from his race, but the tiny girl had a part of him. Children were astounding accidents: his genes ran down with Sarah into a sea of time, their source an anonymous spurt, fateful trickle in the dark. Once Sarah was just *that* size, nearing nothing; and before that just the thump, thump in Lucy. Will put his head against her thump. Why did he like to listen? What was wondrous about a thump, thump, thump . . . ? About the stranger who came out tiny and thumping, an absurd mix of their parts? Will

226

couldn't pretend that passing on a pair of eyes, or a nose, even a whole crew of genes, was a help to him now; couldn't pretend that it gained him a second against an end (his own). He could sow his seed, his tame oats, incorporate his gift for wretchedness into great populaces to come, and it was of no consequence. He was merely inaugurating the process another time: renewing the same old.

Lucy and Will combed the length of the gray beach. The tide was out, and had left its spew behind. Shells, shells of boats, buoys, bits of matter; reflected in the slick, shiny glaze of water left on the sand by the tides. He had held on to one finger of Lucy's hand. Tides.

The day Lucy left was the longest day; the light came into the bathroom, found Will in his bathtub, and finally faded. Neal came in, slouched in the doorframe, and switched the light on. And this day was the other solstice, the shortest day; this afternoon Neal came through the door, smiling, and put the chicken bones on the plate. It was growing dark.

"It could be worse," Neal had told him once: "Lucy might come back." She'd called, and she would come back. Run, rerun. If you run the movie too many times, the film itself becomes brittle, will break. The celluloid spills all over the floor, spun on by the whirling reels, a wriggling mass of plastic. They switched on the light; the film seemed to be struggling down the aisle. Everyone laughed; the projectionist's face reddened. Lucy giggled delightedly, rocked convulsively in her seat, finger leveled at the film pulsing on the floor. The projectionist flipped the switch, and the reels stopped turning, spinning. Will sat quietly, and presently the lights went out again.

My drink was finished. I still held the empty glass.

It was snowing, and it was going to snow. It would be the biggest snowfall in years, the biggest snowfall for years to come. Delsey would give them all dinner (paprika chicken).

227

You and I would share a guest room—you remember the silence between us? I couldn't make jocular chat anymore, no more than you, Will. Nor could I begin to speak.

The next day Neal would dig us out, and we'd go out to Thompson's to get the Christmas tree, as always. Doug fir, as always. Eunice would wait in the car; Neal and Adele throw snowballs at each other, Neal miss with his. You and I would cut it down with the Swedish crosscut saw. You knew as well as I that one man could handle the thing less awkwardly, making the saw the expression of but one will; we worked together, all the same. It was good to get snow into my gloves again, so that my wrists ached, as wrists and ankles always seemed to ache in long childhood winters. Did you like that, Will? Did you think of your child's wrists and ankles, and yours as a child? You must have, no? Correct me if I'm wrong, Will.

That evening we would trim it. The mood lightened; Adele and Eunice even made popcorn together. Adele insisted we put popcorn balls on the tree; I believe Eunice had never made popcorn balls before. We strung them around three times. On tinsel too Adele insisted. We burdened our tree.

That evening Neal would convince me to forsake gin and tonic for hot chocolate, and then he'd burn the milk, as always. A thick brown scab stuck to the pot's bottom. I got my gin and tonic. You helped Neal with the steaks; smoke rose from beneath the broiler, but at last Neal entered, bearing a steak and a smile. He struck strips off the far end, grinning with child's pride, and I watched you, Will—I'd swear you were smiling too. Yes, that will happen: you'll grin with Neal after all, and pile down soft mounds of mashed potatoes. After dinner chestnuts will roast over the fire, in a tin box with a long handle, shaken vigorously by Neal, till flames rise from the box; and Neal will yank the nuts out, cursing lightly, and flip their blackened, smoking remains into a white porcelain bowl. . . .

The next day would be Christmas Eve. Christmas or no, I would have my drink before going to church. Everyone liked the candlelit service: I loved churchly ritual, circumstantial pomp; Neal was allowed to sing (and almost knew the tunes); Will could stay anchored in the past, when Christmas had been important to him; Delsey could finally re*lax;* Eunice adored the candles, the thousand delicate little flames.

And we would go home, and have Christmas—do you remember that Christmas, Will? You'd made us all pots, I think; I got a crooked green one. I still have it somewhere; it's cracked. Just a slow leak. I still have it, Will.

It would be Christmas shortly; and the sun would begin to struggle back in our direction, toward spring, only to leave us again. It would be a long, strangling winter yet. But what do the seasons matter to us? Compared to friends and lovers, brothers, what does it matter whether the leaves are on or off, about to fall or about to bud?

On Christmas Day Lucy would come over; and one day in some spring you would wake to find her pulling a bathrobe from the closet, light shining on the pulled-back mass of her hair. That was all: just the way she stretched on her toes, reached into the closet; the way the sunlight fell on her; the glimpse of her you got, and what you guessed. What did you guess then, Will?—that your love was not dying out, but merely changing shape and shadow, crawling not toward a grave fate but a mute chrysalis?—to break out again, almost unrecognizable in its bright splendor? Yes, Will! You will, if you will.

But Will sat in Neal's easy chair the evening of the winter solstice, remembering what he could. Not without bitterness: he remembered that the film broke, leaving a blank square of light on the screen. He recalled his lively little daughter, the small, hard, dead body of his hawk, the soft sea-large dying one of his father; and then his stream, his wide flat rock in the middle, the blackbird that flew downriver. All that still caught in his craw. Will held up his hand to stop it. Nothing stopped.

There was nothing that Howard could say, could give Will then. I watched him at a distance. I acted slowly, as I tend to do. For a long time I too just sat—on my bench, where I am sitting now; I mulled it over, slowly. Perhaps too late.

Undoubtedly, a gentleman was sitting in the park. What was he doing there, bundled in his coat? He rarely fed squirrels; he never tapped a cane on the pavement. Howard was the type of man who fed the squirrels, who carried a cane; but I carried no cane, fed no squirrels.

I was researching lost time. What did I remember? What I couldn't remember, I made up. Here it is, Will. It's your story. It's for you.

There are no deaths in this story. Except perhaps Howard's. For I'm going to be quiet, now.